ASHER

THE LAROUGE TRIPLETS

ELLIE MASTERS
USA TODAY BESTSELLING AUTHOR

JEM PUBLISHING, LLC

COPYRIGHT

Published by JEM Publishing, LLC.

Published in the United States of America

ISBN: 978-1-952625-93-0

1

ASHER

THE CARNAGE FROM MY YOUNGEST BROTHER'S WELCOME HOME party is everywhere. Empty beer bottles litter the floor. Wine bottles sprawl haphazardly over the countertops. Whiskey bottles—yes, that's plural—are stacked three high on the coffee table, and there's a tequila graveyard where countless crushed limes mourn their fallen gods.

The pain in my head, however, is not due to a hangover.

The swelling in my left eye throbs. My knuckles are a bloody mess. I work my jaw side to side, opening and closing it against a dull ache.

"Brody! Cage!" I yell out for my brothers. I should call them Shit-head and Ass-wipe. "Where the hell are you?" My eyes pinch with pain.

People talk about the twin connection being a thing. I don't know anything about that, but as the eldest of identical triplets, I can testify to the crazy connection between us. That mystical link is how I know Brody is passed out on the porch before I head outside, and how I know Cage is currently working nameless chick number three to her fourth orgasm in the barn.

It's a problem because I need to go out to the barn and I'm not looking forward to walking in on my fucking brother—fucking.

I kick the porch door. It slams against the exterior stone of the house. Brody startles and pops up from the couch he appropriated for the night. His forest green gaze snaps to mine.

"What the fuck, Ace?" He runs his fingers through a mop of midnight black hair. It falls in front of his eyes and he gives a practiced flip, the same one I use to get the hair out of my eyes.

Like I thought, he spent the night curled up outside. Evidence of the party extends out here. More bottles, most of which are empty, tell a tale of heavy drinking and there's more. I scrunch my nose at the used condoms next to the couch.

"Dude, you'd better be picking up that shit." I make a point to kick over a small trash can. "Start with that." My eye catches a third sticking out from under the couch. "Holy crap, three?"

"It was a good night." Brody gives me a cheeky grin.

I shake out my hand and look at the bruising on the back of my knuckles. My nemesis, Felix-fucking-Franklin, got in a couple good swings. I've got the black eye and sore jaw to prove it, but I brought him to his knees. Fucker was no match for me in high school and he's no better now.

Fucking putz.

"You look like crap." Brody yawns and stretches his arms over his head. "Nice shiner. What happened? You run into someone's fist by accident?"

My anger is no less now than a few hours earlier. "Felix-fucking-Franklin's right hook gave me the damn shiner. His left hook did a number on my jaw, but that's all he had time for before I split his lip, bruised his eye, cracked a couple ribs, and kicked him hard enough in the nuts he won't be walking for a week."

"Damn. Way to go. When the fuck did he get back in town?"

"Don't know. Don't fucking care. He looks like shit. If I never see his smug-assed face again, I'll die a happy man."

"Dude's got some balls. La Rouge property is a no-go zone for that asshole, especially after what he tried." Brody leans back on the couch and pinches the bridge of his nose.

"The fucker fucked my girl, under my own goddamn roof, while I was inside doing shots of tequila. I think it's pretty clear what he was thinking."

"He slept with Erin?"

"Fucking putz." Erin's my girlfriend…or was. Shit, I had a ring waiting for the right moment.

"How'd you find out?"

"Knight." I rub the back of my neck and jerk a thumb over my shoulder toward the barn.

"Huh?" Brody glances out toward the barn. The barn door is wide open, almost always is. I think I've closed it maybe once or twice in a year.

"Knight went all batshit crazy last night. When I went to check on him, I found Felix balls deep inside Erin, fucking her brains out right next to Knight's stall. You know how he can be." Knight is a high-strung stallion with attitude, who basically hates every human but me. "Felix gave me a cheeky assed grin, so I punched him."

"Well that's fucked up."

"No shit."

"Told you Erin was shit." Brody gives a satisfied snort. I hear it in his tone, but he doesn't say 'I told you so' out loud. Brody and Cage never liked Erin; said she was trouble, but they tolerated her for my sake.

I'm the fucking asshole with blinders on, thinking she loved me when she was only using me to get to La Rouge money. Too ready to settle down, I missed all the signs.

"Glad you found out now, instead of later." He gives me a long look. "You good?"

"I kicked her out right after I shoved Felix's balls so far up his ass that he might as well have swallowed them."

Brody tips his head back and laughs. "Now that's a visual."

"Well, Felix won't be showing his face around here anytime soon."

"I'm surprised he showed at all, considering…"

"I agree. Fucking-Felix can rot in hell with his bruised testicles. As for Erin, she can cry her eyes out. I'm done with relationships."

"About damn time you came to your senses." Brody spreads his arms out wide. "We're young, wild, and free. No need to go tying ourselves down."

Except we're not as young as we used to be. In two years, we'll be thirty. Eventually, one of us is going to crack and give our mother the daughter-in-law she always wanted and those grand-babies she's been waiting on forever. Hell, when she was our age, we were little hellions in second grade.

I palm my face and drag it over the stubble of my jaw. It's too damn early and I'm getting tired of these all-nighters and the name-less women who flock to a La Rouge brothers' party. Our events are memorable. Always have been, but I'm tired of this shit.

The backbreaking work to keep this place going, and the constant pressure not to lose it all, is getting to me.

I'm grouchy.

It's an hour before the ass-crack of dawn.

And I have work to do.

It begins in the barn where there's shit to shovel out of the horse stalls, where memories of Erin's betrayal linger, and where the youngest La Rouge triplet is currently getting it on.

Unlike Brody, I don't have the day off. There's shit to do, and from the look on his face, I'm not getting any brotherly help.

Brody shifts on the couch and swings his legs around. He reaches down and swipes up the used condoms to toss them at the trash can. Only one of the three actually makes it inside.

"Your aim sucks." I shake my head, then glance out at the barn. Brody follows the direction of my gaze and his mouth twists into a grin.

"He's out there, isn't he?"

"Yeah." Brody huffs a laugh. "Took two with him."

"I'm surprised it wasn't three. Shit, you guys come down for a long weekend, chase tail, and fuck anything with two legs, while I…"

"Whoa! Slow down there. We don't fuck anything with two legs. There needs to be pussy attached and the longer the legs the better. Which is exactly what you need."

"What's that?"

"A little pussy action, idiot. You need to get laid; the sooner, the better. A little pussy will make you forget all about that bitch. Erin is trash, and speaking of trash, you know Felix is just going to go stirring shit up."

"Yeah." Felix always had it in for us. I'll be looking over my shoulder waiting for whatever revenge he has in mind.

As for forgetting Erin? I'm not sure keeping my dick wet is the best idea.

First off, my reputation around town is legendary. Brody and Cage fly in and fly out. They sleep with women all over the globe and only occasionally come home. I've been sticking my dick in the same local waters for the past decade and, except for Erin, scared off any potential interest years ago. I'm known as the fuck-them-and-forget-them-man.

"Tell me, aren't you tired of a new girl in your bed every night?"

"No." His brow quirks up. "I like having options. No strings. No commitments. Just fun." As an investment banker, Brody's killing it in the city, but he's never been in a relationship that lasted through the night.

I cringe thinking about all the places he's dipped his dick. Despite his aversion to relationships, he's never without some model-gorgeous catch of the day hanging from his arm. He has those rugged good looks girls go crazy for and a panty-melting grin which never fails to seal the deal.

I should know, I have the same looks. That same smile. Those same arresting forest-green eyes which never fail to get me laid.

When people look at us, they only see the similarities. I see the differences.

Brody spends his life behind a desk. He's got the same wide shoulders and powerful legs, but he's leaner than me. When not at the office, he bikes hundred-mile days, or is on one of his insane ultra-marathon training sessions. I'm bulky, packed with muscles honed by rough, rugged work. Cage is a mix between us. A nature photographer, he travels the world and lives an active outdoor lifestyle.

We all take advantage of our looks.

Brody is simply looking for the next great lay.

And Cage?

Littlest brother is a beast.

I turn to Brody. "Wanna saddle up and make the rounds?" I try enticing him with a little bit of fun. La Rouge Vineyard is situated outside Napa Valley, nestled against state forest land.

"Naw, it's too fucking early." He squints at the pre-dawn twilight. "What time is it anyway?"

"Mom's expecting us to make an appearance." I try to entice him. "We can be there in time for pancakes."

Our mother moved out of the sprawling family estate to a small cottage when I took over operations eight years ago. With our father's passing, she said the house held too many memories. The small, single bedroom home we built for her snuggles up against state forest land and is perfect for her.

"Seriously, the thought of riding makes my head swim." He glances at the sky. It's covered in pale, pastel pinks, yellows, and greens, a pre-dawn show put on by the sun every day. Brody gives a wistful sigh. "Don't see much of that in the city."

"You miss it?"

"Sometimes."

"Enough to move back and help me out?"

"Ha-ha. You'd just spend your time bossing me around, and as fun as that might sound, it's not going to work."

He's the CFO of our little slice of heaven. Cage is our marketing genius. As the eldest, I'm CEO of La Rouge Vineyards, which makes me their boss.

I came into this world first, making sure it was safe for them, while they hung out inside mom for a little bit longer and fought to be second. Brody won that exchange with Cage entering the world last. He was born seconds after Brody, but last is last, and we never let him forget it.

"Well, if you're not going to come…" My frustration shows as I bark orders at him. "Clean this place up."

"Why? You're just going to hire a cleaning crew." He cups his head in his hands and rubs his temples.

"A cleaning crew I depend on. They won't be cleaning up your discarded condoms."

Brody plops back down on the couch and covers his eyes. "You really think mom will make pancakes?"

"For her favorite son, she will."

He grabs one of the throw pillows and aims it at my face. "Give me five minutes. I need to piss and brush my teeth."

"I'll meet you in the barn."

2

EVELYN

Sweat drips into my eyes. It stings and blurs my vision. Late morning, the sun is busy heating the air, and I'm on a mission to slay this trail.

I turn up another switchback, heading deeper into the state forest, arms pumping, legs burning, breaths surging in and out of my lungs. Each pull brings earthy smells deep into my lungs where the rich aromas of juniper and pine flood my senses.

I'm hot, tired, and hiking on a trail thousands of miles from my past.

Forget the past.

Live in the present.

It's my new motto.

And much harder than it sounds.

I'll never take another day for granted.

I savor each sensation. Drink in the sun baking my skin. Listen to the wind whispering between the pines. It's a soft, lonely sound. Much like me.

My muscles ache.

My heart pumps.

I breathe hard.

I'm alive and living.

And my cellphone rings.

Dammit!

The hardest thing about living in the present is when the past refuses to let go.

No need to look at who the caller might be.

My initial thought is to let Prescott's call hit voicemail. He'll leave a message I don't care to hear, but the thing about Prescott is he'll keep calling. He's a persistent bastard when he wants something.

I let the phone ring. I want him to know he's intruding. On the sixth ring, I accept.

"Evie, where are you?" He still calls me by my childhood nickname and it grates on my nerves. I'm a grown woman, not the five-year-old he used to bounce on his knee.

"Out and about." My answer is as vague as I can make it.

"You need to come home."

"I have no home."

Thank you, Past for intruding on the Present. I want to tell Prescott to fuck off and go away, but he's my father's best friend.

Correction.

He was my father's best friend.

"Evie, you have a home."

Technically, I don't.

I'd hang up, but Prescott wouldn't call if he didn't have a reason. I ignore his comment about home and hurry this conversation along.

"Do you need something?" Some other document I need to sign?

"We're worried about you." Prescott and his wife, Gracie, care about me, but their sympathy suffocate me.

"Don't be."

"When are you coming home?"

Never.

"We talked about this." I told him to give me time.

"It's been two months." The tone of his voice shifts, talking to me like a moody teenager instead of a grown woman.

It'll be two more months, two years, maybe two decades. I have no intention of ever going back.

"Stop worrying about me."

"Where are you?"

I take in a steadying breath. He frustrates me with his need to keep tabs on my whereabouts.

"I'm on a forest trail somewhere in wine country."

"California?"

"Yes."

"How did you get to California from Colorado?"

I cringe, because this is going to lead to questions I don't want to answer.

"I don't see any transactions." As executer of my trust, he has access to my accounts. In two months, when I hit twenty-five, I'll gain access to the Thornton estate worth hundreds of millions. Frankly, I'd rather have my parents, and my brother, than the money.

Do I admit I hitchhiked? He'll have a cow.

I glance around, eager to get on with my hike. There's another six miles before I reach my camping spot for the day and I'd like to be settled long before sunset. I've learned the hard way not to wait for dark to make camp.

Late summer, the grass is brown, crisped by the sun, and starved of rain. Junipers sprawl across the ground, thickening further up the ridge where they join drought resistant pines. Prescott is ruining my perfect day.

My world consists of browns and greens and intrusive phone calls making it impossible to live in the present.

"Look, I promised I'd check in, but if you don't need me…"

"Gracie is beside herself. We don't know where you are. You're not even in the same state anymore. It's not safe out there."

And here we go with the blah-blah-blah crap about the dangers of a young woman traveling on her own.

According to him, I'm more likely to wind up dead in a ditch than…well, I don't know where I'm more likely to wind up. On some trail in butt-fuck nowhere would be nice, preferably without cellphone reception.

"I'm not going to check in every day. I appreciate your concern, but I need space."

I need time to grieve.

"It's just—a young woman hiking alone. It's dangerous. We worry. Could you just turn on the tracker?"

"No. We talked about that." I don't need them tracking my whereabouts. "I'm good and I promise I'm being safe."

I have a knife, a pistol, a taser, and bear repellant. Although, I don't think bear repellant does anything to keep bears away.

I ask questions. I learn. Other than wearing full body armor, I can't be any safer.

I come from a life of excess, where I did nothing for myself. Look what that got me?

Now, I rely only on myself.

Granted, I make rookie mistakes. I'm not an outdoorsy kind of girl, but I will be. All the hustle and bustle that came with being a New York socialite is behind me forever. I'm never going back to that life.

"Please, Evie. You have so much left here. Let me send a jet…"

"No." We've gone over this.

"You can't just walk away."

He's wrong. Two months ago, I did just that. I'm a city girl slowly becoming an outdoor enthusiast, and I don't regret turning my back on that life. I'm rediscovering who I am.

An outcropping of rock comes into view. I'm out of breath. Hiking and talking take the wind out of me. I stop and decide to scramble to the top.

"Look, I gotta go."

"Evie…" He knows I don't need to do anything. My time is mine.

"I promise to check in. I'm spending a few days here. There's a bunch of really great hikes around here, but fair warning, I'm headed to the Sierra's next. I'll be out of contact for a couple weeks at least."

"We could send you a satellite phone."

"I don't want it." I'm a strong, independent woman, and while I may be a little lost in life right now, I've got this. "I'll call you in a few days, okay?" I stare at the boulders, itching to climb them. I take off my pack and prop it at the base of the towering rock.

"Promise?" He's frustrated. I can tell by the tone of his voice.

"I promise, and tell Gracie not to worry about me, please."

"Take care, Evie, and please check in more often."

I end the call and climb the boulders, eager to take in the view.

I'm not disappointed.

Wine country extends as far as I can see. The vineyards pop with green. Beyond them, the Sierras rise out of the ground and wait for me. From here, there's little to see of their majesty other than a faint purple haze on the horizon.

I intend to hike the length of the rugged Sierra's, at least after I'm a bit more confident of my backpacking and survival skills. Mistakes can mean the difference between life and death in the wilderness, especially for a woman all alone.

Although, do I care?

I have all the time in the world to do nothing and no one to share it with. I continue on up the trail, headed to the primitive campsite which will be my home for the night.

Live in the moment. That insistent voice in my head reminds me of my new motto.

As for dealing with the past, I'm not doing so well with that.

I'm terribly and brutally…alone.

I climb up the last steep switchback and emerge onto the ridge where I plan to spend the night.

Except I'm not alone.

Movement near the primitive campsite draws my eye. In my very limited experience, hikers are social creatures. We may look like loners, especially those of us who hike solo, but I've spent many nights sharing a campsite with strangers where we gathered around the fire, traded stories, and laughed until sleep found us beneath a canopy of stars.

More often than not, they share their tips and tricks with me, the inquisitive newbie. Incredibly supportive and helpful, most of what I learn about backpacking comes from people on the trails. There's no reason to think this man will be any different, but for some reason, I pull out my phone and snap a picture. I tuck my phone into one of my cargo pockets and take a breath.

In and of itself, running into someone isn't unusual, but I've been alone all day. For some reason, I'm a little on edge. I blame this on Prescott. His intrusive phone call connected me to a past I've spent months running away from.

The man's erratic movements bring me to a stop. Dressed in baggy clothing with a bushy beard and oily, shoulder-length hair, my first thought is he's homeless.

Not usually this paranoid, I try to calm down.

The man stops at a bush at the edge of the campsite and fluffs it?

I don't know what else to call it.

What is he doing?

There he goes and does it again. It's weird.

He squats down—his back is to me—and the bush gives a little wiggle. Is he hugging it? Have I found some weird bush-hugging freak? Is that even a thing? Although, this is California. There's lots of tree huggers around here. Why not a bush hugger as well?

There's a revolver tucked into the pack at my waist. A knife strapped to my shin. And I have that super effective bear spray that might take out a house cat, if I'm lucky. It should work on a man, right?

I should be totally safe.

Which is a good thing because the man notices me. I lift my arm and wave. Best to present a friendly face and take it from there.

He stretches to his full height, hands pressed to the small of his back, and squints. There's no friendly wave. No hello shouted in greeting.

Well, I'm pretty good in social situations. I can charm a rock with my smile. It doesn't hurt that I have the looks to stop a man in his tracks, but this may not be the best time to play that card.

Carefully, I make my way down.

"Boy, it's a hot one today." Talking about the weather always kickstarts a conversation.

The man stares at me.

Okay, next.

"Are you from around here?" People love talking about themselves. I just need to open him up a crack. Do that, and he'll be my best friend in less than an hour.

His eyes narrow.

Okay, next.

"My name's Evelyn Thornton. My friends call me Evie." I flash him my biggest, brightest smile. It's one that comes with a ninety-nine percent success rate in winning over men.

The man is unimpressed. He returns a scowl.

A tough nut to crack, I step it up a notch and bring out my skills as a socialite.

Megawatt smile engaged.

Bouncing boobs on point.

A little flick of my lashes?

He checks me out.

I prop my hand on the top of my bear spray. "Are you camping for the night?" My tone remains bubbly, cheerful, and light. My gaze darts around, looking for something which might tell me more about this stranger.

There's not much to the campsite. It's a bare patch of ground cleared of vegetation and most large rocks. There's a fire ring in the center with the remains of ash and a blackened piece of wood that failed to burn.

I catch a bag sitting off in the bushes, something I'd expect from someone in the military. Maybe he's a homeless veteran?

A bunch of rags spill from the opening, along with the tip of a white plastic container.

He's tall and fit. Broad in the shoulders, with a thick waist, thicker legs, and biceps which are stacked with muscle. If he wants to overpower me, there's not much other than a can of bear spray, the taser, my knife, and the gun in my pouch, to stop him.

Fortunately, I know how to use them all.

I take my hand off the bear spray and move it over the pouch where I keep my revolver. The knife on my shin remains hidden. It's my weapon of last resort.

"What are you doing out here?" He finally speaks.

"Hiking. Backpacking. Camping. You know, loving the outdoors."

I decide to ditch this campsite and make it clear I'm not hanging around.

There's another primitive site three miles up the trail. It'll be past dark, but this guy is throwing wicked-bad vibes.

"Well, enjoy the rest of your day." I skirt around the cleared area, keeping as much distance between him and myself as possible, without looking like I'm keeping my distance.

A pile of rags tucked under a bush catches my eye. Not so strange in and of itself, except the rags are damp, as if soaked in water. Seeing how it hasn't rained all week, that raises a red flag. His eyes are on me as I move around the campsite. My attention should be glued to the trail, but I can't help but look around. Sure enough, under another bush, a pile of rags wraps around the gnarled trunk. They are also damp.

I stop and turn toward the stranger.

He stares at me and I bite my lower lip as a feeling of unease comes over me.

"You're alone?" He cocks his head.

"Yeah." I rock back on my heels.

I see Prescott's point. I slide my hand into my fanny pack and place my palm over the pistol grip of my revolver; six shots, no racking the slide, it packs a punch.

Point, aim, and shoot. It's fast, lethal, and I'm an expert shot.

I edge away. We're on a narrow ridge with steep slopes to other side and deep ravines at the bottom. I'm headed up. He moves to intercept me.

"Well, no one is truly alone," I say.

I'm hedging here and hold up my phone. Giving it a little shake, I snap a selfie, making sure he's in the frame of the photo. If they find my dead body, they'll know who the bastard was who killed me. It's the best I can do and I'm really hoping the picture is a deterrent to whatever is going on in this guy's head.

"I post all about my hikes on social media. I've got thousands of followers."

I'm not on social media. I have zero followers.

He keeps one arm tucked behind his back and rolls his lips inward. It makes the hair on his chin stick out. Not a good look.

"Reception sucks up here." He gives a little nibble of his lower lip which makes the hairs of his beard wiggle.

My gaze casts down to the bush he just squatted next to. Another pile of dirty rags; also wet. When I look back at him, a can of lighter fluid is in his hand.

I step back and stumble over a rock. It's all the distraction he needs. As I fall back, he launches forward. Rather than keeping my hand my revolver, it falls out of my grip when I try to break my fall. The breath is knocked from me as I land on my back.

I don't see the rock, but I feel it crash into the side of my skull.

3

ASHER

If I can get all three of us to mom's for breakfast, I'll be her favorite son. That means extra butter and syrup, not to mention I'll be able to lord that over my brothers for days.

I head to the barn, leaving Brody to get ready. As expected, noises come from inside. I barge in as if I own the place, which technically I do.

The low moans of two women come to a sudden halt.

"What's that?" One of them says.

Cage's deep grunts don't let up. He's a man on task.

Another woman cries out. "Oh, yes! Right there. I'm going to come." She adds her moans to the ménage; sounds totally fake.

I tried a ménage once. Too much work.

I don't see Cage and his women, not that I'm eager to catch a glimpse of my naked brother's ass. I head to the tack room where I check everything out and I'm not quiet about it. Not that it matters to the threesome who return to their amorous activities. Like, hello, I'm right here.

I grab Knight's bridle. He's a gorgeous, black stallion, with all the attitude and spitfire that comes with his name. I'm the only one he allows to ride him. He's unseated every other rider, but then, I bring him treats.

I dip my hand into the bucket holding the apples and flip open the box with a stash of sugar cubes. It's my secret weapon.

Slinging the bridle over my shoulder, I head down the long row of stalls. We have twenty slow, plodding mares for our trail ride business. They're in the back pasture, hanging out together. Then there's Knight. He's a lot to handle and I don't let him out with the girls. He gets too frisky. Brody's Arabian is next to Knight and Cage's chestnut mare, aptly named Chesty, is across from him. There are several more stalls leading to the back of the barn, all empty for now.

The sound of sex escalates. The main event is drawing near if the change of pitch in the cries of the woman is any indication. One of them expounds Cage's godlike status, and then there's the deep chugging of my brother's breath as he does his thing.

I go about my business, not trying to be quiet. In fact, I may let the stall door bang a little louder than it needed to. Knight's excitement grows and he bucks a little, kicking at the side of his stall. There's a gasp from a couple stalls down.

"Who's that?" a woman asks.

"Ignore it," Cage says with a growl. "I'm almost there."

"Harder, Cage, fuck me harder." The second woman cries.

The sound of flesh slapping on flesh makes me cringe. I can imagine what's going through my brother's head. He's probably wondering if I'm going to be a dick and break up the final act. I'm giving him a pass on this one. As much fun as that sounds, I really do have shit to do. I lead Knight to the front of the barn where I grab his saddle and cinch it down tight around his flanks. Just as I finish up, the long keening cry of a woman rips through the air.

Attaboy, Cage!

I feel like cheering him on.

His low groan follows and I give him a few seconds to recover before cupping my hand over my mouth.

"If you're done fucking around, get your hairy ass out here."

"Fuck you." My brother's panting makes me grin. He's out of practice if he's that out of breath.

"Who's that?" One of the women gives a screechy shout. It pulls my shoulders up to my ears.

"My brother."

"Your brother?" There's a little scrambling sound. I imagine she's trying to find her clothes.

Cage sticks his head out of one of the nearby stalls, then glances back inside. "Yeah, my fucking brother."

"Oh…" Excited giggles follow as the girls discuss us. "I've never done it with twins."

I roll my eyes. "We're not fucking twins." And I'm not into Cage's sloppy seconds.

One of the girls peeks out of the stall. She holds her shirt to her chest and gives me a long, hard look. "Now, don't you look fine. Wanna join us?"

The thought makes me want to gag, but I'm too much of a gentleman to insult this poor, eager, and soon to be disappointed girl. I do the next best thing and treat her as if she's not even there.

Cage yanks on his pants and shoves his arms in the sleeves of his shirt.

"Brody and I are riding out to mom's. You coming?"

"Pancakes?"

"Only for her favorite."

He gives a smirk. "Good thing that's me." Without another thought for the girls, he saunters away from the stall, leaving them to fend for themselves. The girl gives a little pout, but when she realizes he's already forgotten her, the look she gives could kill.

I turn away, not interested in getting dragged into that shit-storm.

Cage greets his chestnut mare, Chesty. "You want to go for a ride, girl?"

She gives a soft whinny and rubs her nose against his hand. Cage strolls to the tack room, grabs a bridle, and heads back to Chesty while I lead Knight outside.

Brody rushes out of the house. He's dressed in worn jeans and a plaid shirt. We look nearly identical, except my shirt is red and black. His is green and black. Cage looks just like us, except his shirt is yellow and black.

It's the triplet curse.

We try to never dress alike. That shit is for girls, but somehow, we always manage to wear something that ties us together. Not much to do about the jeans, but our shirts? Yeah, we didn't plan that.

"Hurry up." I put my foot in the stirrup and climb into the saddle. Knight is ready, but I keep him in check with the steady pressure of my thighs.

We ride together every day, in tune with each other. The reins are more for show. I don't need them to control him. The gentle pressure of my legs, the soft nudges of my knees, and the tiny kicks of my heels, tell him exactly where I want to go.

For the most part, he allows me to lead.

Knight can be an ornery shit.

Brody heads into the barn as the two girls exit. They look barely legal as they hold their heads together and whisper. Their eyes are wide and their mouths gape when they realize there are three of us. I shake my head because I know exactly what they're thinking.

We tried that once. It doesn't matter how hot the girls, getting naked with your brothers and trying to get, and stay hard, is impossible. Banging the La Rouge triplets may be a bucket list item for many local girls, but none have ever managed it.

Cage saunters out, leading Chesty by her bridle. He vaults into the saddle and stares down at the girls.

"Ladies, thanks for a memorable morning." He tips his hat then turns Chesty in a circle and speaks to me. "Last one there is a rotten egg."

Chesty launches and Knight isn't letting a mare get the best of him. Before I realize it, we're racing down the lawn and barreling between the vines stretching out before us. Cage gives a hoot and glances over his shoulder.

I give him his lead and slow down to wait for Brody.

I'm so far behind in chores, there's no way I'll catch up. What I should do is turn around and leave Cage and Brody to mom's fluffy pancakes, while I deal with the family business.

But I don't.

As much as my brothers can be shitheads, we rarely get time alone together. Brody's horse trots up behind me and I flash a grin. Cage is nowhere to be seen, but that's okay. We're taking a shortcut. Brody and I zip around the vineyard and head to the road leading to mom's tiny cottage. We're in an all-out race.

A hundred yards behind us, Cage's garbled curse is too low to make out, but the thundering of Chesty's hooves prove she's not going to let the stallions win. She eats up the distance, but it's too late.

Brody and I thunder down the road and turn into the small lane leading to mom's house. Neck and neck, we race. There is no finish line and we don't care. All that matters is getting there ahead of Cage.

Brody laughs as his horse pulls up short of mom's porch. I vault to the ground as Cage draws to a stop.

"You cheated." He dismounts and comes at me, fists swinging.

I meet him head on. We go down in a pile of limbs and laugh while we wrestle. He pulls his punches, as do I, and we wind up turning to our backs and laughing into the sky. Brody stands over us as our mother comes outside. She holds an earthenware bowl on her hip and stirs the thick batter inside.

"Pancakes?" Her bright green eyes twinkle as she takes us in.

"Yes, ma'am." We speak in unison. Cage and I pop to our feet.

"Wash up." Her voice is stern, but filled with love. "I've been expecting you."

Our mother has a sixth sense about us.

Bacon crisps on the stove. Stacks of fluffy pancakes sit in the middle of a fully set table. It's like she knew we were coming and exactly when we'd arrive.

While I pull out milk and OJ from the fridge, Cage snags the bottle of syrup. Brody gives Mom a kiss on the cheek and takes over at the stove while Cage and I sit at the table.

"How was the party?" Mom wipes her hands on her apron and ruffles Cage's hair.

"Nice." Cage smiles at her. "Wish you'd been there."

"Oh, you don't want some old lady crashing your party." She threads her fingers in his hair and gives a slight tug. "I hope you behaved." She looks to me for confirmation.

Mom knows us all too well.

I lie through my teeth. "They behaved like angels."

"Devils are more like it." She gives another yank.

"Ow!" Cage sits straighter and grabs at her wrist.

"As much as I can't wait for the blessing of grandchildren, it will be after you're married. You'd better have used protection."

Our mother is incredibly old fashioned. If it were up to her, we'd all be celibate monks up and until the night of our wedding. Fortunately, or unfortunately, she's well aware of our reputations around town. We're no angels.

She releases Cage and turns. Before I can blink, her towel snaps out and bites Brody on the ass.

"Mom!" Brody rubs his ass where she smacked him.

"And you as well. If you sleep with them, wear protection."

"We always use protection." Brody gives a grumble.

"And do you treat them with respect?"

His cheeky grin flashes for half a second, then disappears when she turns the full force of her disapproving frown at him. I hold back a chuckle while Brody withers under that glare.

"As much as they give me. They use me as much as I use them. It's a dog eat dog world out there. Not like when you were young."

"You can't afford a surprise baby." She jabs her finger at him. "And I'm not raising your rug-rat because you forgot to tie its mother to you with a ring." She props her hands on her hips and spins to Cage and me. "That goes for the two of you as well. I want grandbabies, but not before you give me daughters-in-law."

I can't help but laugh. "You have nothing to worry about from me."

"Bullshit." Cage punches me in the arm.

I rub out the sting. "It's true. I've sworn off women. I'm done with them."

"Ah, my poor boy, Erin really did a number on you."

How the fuck does she know about Erin? I glance at my brothers but they return identical shrugs. Mom's sixth sense is scary.

"Don't worry, you'll find someone. It's always when you're not looking that the one you're meant to be with walks into your life."

I shrug off her maternal pep talk. I really am done with women. I need a break from all of it, besides, it's the busiest time of year and there are plenty of things to keep me occupied.

"Ace is just pouting. Give him a week, or two, and he'll be fucking anything with two legs." Brody throws my words back at me, but I'm not dumb enough to take the bait. Not when Mom stomps over to him and smacks him upside the head.

"You will not speak like that in my house." She follows the smack to his head with a swat to his ass. We may be closing in on thirty, but we'll always be her little boys.

Cage snickers and I thread my fingers together behind my head in smug satisfaction.

"Sorry, mom." Brody rubs the back of his neck.

"Sit at the table. You're incorrigible, and I'm serious about using condoms."

We give a communal groan as she goes on a tirade about condoms, sexually transmitted diseases, and respecting the sanctity of our bodies as well as the women we sleep with.

Her boys don't have sex.

We sleep with the women we fuck.

Cage, Brody, and I exchange looks. We'd change the conversation, but when she gets like this, it's best to let the tirade run its course.

We shovel pancakes and bacon into our mouths while Cage tells her all about his latest assignment. We spend all day with our mother, taking time to fix things up around the house. Brody makes his famous burgers for lunch and Cage digs deep in the freezer and finds ribs to thaw for dinner.

We shoot the shit all day, loving this time we get to hang out.

Mom is beside herself, fussing over us, grilling us about life and our plans. She's a mother hen, but she's our mother hen. We play cards with her, put together one of her favorite puzzles, and let the long day pass.

It's been a long time since we've all been in the same place, and I miss my brothers more than I'm willing to admit. With Brody living in the city, and Cage gallivanting around the globe, home feels lonely.

I field a few calls from my foreman, George, managing operations from my phone. The work never stops. Then, I clear the dinner dishes while Brody and Cage take up stations at the sink. They do the dishes while I head into the living room.

"You seem distracted." My mother places her hand on my arm. "And you've lost your smile."

"My smile is fine."

"Is it?"

She wants to talk about Erin and make sure my heart is on the mend. I want to forget all of it and have been successful in avoiding that topic all day.

"I need to take this." I lift my phone. There's no one calling, but that's not the point. I need a moment away from the memories my mom won't let me forget.

When I step outside, the sun is down and woodsmoke curls in the air. I pinch my brows together and look around. It's the end of the summer, dry season in California, and we're on a burn ban.

A tendril of smoke lifts off the hill behind my mother's cottage and a shiver worms its way down my spine. I dial my longtime friend Brandon Bingham. He's a firefighter in our hometown just down the road.

He picks up on the first ring. "Hey, Ace, what's up?"

"Are you guys doing any controlled burns?"

"Not that I know of." Concern edges Brandon's voice. I'm not one to call out of the blue. "Why?"

"I've got smoke on the hill behind my mother's house."

"Campfire?" There are primitive permits issued by the federal and state park services. It could be a camper setting a fire for the night, but I shake my head.

"No, the column of smoke is too thick. I think we have a problem."

"I'll call it in." Brandon is a firefighter in Sequoia Springs, and I'm part of a tight crew of wildland firefighters. Most are volunteers like myself, and we provide manpower for the initial-attack on wildland fires across the nation. It's one of the things I do when not trying to manage the family business.

There's no time to dick around. I call in the fire, knowing Brandon is doing the same. All my gear is at home. I need to report to our staging area as quickly as possible, but first, I need to evacuate my mother. The winds are shifting, which means fire is coming down that hill.

4

EVELYN

MY HEAD THROBS WITH SKULL-CRUSHING PAIN, AND IT'S HOT, seriously hot. Awareness returns as acrid smoke fills my nostrils. Slowly, I raise my hand, or try to, but it doesn't move. There's tremendous pressure on my shoulders, and that's when I realize my hands are bound behind my back. When I open my eyes, gray fog surrounds me.

Not fog.

There's crackling all around me, a ruddy glow, and intense heat against my face. I blink against the caustic smoke and suck it into my lungs. This makes me cough until I feel as if I'll hack up a lung. Flames surround me and panic sets in.

I flop on the ground, struggling to get up, but with my arms tied behind my back, that's not easy. I make it to my knees and gag against the thick smoke.

I'm alone.

Vulnerable.

Scared.

And in terrible danger.

Most of the smoke heads up, but some of it swirls down where it lingers along the ground hugging burning bushes and rolling over rocks. It fills my mouth with the sharp, caustic taste of burning wood. My eyes sting and tears run down my cheeks. Everything is blurry. I cough against the irritating smoke, but there's no getting away from it and it's worse now that I'm on my knees.

Flames crackle and pop all around me, devouring the dry scrub as it licks along bone dry limbs, crisps leaves to ash, and obliterates parched grass. The heat is unbearable.

I don't know where I am and it's hard to see. I suck in a scalding breath and peer through the smoke.

I'm in the middle of the primitive campsite, next to the fire ring. It's the only reason I'm alive. For about twenty feet all around me, the ground is clear of vegetation, which gives me a fighting chance.

But not with my hands tied behind my back.

I'm in full on panic mode, but there's a small part of my brain which slows down. It's thinking, solving problems, and not giving up.

It tells me to cut the rope binding my wrists.

My panicked-self freaks out, but that small voice in my head is calm and tells me what to do.

I lean back, arching awkwardly, coughing with every breath, until I find the knife strapped to my shin. It takes several tries, but I finally get it free of its sheath. With hacking breaths and blurry vision, I saw at the rope until my hands are free.

The first thing I do is rub at my eyes. That's a mistake, because it grinds soot into the delicate tissues of my eyes. But I need to see.

A quick look reveals the impossible. My tent is pitched. It billows in the wind. My camping gear's set up, as if I made camp, but I'm virtually certain I did no such thing. The fabric of my tent melts, disappearing slowly as the heat consumes it.

Memories return.

A man with the beard.

He hit me in the head with a rock, but why did he set up my gear? That makes no sense, and I don't have time to think because I'm surrounded by fire. The prevailing wind blows downhill, which sucks. There's nowhere to go except up...into the thickest of the smoke. Smoke which will kill me before the flames, but if I stay, I'm toast; crispy, burnt, Evie toast.

The fire gains strength, fueled by dry grass and scrub oak. I'm in a tinder box rapidly turning into a firestorm.

I very much want to live, but I can barely breathe.

My gear.

The bastard went through my gear, setting up camp down to the last detail. Then I glimpse my hydration pack. I grab the water and a spare shirt out of my pack. After I take a quick pull of water, I wet the shirt and wrap it around my head, leaving only my eyes exposed. I grab another shirt, rip it in two, wet that, then wrap it around my hands. I'm trying to cover every inch of exposed skin because I'm going to have to leap over the small scrub which is on fire. My boots are thick and I hope that's enough protection from the flames along the ground.

If I move quickly enough, I might be able to escape this blaze.

My heart thumps wildly as adrenaline surges in my body.

It's going to be okay.

I'm strong. I can run. But I've already spent the day hiking up the hill. My muscles are sore, exhausted, and fatigue is settling in. A quick check of my things reveals I still have the bear spray, my fannypack but no revolver, and my knife. I don't see my phone.

Less than a third of my water remains and I douse myself with all of it.

Then I run.

There's one tiny gap in the flames and I make a break for it. Most of the fire flows downhill, spurred by the wind coming up over the ridge and flowing down into the valley below. I have what looks like twenty feet of burning brush to cross before reaching the leading edge of the fire.

I keep my arms tucked tight, my steps high, and sprint as fast as I can.

Heat encapsulates me. I'm literally running into what feels like a furnace, but I don't stop. Every instinct in my body says to turn around, seek the safety of the campsite, but I'll suffocate if I do that.

My boot catches a root. I stumble and my arms windmill, but

panic is my friend and it powers my body as I regain my balance and keep going.

Smoke sears my lungs. Tears blur my vision, but I don't stop.

I run.

I run until I'm out of breath. My eyes sting and I'm blinded by tears. I hack against the smoke that makes it through my makeshift mask, and catapult myself right over the side of the ridge.

The ground drops out from beneath me. My legs bicycle in the air.

I fall.

Dry limbs crack as I smack into the side of the steep slope. A rock digs into my hip. A bush slaps my face, slowing my fall, but I'm tumbling.

Completely out of control, I flip end over end down the rocky scree where I take out every bush and small tree along the way until I come to a bone-jarring halt.

The only good thing is there's less smoke down here, but I'm in a small ravine and see no way to make it back up the ragged slope. I can see where I fell. My body dug a line in the rock scree as I bounced to a stop.

I do a quick check for injuries. I'm scraped, bleeding, and sliced from the fall. My arms are a little burned, but I'm alive. Nothing's broken, but my ankle is tweaked. I pray it's not a sprain.

And I'm trapped.

As long as the winds don't change, I should be safe, but it won't take much to change that. A pillar of smoke rises into the air and wind rushes over my skin. The hot column of air is sucking in fresh oxygen to fuel the burn.

I'm not safe.

I test my ankle, but it's sprained. To get out of here, I have to hobble or hop on one foot, and I see nothing I can use as a cane. All the bushes are scrawny things, gnarled, twisted, brittle, and dry.

So, how does one survive a firestorm?

They don't do it by sitting still. I'm in serious trouble. If I can't get out of this little ravine, the fire will overtake me, suffocate me, and kill me.

But what can I do?

I take the wet fabric covering my head and rub at the burning sting in my eyes. I need to see. To think.

I need to survive.

Flames lick less than twenty feet above my head. The fire followed my mad dash. There's not much here to burn, but the tiny scrub won't put up much of a fight.

Knowing nothing about wildfires, I have no idea what to do. I don't have time to look it up in my wildlife survival guide. It's up that ridge, probably burning by now.

My stuff.

Why did that guy put up all my stuff?

The wind kicks up, drawn inward to feed the fire. Its low roar fills the air. At least it brings fresh oxygen. I have this to be grateful for as I scramble along the bottom of the ravine. I need someplace to hunker down, let the fire around me burn itself out.

I need shelter.

Then I notice a group of rocks, boulders about chest high, which tumbled down into this ravine eons ago. They squat together and I scramble to them because there's a small opening. Several times, I attempt to bear weight on my injured foot, but my ankle gives out beneath me.

Above the crackling noise, trees ignite with a popping sound. The column of smoke extends to the sky, a blight against a sunset of fiery orange and red.

The fire roars and flames shoot thirty feet into the air.

My tiny ravine feels very inadequate. But what else can I do? I can't climb out.

I need options if things get too bad.

Too bad?

Who the hell am I kidding? I'm up shit creek and the damn water is on fire.

Think, Evie. Think! How do you survive?

I think back to a campfire I shared with a pair of hikers, Seth and George. I met them over a month ago in Colorado. They taught me how to build a fire and gave me tips and tricks, like the best way to build a fire for cooking and the best fire for warmth. They said something about wildfires.

All I can remember is them saying to keep your wits about you. Well, I'm pretty much at my wits end. What else? What did they say?

Be aware of your surroundings.

This applies in every situation.

Attempt to evacuate.

I tried that and did well until I launched myself over the edge of the ridge. Now, I'm paying for that mistake with an injury which makes getting out impossible.

Seth mentioned the wind. But what did he say? Something about traveling with the wind, or against it? It doesn't make sense to travel with the wind. Wind feeds fires. So, I need to head into the wind?

Canyons and gullies are exactly where I'm not supposed to be. George said they could act like a chimney, funneling deadly heat upward.

Well, shit. Now I'm trapped inside a fire-funneling chimney.

Keep your wits about you, Evie. Don't let panic set in.

That damn, rational side of my brain tries to make sense. I need to listen to it.

Look for natural firebreaks. Seth's words poke through my panic.

Well, I've done that. The grouping of boulders isn't a firebreak, but it will shield me from the flames, reducing the radiant heat to a life-surviving level.

Despite my ravine being a potential fire-funneling chimney, the lack of vegetation and rocky ground are a win.

You can't outrun a fire.

Everybody knows fire travels faster than humans can run. It travels faster than deer can run, and now my heart hurts for all the animals trapped in the fire without a way to escape.

Focus!

I can't allow my soft heart to distract me from survival. Seth said something about digging a ditch. Or am I thinking about surviving a tornado? I've learned too much about the outdoors that it's all getting muddled in my head.

But then, I remember George showing me how to lay face down, feet pointed toward the fire. He told me to cover myself with dirt or rock and let the fire pass.

Let it pass?

Like, let it pass over me?

I'm so terrified I can barely breathe, but I am breathing. The choking smoke is above me. Not that my situation can't change with a shift in the winds. I keep thinking about canyons funneling hot winds.

I make it to the boulders and there's the tiniest opening big enough to fit my head and shoulders. It's dark inside and it's getting darker outside.

That red glow? It's not from the sun. The fire is growing. Roaring. The fearsome sound is straight out of a nightmare.

I wiggle into the space between the boulders, but there's not a lot of room and my legs stick out from the knee down. I pull out and dig a trench, keeping George's words in mind.

Dig a trench. Cover yourself with dirt and rock.

I have nothing but my hands. I unwrap the cloth from around them and set it to the side. Then I dig and prop rocks along my little trench. It's not much, but I cover my legs with dirt while trying to twist back around to lay on my stomach. I used all the water during my mad dash, but the rags for my hands, and the one around my head, are still damp.

It's the best I can do.

With boulders overhead, and my feet sticking out, I hunker down and pray.

5

ASHER

I LEAVE BRODY AND CAGE WITH MOM AND RACE BACK TO THE HOUSE. It's too early to think about evacuation, but I know fire. The wind blows toward us. I'm not taking chances with mom's house. As for the vineyard? If that fire spills down the hill, our entire livelihood will be at risk.

My brothers will extend the clear space surrounding mom's house. She keeps a fire break, or rather I do, one of my obsessive compulsions after seeing far too many homes destroyed by wildfires.

The thin column of smoke behind me grows.

That's bad.

The drought doesn't help. All the vegetation is dry; primed to feed a fire's hunger. If we're not careful, we'll have a firestorm on our hands. As I gallop away, Brody fires up the chainsaw while Cage goes to town with the rake. They'll do what they can to protect the house.

When I get to the barn, George is waiting. Brody must have called ahead.

"Get him inside and gather the mares from the fields." I turn over Knight's reins.

"Already on it. Juan and Miguel are getting them now." George steadies Knight. "I've got Andy on the tractor clearing the road."

My foreman is amazing. He's got our men already at work. Juan and Miguel will keep the horses safe, corralling them in small fenced enclosure next to the barn. If we need to evacuate, it'll be easiest having them contained rather than chasing them across a field. Terrified horses fleeing fire is not a good thing.

"I'm hooking up the trailers, just in case," George adds. "You think I should move them now?"

"Hopefully not." We have twenty-five horses to evacuate if the need arises, and barely enough hauling capacity to do it.

With Andy working the roads to push back any vegetation which may have overgrown from our last pass at the beginning of spring, I'm hopeful. Our vines should be safe. The main house, barn, and working buildings are in the center of our property with a large clear space around them. Even if we lose the vines, chances are the main structures will endure. With the exception of the barn, the buildings are constructed mostly of stone. We'll survive and rebuild.

It's my hope this is nothing more than an exercise in preparedness.

Always ready to respond at a moment's notice, I sling my go-bag over my shoulder after pulling on my protective gear. A quick stop at the sink to fill the bladders of my hydration packs, and I race out of the house.

Over my shoulder, the faintest ruddy glow is visible at the base of the smoke. The damn fire is establishing herself. She's going to be a feisty bitch. I feel it in my bones, but that's not why I curse. Wind rolls over the ridge and pushes the angry flames down toward the valley.

It's coming right for us.

Less than ten minutes later, I report for duty at the airstrip. Fear mixes with adrenaline until they blend into one and the same, making me feel alive. If this job was easy, everyone would do it, but it's not. The men in my helitack crew are a tough breed, hardened by Mother Nature's crucible to endure and survive. Half the team is present. The others are minutes away. Our pilot inspects the helicopter while I head to the briefing room.

We're a part of a large organization. Unlike my best bud, Brandon Bingham, who's a professional firefighter, most of us are seasonal employees and volunteers. Over the years, I've worked several jobs within the Forest Service. I served on a hand crew for three seasons before becoming a hotshot, crews who work the hottest part of wildfires, then I hired on as a smokejumper the following season.

An insane job, we parachuted into remote and inaccessible areas to fight wildfires. I'd still have that job, except it's not compatible with work. Last season, I switched to a local helitack crew.

It fits me.

Fighting wildfires is a kickass job, but family responsibilities tie me to home. Until my brothers step up to help out, it's just me.

My helitack crew uses helicopters to rapidly deploy into trouble spots. Often, we're the first responders to a wildfire. Let's face it, rappelling out of a hovering helicopter is pretty fucking badass. It almost makes Cage's ascent of Mount Everest look like child's play —almost.

Joe 'Tarzan' Bradley looks up as I walk in and gives a chin bump. "Hey, Ace."

Freddy 'Highball' Jameson does the same. "You ready to give this bitch your all?"

"Damn straight." I smile at the banter.

Like me, Tarzan and Highball are seasonal employees, temporary hires for the late summer fire season.

Pete 'Smokey' Larson is our lead. He does this full time and gives a long pull of his scruffy beard.

"Hey, Ace." Smokey waves me over. "You called this one in?"

"I did."

"We're waiting on Dice and Cosmo, then we'll load up." Chance 'Dice' Houston is a new addition to our crew. Tyler 'Cosmo' Andrews started with me, and he hates his nickname. Smokey turns his gray gaze on me. "You got your gear?"

Of course I have my gear, but it's his job to ask.

"I'm ready."

Smokey peers at the map spread out on the card table. Four empty coffee mugs anchor the corners. He gives another rub of his scruff. "It's right by your place." His brows draw together. "Spilling down from the ridge…"

"Moving downslope last I looked."

He turns his heavy gaze to me. "Damn winds aren't doing us any favors. Not that I'm saying it, but I wish the winds pushed it the other way. With all the new construction…" He gives a shake of his head.

He doesn't need to say anything else. We all look at each other. This new breed of environmentalists refuse to clear the brush around their homes, claiming minimal impact, but they don't respect nature. Their refusal to clear the vegetation around their homes places not only their property in danger but their lives as well.

"Well, that's not our problem. Local fire assets are managing that." He points to the top of the ridge, at the leading edge of the fire. "We're assigned here. Firebreaks in case the wind shifts."

I give a nod. It's a solid plan. We have the training and resources to reach the ridge. Our pilot will set us down and we'll get to work making sure if the wind does shift, that fire won't have anything to burn, stopping her right in her tracks.

My buddy, Brandon, and the rest of his team from Fire Station 13 will be on the lower fire roads doing pretty much the same thing, expanding the fire breaks put in by the forest service for precisely this reason.

We're different legs of a multi-legged stool, providing safe and effective wildfire response.

The last of our crew rush in. Chance and Tyler are out of breath, but kitted out in their gear. We all are.

Smokey greets Chance and Tyler as the rest of us hover over the map. We're imprinting the terrain into our brains because we're going to be in the thick of things just as soon as we can load into the helicopter and fly into position.

The epicenter of the fire is marked in a big red X, along with its current spread. From there, predictive models attempt to guess where it will spread and how fast.

It's peak fire season in northern California. Months with little to no rain make conditions ripe for fire. Add to that the hot Santa Anna winds and we're looking at a long hard night of backbreaking work. Our shift is slated at twelve-hours, but we've been known to pull thirty- and forty-hour stretches.

Sometimes longer

If it weren't for George, I wouldn't be able to volunteer. He runs the estate when helitack and firefighter training pulls me away for days on end.

This job is grueling, but I love it. Some say we're everyday heroes, but we're really adrenaline junkies looking for our next fix. As for our workplace? It sometimes looks like the jaws of hell have opened before us, but we love staring down death and walk into that without fear.

Smokey completes our briefing, then we're off. Grabbing chainsaws, axes, rakes, and other firefighting tools, we're ready to fight the flames.

Twenty minutes later, we rappel out of the helicopter in advance of the line of fire. She's spreading fast, gaining speed as the dry brush fuels her lust to consume and destroy.

Our goal is to keep the fire from destroying more forest land. Brandon's job is to keep it from reaching the town. I'm not sure which of us has the worst job.

The greedy bitch sucks air in to fuel her destructive blaze. The resulting wind makes for one hell of a choppy flight. Our insertion is insane and we circle around the fire and come back at it from the side.

It's clear where the fire started and I wonder at the idiot responsible. This fire is clearly the result of human carelessness. It's not due to lightning. The skies have been clear for days, which means there's probably some hiker who thought the rules about fire didn't apply to them.

The ridge is a blackened crisp. Charred scrub and ash twist in a mockery of life. Devoured by the fire, it's a deadman's land. The fire is done with this patch of ground. She's moving on, seeking nourishment in the valley below.

The roar of the fire drowns out the hissing of the rope as I rappel down the line. We carry heavy equipment, chainsaws, axes, and shovels. I'm on the shovel crew, assigned to dig a trench as a fire break in case the winds shift.

Most of the smoke blows eastward, following the path of the inferno, but we're still choked out and wear masks to protect our lungs from smoke. Our heavy protective gear hampers our movements, but we take no chances.

I'm the last man down and give the all clear signal to our pilot. The nose of the helicopter dips forward, then he takes off, returning to base to pick up the bucket.

His primary job is to support our crew, but he'll head back to headquarters to grab a tough, lightweight, collapsible bucket which allows him to pick up water and deliver it on target while we slave away with shovels and chainsaws.

We all multitask.

I free my shovel from where it hangs on my back and join Tyler at the blackened edge of the ridge. In some ways, we're lucky. The fire did the initial job for us. All we need is to turn the earth and create a ten-foot swath of land stripped down to bare soil. It's the barrier which will save the forest behind us.

Once we finish, we'll work the leading edge of the fire, following it downhill until we meet up with local firefighting support crews.

Tyler gives a grin and shoves the blade of his shovel into the soil. "Ten bucks I win."

It's a standing bet between us and I take him on. The first to clear fifty yards wins. The loser buys the first two rounds for the team. I've only lost once and might be more proud of that than wise.

"You're on, Cosmo."

He grimaces at the nickname, but says nothing. He can't, and while he's on us to change it, he knows it's a lost cause. The thing with nicknames is once bestowed they stick. I should know, not that

I mind mine. Ace is kind of a cool nickname and I prefer it to the name my mother gave me.

He got his after a particularly grueling job. It was his first with our helitack crew and Smokey bought him a drink afterward for a job well done. The bartender put his whiskey down on the bar while Tyler got distracted by a hot chick. Turned on by the smell of burnt ash and sweat, she clung to the tired Tyler, then complained about the soot on his face. Eager to seal the deal, he rushed to the bathroom to clean up.

Full of himself, and what he thought would be an easy lay, he strutted back, making a big deal of himself, and absently grabbed his drink. He tossed it back in one gulp, then spewed it back out all over the girl's slinky sequin dress. He lost the girl, claimed a name, and is now known as Cosmo amongst the guys.

We go to it, scraping burnt vegetation to expose the bare soil underneath. He moves to the left while I work along the ridge to the right. I clear nearly the full fifty yards when an irregularity catches my eye. Leaning on the handle of my shovel, I peer at the burnt ground and the odd indentations in the soot. I drop the shovel and take a closer look.

It looks like bootprints.

On top of the burn?

I radio Smokey.

"I've got something." The radio crackles and static is returned while I wait for Smokey to respond.

"What's up, Ace?"

"Bootprints." I peer at the tracks. It looks like a kid, but what would a kid be doing up here?

The allure of illegal fireworks comes to mind. My brothers and I are guilty of that. Our father tanned our hides after we lit leftover bottle rockets in the vineyards and set fire to half an acre of his prize-winning grapes.

Needless to say, that was the first and last time we ever did that.

"On my way." As lead of our team, any irregularities are his to deal with.

While waiting, I check out the area. Sure enough, the tracks point out from the hot zone. Whoever those belonged to fled the fire. There's charred matter beneath the footprints which means it was burning when this person ran.

But where are they now?

I scratch my head and follow the tracks to the edge of the ridge where they disappear. Am I following a ghost?

Smokey comes up behind me. "Hey, Ace, whatcha looking at?"

I gesture for him to follow me and take him to the tracks. "Look. They head out of the fire, while it was burning."

Smokey squats and examines the bootprints. An old-timer, he's been doing this for over twenty years. I've been fighting fires as a volunteer since I was eighteen. It's been nearly a decade and he still makes me feel like the young buck on the team. I'm not, but that's beside the point.

"Not a man." He places the span of his hand over the boot print. "I think it's a woman."

"I was thinking a teenager firing off fireworks."

"Could be, but we won't know until after the investigation. Did you see where they were headed?"

"The tracks disappear over the edge of the ridge."

He follows me to the ridge line and we peer down the rocky scree.

"What do you think?" I ask, honestly at a loss with what to do.

He's my boss. Our primary edict is the preservation of human life. The second is putting out the fire. Sadly, the third is the wildlife and forests we serve.

6

ASHER

Asher

"What do you think?" I pull at the scruff of my beard which only smears soot all over my face. It's oily and the acrid smell burns my nostrils. My breathing mask is no longer required because the wind pushes the smoke over the ridge, giving us fresh air. Fresh air, which urges the fire to race toward my mother's home.

Smoke billows back and forth, most of it blowing away from us, but the air is inherently unstable. Flames split wood with a crack. Dry tinder snaps as it pops in the heat. We work in a thick haze as the fire draws in fresh oxygen, devours it, and spits it into the air as acrid smoke. Flames down the hillside spin and whip in a vortex formed by the heated gas.

And we've lost the sun which make things ten times harder.

I spare a moment to pray my brothers are helping George prep the estate. Our mom probably gave them grief about leaving, but I'm certain they took her with them. We can rebuild her home, but we can't afford to lose her. She's too damn precious. She's also incredibly stubborn. I don't envy my brothers' task.

Smokey peers over the edge and gives a shake of his head. He doesn't like what he sees.

"Whoever it was…" He gives a sharp shake of his head. "They went over, that's for damn sure." He examines the scree. "I don't see any tracks."

"You think they ran over?" I turn to him, remembering what he said about the space between the prints. "Not up or down the trail?"

"The tracks say they went over." Smokey runs a filthy hand through his smoky-gray hair. He leans out a little, but it doesn't help. The look on his face reveals his frustration.

We don't have time for a rescue, but we'll do whatever's required to save a human life, which also means the two of us aren't supporting the fire-line.

I'm taller than him, but those few inches don't help me to make out any sign of someone climbing down.

"Maybe they headed up?" He glances over his shoulder where the trail heads further up the ridge. He's mulling through the options like me.

"How would they breathe? If the fire started here, and we have every reason to believe it did, the smoke would've been blinding— suffocating."

"Good point." He calls in a status update.

I've lost my bet with Cosmo. He's nearly finished with his second fifty yards. The rest of the team calls in with similar results. I'm the only one slacking, but it's for a good reason. There may be a life at risk. We can't ignore the possibility this person is still alive.

Smokey drops the rope coiled over his shoulder and shakes it out. He gestures over the edge. "I'll belay you. See if you can make anything out, but don't dick around. Get in and get out."

"On it." I don't need to be told twice. Getting down will be a piece of cake, but I'm not looking forward to climbing back out.

As he sets an anchor to belay me, I check my harness and loop into the rope with a figure-8 carabiner. On his signal, I head over the edge. It's steep, and while I could scrabble down, it's more efficient to rappel down the line in long, smooth bounces. I slowly place weight on the line, letting Smokey brace himself. He'll mind the line as I head down.

Ten feet down, a fresh gouge tells a horrifying story.

"Someone fell, that's for sure." I radio back to Smokey.

"What do you see?"

"Huge gouge in the scree scraped down to soil." I glance over my shoulder, making sure not to twist too far around and lose my footing. "Broken branches. Uprooted an entire bush" Several actually. "Whoever went over had a rough go of it."

I bounce down the steep slope, using my quads to push outward while letting the rope slide through my hands as I drop quickly down.

"It wasn't controlled." I keep a running commentary for Smokey's benefit.

The fall looks freakishly severe and I have the sinking suspicion I'm on a body recovery mission instead of a rescue. However, there's no body at the bottom.

"Ace, what's going on down there? I feel slack on the rope."

"Yeah, sorry. I'm at the bottom. No body." I see little in the growing gloom.

The glow of the fire on the ridge made it seem as if it's midday. With the blaze hidden by the ridge above, it's dark. I flick on my headlamp and peer around. Smoke drifts in faint curtains, wandering aimlessly down the ravine.

"I'm getting off the rope to look around." I call up to him.

"Okay, I'm going to pull it up and finish up with the others. Keep me posted, and don't waste time."

"That's the plan."

Smokey isn't happy splitting me up from the team, but it's not like we don't do that when the situation demands it. I'm in agreement about one thing. I'm not shooting the shit down here and have little interest in spending more time than required.

There's no body at the base of the slope. Whoever fell, moved away from here. I do a quick check in a wide perimeter. Bodies can bounce. Then I see an irregularity in the soil. A long scrape, as if something dragged across the soil. I bend down to investigate.

Whoever fell, survived. Unfortunately, they're on the move, but they're injured. I follow the tracks to the base of several boulders and scrunch my brows when I see a pair of boots sticking out from beneath the rocks.

I'm reminded of a scene from the Wizard of Oz, except instead of a house that dropped on a witch, I have a collection of boulders piled on top of a body. There's no way they fell on whoever this is. I pick at the rocks covering the legs and find myself impressed.

Whoever this is, they dug a trench—a fucking trench! Then covered themselves with rocks and dirt.

I give a closer look and sure enough there's a person crammed in the cleft between the rocks.

What the ever-loving fuck?

"Hello." I give the legs a little wiggle.

These hills are normally peaceful places, their quiet interrupted only by the whistling of the wind through and the incessant cicadas who buzz through the night.

Tonight, quiet is not the flavor of the day. There's no soft rustling of pine needles on a gentle breeze. No chirping of birds. No scratching in the weeds as squirrels hunt for nuts buried last fall. No cicadas droning on and on.

We're in a pressure cooker with the wind acting as the bellows to feed the fire overhead. The roar of it sounds like a freight train barreling down on us.

Whoever this is, they aren't answering and they're unresponsive to me tapping on their leg.

"Hey, boss." I call out to Smokey. "Found someone."

"Alive?"

"Unresponsive."

"Hurry up." There's strain in his voice.

"What's wrong?"

"Wind is shifting. I want us out of here. Helo is on the way."

Well, shit.

No more polite tapping.

I push the rock and dirt off whoever this is and try to drag them out. Only, that does me shit good. They're some sort of contortionist because I have no fucking clue how they wedged themselves in there.

Correction, how she got in there. My hiker is a woman. Long, blonde hair spills around her face, which happens to be completely wrapped in cloth. Wet cloth.

Wet cloth? A trench? I'm seriously impressed with her survival know-how.

But, what the hell is she doing here? And is there anyone else with her? I don't like this at all. Not with the urgency threading through Smokey's tone. Nothing riles that old man.

Nothing to do about it, I need to extricate the woman. Unresponsive, I don't know if it's from injury, asphyxiation, or smoke inhalation. That fall likely gave her a concussion.

"Hey, boss?"

"Yeah? How's it going?"

"She wedged herself between some boulders. I'm trying to get her out."

"Still unresponsive?"

"Yeah." I might wake her as I try to get her out from under the boulders. "We need medevac." I'm not getting this hiker back up that steep slope, but I can carry her out. "You want to call it in?"

"You sure?"

"Yes." I give a good long look at the thin crack she wedged herself inside.

"You get to work. We're moving down the line. I'm not happy with the winds."

"Gotcha." There's no need to ask. I know exactly what he's worried about.

I am too.

Ravines, such as this one, have a nasty habit of turning into wind tunnels. With the fire moving down below us, there's a very good chance we'll be caught inside a chimney of superheated gas.

I cut the chatter and focus on the woman. If she's unconscious due to a head injury, there's nothing I can do about that, but if it's smoke inhalation, fresh oxygen might rouse her enough so she can help me help her out from under the boulders.

My oxygen canister is fully charged. I pull it from my belt and contort my head and shoulders through the gap until I can fit the mask around her head.

"Miss." Gently, I shake her as I press the mask tight to her face. "Miss, my name is Asher La Rouge and I'm here to help." A quick check reveals she is in fact breathing.

My job is now a rescue instead of body recovery. I'll take that any day.

Her body gives a little twitch. I gently nudge her on the shoulder and repeat myself. Most people, when they come around in unfamiliar surroundings, can be quite combative. A firm, calming tone generally works wonders. I keep repeating myself, letting her know my name and my intent.

"Miss, my name is Asher La Rouge. You fell down a ravine. I'm here to help."

Her body convulses and a tiny cry escapes from her mouth. It's a sign of life, and I cheer. I press against her shoulder, and repeat myself a third time.

She comes around with a screech, drawing her arms in a defensive move to cover her face.

How the hell did she manage to survive?

It's a question I'm dying to ask, but it needs to wait. I'm very impressed by what she's done.

Very few people survive wildfires in the open.

There are a few hard and fast rules. First, create a barrier between you and the fire, something to protect yourself from radiant heat.

The heat of a wildfire easily reaches several thousand degrees. It's a death sentence for those caught out in the open, but place a few inches of rock between yourself and the flames and the deadly heat can be survivable.

After that, it's all about whether there's enough oxygen and minimizing the damaging effects of smoke inhalation.

This woman has her entire head covered in wet cloth. She's a damn survivor and I find that not only impressive, but insanely attractive.

A woman with a head on her shoulders?

How often does that happen?

I'm nearly done clearing the rock from her legs when she wakes up, bucking and screeching at the top of her lungs.

"Get off of me!" The woman turns feral, fighting me off as if I'm attacking her rather than saving her ass.

I lift my hands and back off.

"Miss...Miss!" I try to break through her panic.

She crawls further into the tiny cleft, but there's no place to go. Her panic is palpable as her breaths deepen and the pitch of her voice rises.

"Miss! I need you to calm down. I'm here to help."

My shout stills her frantic movements and I don't know if it's because she's given up, realizing there is nowhere to run, or because she realizes I'm here to help.

"My name is Asher, Asher La Rouge, I'm a member of a fire fighting crew. You fell into a ravine. I'm here to rescue you." My words are slow, measured, and project calm.

Unlike my friend, Brandon Bingham, in my job as a wildland firefighter, we rarely run into civilians. Our job is on the front lines putting out forest fires. Brandon knows how to talk to panicked civilians so he can get them out of burning buildings. This part of the job is very unfamiliar to me.

Fortunately, she stops struggling and peers up through the cleft. I remove my yellow helmet to let her see my face.

"Rescue me?" Her voice is soft, breathy, exquisitely feminine.

"Yes." I flash a grin, it's my best quality, and I hope it helps her to relax. "Are you injured? Do you need help getting out of there?" I'm still confused as to how she got in there in the first place.

"What...happened?" She's a little out of breath.

"I was hoping you could tell me." I glance up at the hill.

Did she start this fire?

Chances are good and my gut twists in anger. Too many people disrespect the wilderness, thinking they can do whatever the hell they want without regard to the consequences of their actions. She probably set the damn blaze. It's all I can do not to reach out and strangle her, but I'm a fucking professional, a veritable saint, and right now, that means I'm her savior.

The strangulation can wait until she's safe.

It's fully dark now. The thick smoke blots out the moon and stars. Up and to my left, over my shoulder, a ruddy glow fills the sky. Yellow flames dance in the churning column of smoke.

For me to see flames, they have to be shooting thirty to forty feet in the air.

Maybe more.

Our little blaze is all grown up and now qualifies as a full-scale forest fire.

My headlamp provides the only illumination down in this ravine, accentuating the shadows, making things indistinct. But I can see what's right in front of my face, in fact, I'm looking at something incredible right now, breathtaking even, as she squirms and wiggles her way free of her makeshift shelter.

"I think…" My jaw drops as the most perfect ass I've ever seen wiggles out from between the rocks.

Covered in dirt and soot, she's a mess, but what a damn fine mess she is.

More than fine. The woman is stunning.

When she removes the mask and hands it to me, silky hair spills around her shoulders in flowing golden curls, but that's nothing compared to the brilliant blue radiance of her eyes, or her full rosebud lips which I swear were made to suck dick.

Holy fuck, my mind twisted sideways fast.

I feel like a love-struck, horny, teen-aged kid who got his first look at a pair of boobs and doesn't know what to do next. Swallowing thickly, I remind myself why I'm here, and it's most definitely not for any of the fantasies spilling through my head.

Get a grip, Ace.

She struggles a little, which makes her ass wiggle. There's no avoiding it. I lean in and steady her hips, planting my hands right above where my inappropriate thoughts want to put them.

Her ass is now front and center and my dick gives a little nod of appreciation. Shit, I don't have time for this. Not now.

Out of habit, my attention shifts to her hand where I look for rings.

Score! There are none.

She slips, and I catch her, lifting her easily. She's far enough out of her little hidey-hole that I pull her free. When I place her on her feet, her left leg crumples and she cries out, clutching at me for support.

"What's wrong?" I glance down at her leg, but see no obvious injuries. This chick is scratched and bruised, looking worse for wear, but I don't see blood or broken bones.

"It's my ankle."

Her hold on my upper arm is unrelenting as she steadies herself. That brief contact is all it takes for blood to surge straight to my eager cock.

I stand stiffly, praying she doesn't look down, even though my bulky protective gear hides the woody I'm painfully sporting. I resist the urge to adjust myself and bite down as I try to get a grip. I need to focus, not gawk.

"Your ankle?" I peer down at her boots.

"I sprained it on the way down. I can't walk."

"Does that explain why you took shelter in the rocks?"

"Yeah, I didn't know what to do and there was no way I could hobble out of here. I just figured I'd hunker down and pray." She gives a sheepish grin. Her eyelids flutter as she glances down. I can't stop staring at the perfection of her face, but I remind myself I'm a professional. Not that it helps.

Every time her mouth moves, I wonder what she might taste like, or how I'd love to see her lips wrap around my very insistent cock. It's giving her the full salute.

"Not many people would have thought to do that," I say, trying to focus on the present and not the thoughts swirling in my head. "It's one of the techniques my crew is taught if we're ever caught in a fire." I'm surprised she thought of it at all.

"Honestly, I didn't know if it was worth it, but the idea of being caught out in the open wasn't top on my list." She glances over her shoulder at the boulders. "Although…I have to say…it felt like…

crawling inside an oven. I just kept thinking…I was going to get cooked in there." She's a bit breathless, which is a cause for concern.

I try to dispel some of her fear while she catches her breath. "I can definitely see that, but much better getting a little cooked in there than burnt to a crisp out here. Mind telling me how you got down here?"

"Pure panic."

Emotions march across her innocent face. Pain creases her lovely brow. Fear lingers in the down-turning of her full lips. But her eyes show grit, and the determination to survive the unthinkable.

This is no fragile thing.

She's a fighter, a survivor, and damn if that doesn't turn me on more than her perfect ass.

Maybe it's in the set of her jaw, or the firelight flickering in her eyes, but I sense the soul of a survivor. Her fierceness, more than her eloquent beauty, steals my breath.

"Panic?" I give a shake of my head to erase the spell this woman weaves over me.

"Yes. When I came to…there was fire…all around me. I didn't know what to do…and…I ran." Her voice rises in pitch. "I ran right over that cliff." She rubs at her temple and that's when I see the bruise.

"You ran over the edge?"

"Not on purpose." She props her tiny fist on her hip.

"Is that how you hit your head?"

She's scratched and bruised. Her ankle is tweaked, but she's surprisingly unharmed from her fall.

"No." She points to her temple emphatically. "That's from the rock that man used to knock me out."

"What man?"

"The one who put the rags under the bushes and started the fire."

"What?" My brows pinch together.

My radio squawks. "Ace?"

"Excuse me." I press the call button. "Got her, Smokey, but she's injured. I'm going to walk her out."

"I can't walk…" she says, but I brush aside her concerns.

"I'm headed down the ravine. Is it still clear?"

"Yeah, the blaze angles away from your position. You should be good. Bingham is bringing his chopper in to a clearing." Smokey rattles off coordinates. "Stay in contact."

"Will do." I'm going to walk her out of here. She doesn't know I'll be doing that with her strapped to my back.

"There's a clearing about a click downhill. You think you can make it?"

"That depends on this fire." I know what he said, but I respect fire and I'm not convinced we have control of the blaze.

"We're cutting firebreaks downhill as we go. You should be good." He repeats the coordinates, which I write down on my scratchboard. Familiar with the local area, I have a good idea where Smokey is sending me.

I turn to the girl.

"You ready to get out of here?"

"I told you, I can't walk."

"You're not going to walk, honey. You're going to ride me." I flash her a grin, implying the double entendre and search her expression for any interest.

She stares at me, then her eyes widen when it hits. Taking a step back, she cries out as she inadvertently places weight on her bad foot.

I reach for her. "Easy! I've got you."

But she jerks out of my grip.

I don't have time for this shit and pinch the bridge of my nose. After signing out with Smokey, I grab the length of rope strapped to the webbing at my belt.

"I mean, I'll carry you on my back—like a backpack."

7

EVELYN

EITHER FROM THE ROCK THAT ASSHOLE HIT ME IN THE HEAD WITH, or from smacking my head on the way down the hill, I'm pretty sure I'm hallucinating. Or maybe the universe is apologizing for dealing me such a shit hand lately.

Naw, I'm delirious.

I must be, because my rescuer is drop dead gorgeous. Kitted out in firefighter gear, soot smears across his face, dirt clings to every square inch of him, a yellow helmet sits on top his head, and all I can do is stare, slack jawed, eyes wide, with a flutter in my belly, and licks of pleasure tickling me in my lady bits.

I'm serious.

Nobody looks this good.

He's every woman's wet dream, or mine at least if that tingling between my legs is any indication.

When I go to bed, hoping for a little nighttime fantasy, he's what I imagine. A man with mussed up hair, the darker the better, raven-colored is best, and arresting forest green eyes that steal my breath. His eyes are so vividly green they practically glow.

They're mesmerizing.

I lick my lips for what feels like the millionth time, because I'm terribly afraid I'm drooling. He's sexy in so many ways, and I'm not even going to start with the whole rough and rugged, Hey-I'm-your-rescuer obvious kind of crap.

Hell, he can rescue me all damn day.

It's not that he's perfect. The man has flaws, but it's in the grit of his perfection where he shines. Every time he looks at me, those magnetic eyes pin me down. He said something about riding him and my mind went to the filthiest place. I'm so far down the gutter, there's no escape.

Fortunately, he appears to be oblivious to my gaping mouth as he measures out his rope.

Or is he?

I swear my rugged stranger's oh-so-expressive face transforms into an impish grin.

And he has dimples.

Just kill me now.

I bet he knows I imagined riding him just like he said.

I'm a total fool and acting like a star-struck teen, not caring we're in the middle of a raging inferno. I'm ready to climb his towering form, wrap my legs around his hips, and ride him through dawn.

Holy mother of God, it just got hot down here, and I'm a little out of breath.

Actually, I'm a lot out of breath. I can't breathe deeply enough and I'm a bit dizzy.

"Hello?" He snaps his fingers in front of my face.

"Excuse me?"

"I asked what your name was?"

I totally missed his question.

My cheeks heat with a sudden flush of shame.

"Um..."

"Um...you don't know your name? Or um...you got knocked in the head and don't understand me?" Amusement fills his voice and he flashes a cocky smirk. He's having too much fun with me, and damn if I don't love it.

All I'm thinking about is knocking boots with this gorgeous firefighter, climbing his towering frame, and yes, I'm thinking about riding him.

In my defense, his words blindside me, but nowhere near as much as the fact he looks like he means exactly what he said. Not the getting knocked on the head bit, but rather the thing about me riding him. I'm still a little confused how that's going to happen.

I can't see him slinging me over his shoulder in a fireman's carry and walking any distance in this rough terrain. Carrying me in his arms isn't feasible, not for the distance he'll need to walk. I don't care how bulky those biceps of his look; no man can carry that much weight that far. Not that I weigh a lot.

His soft laugh is arresting. "Cat got your tongue?"

"Sorry. I'm a bit—overwhelmed. My name is Evie, um Evelyn Thornton." I close my eyes and let my hair cover my face. I'm embarrassed by how awkward I'm acting.

He shoves out his hand. I take it hesitantly then give a little jerk at the spark of electricity jolting through my body.

There's too much of this man to process. He's tall, broad-shouldered, and muscular. He might be wearing bulky firefighting gear, but there's no denying what lies beneath.

My fingers itch to explore the skin beneath his gear. I want to walk my fingers all along the six-pack abs I know he's hiding and dance along his pecs. Add in his chiseled jaw and those penetrating, mesmerizing, arresting eyes? Shit, I'm staring, again.

Am I drooling?

God, I hope not.

"Well, it's nice to meet you. Like I said, my name is Asher, although my friends call me Ace."

"Ace?"

"Yeah." He gives a shake of his head, and there's something about the roguish look in his eyes, like he's teasing me, testing me, maybe trying to see if I'm interested? Well, I am, even if I'm too awestruck to do anything other than act like a fool. "Anyway, it's an old nickname. You can call me Asher, if you want."

"It's nice to meet you, Asher."

"Likewise, it's nice to meet you, Evelyn." The way he says my name, as if he's tasting each syllable, is sexy as fuck. He gives a sharp nod, as if coming to some decision. "That's a pretty name, Ev-e-lyn."

My heart about stops. I'm not sure why I keep blushing. Maybe it's the way he looks at me, like he sees right through me, but I dip my head and stammer. "Uh, thanks."

The whole time, he runs a length of rope through his hands, finding the midpoint. He points at my waist.

"Now, as for the riding part." His wink is arresting, as in heart-stopping, breath-taking, full cardiac arrest arresting. I bet he gives great mouth-to-mouth. "First, I need to tie you up." His eyes crinkle with that comment, and I have a sinking suspicion I'm not the first woman he's ever tied up.

"Um, what did you say?"

"Tie you up." He gives a soft laugh. "Not the fun stuff, but I need to tie a harness around you."

"A what?"

"It's called a Swiss Seat, and it'll let me secure you to my back. You know, for the getting out of the forest fire part of our journey."

Ah! My eyes widen when I realize what he intends. I've only recently learned about bouldering and climbing. I'm not into rock climbing, but I met several hikers on the trails that were. They had fancy harnesses, kind of like the one Asher wears. I like the way the canvas straps mold around his groin, suggesting more impressiveness for a girl lucky enough to get him out of his clothes.

But how is he going to make a harness out of a length of rope?

"Did I hear you right? You're going to carry me on your back?"

"I did. How else are we getting you out of here?"

"You can't carry me."

"I'm pretty sure I can." He sounds a little offended.

No, he's not offended. That cocky grin of his makes another appearance. He's having fun with me.

"I'm not doubting your strength, just… Carry me?"

"It works really well. I tie a harness around you, then secure you to my back. You'll be wrapped tight against me, so your bodyweight doesn't shift. It lets me move freely, like carrying a backpack."

"Great, I'm a backpack."

"Or a cling-on."

"A what?"

"Never mind." He glances up at the ridge and his lips twist. "We should probably get a move on. This isn't the best place to be with a fire raging over our heads, and if the winds shift…"

"I don't want to think about the winds shifting. Did you know ravines like this can act as a chimney?" Why do I say that?

He arches a brow and gives me a look like I'm stupid.

"I may know a little bit about wildfires, hun."

"Sorry. I didn't mean…"

"It's okay, I'm teasing, and you're right about ravines." He lifts up the rope. "So, about this Swiss Seat thing, just let me do all the work. I'm going to have to touch you around your waist and legs. I'm a professional, so no worries, right?"

Knowing what little I do about harnesses, I understand what he means.

He averts his gaze and his attention drops to my waist. I wobble a little. I've been standing on my one good foot for too long, and the muscles in that leg are beginning to protest. I try to take some of the weight off my good foot, but the slight pressure on my twisted ankle makes me grab for the nearest support. That happens to be Asher's arm and there's no longer any doubt about his ability to carry me.

Holy hard muscles alert. This man is stacked.

He takes the midpoint of the rope and places it at the center of my waist.

"Here, hold this for me please."

Before I realize what's happening, he crouches before me, which places his face eye level with my private parts, right where all those delicious fantasies want his face to be. I bite my lower lip and stare up at the sky. There's nothing to see except the amorphous haze of smoke. No moon. No stars. No nothing.

But there's lots to hear. A dull roar. The popping of wood as the flames consume the dry tinder. The whistling of wind as it's drawn into the blaze. I hear nothing else, except for my ragged breathing.

Asher's hands work the rope. He wraps it around my back, crosses the ends and brings the rope back to center. His nose is inches from my belly. I hold the center of the rope while he ties an intricate knot. Then I practically levitate when he passes his hands between my legs, moving efficiently, brusquely, and practically touches my most intimate parts.

He avoids putting his hands on me, unnecessarily. Despite the intimate contact, he remains a consummate professional. Although, if he wanted to cop a feel, there would be nothing I could do to stop him.

But he doesn't touch me that way. He does only what's necessary to rig the Swiss Seat, but that damn rope drags between my legs as he draws it up to my back and I have to bite my lower lip because this is easily the most sensual experience I've ever experienced.

He makes quick work of the rope. I dare to look down and give a little gasp at the intricate harness he constructed around my legs and waist.

"You ready to ride me?" He presses on his knees and stands to his full height. We're close, like if I take a deep breath, the tips of my nipples will drag against his chest.

"Um…" I can't help but nibble at my lower lip. "Does that line work on all the girls, or just those who fall in a ravine in the middle of a forest fire?"

He gives a low, throaty chuckle. "Naw, my pick-up lines are much better than that." He twists around and takes a knee. "Now bend over…"

I swear this man is going to be the death of me. He ties me in rope, then tells me to bend over? How is this not every woman's fantasy?

"Wrap your arms around my neck, but not too tight. Once I have you secured, you won't have to hold on at all."

"I've never been tied up before."

He laughs. "Do you like it?"

"Hmm," I tease. "It's a little scratchy."

"We'll use a different kind of rope later. Right now, do as you're told. Wrap your arms around my neck and lean against my back. I need to secure you to my harness so we can get out of here."

"And what about my legs? Do I wrap those around you too?"

"You'll see." He gives another low laugh. "How about you stop distracting me and let me work?"

He does something with the loose ends of rope, knotting them into the harness he wears. Without a word, he stands, and I give a little screech as my world tilts. I grab at his neck and he gives a choked sound. Then he peels my hands from around his throat.

"Seriously, you don't have to hang on. In fact, it'll make it much easier to breathe if you're not crushing my windpipe."

"Sorry." Then I realize what he's done with the rope.

My legs wrap around his hips, but not because I'm doing anything. He's somehow rigged the Swiss Seat so it holds all my weight. I'm literally strapped to his body. I try it out and release his neck. My expectation is that I'll tumble off his back, but I'm surprised how secure and steady I feel.

"I'm a backpack!"

"Oh, you're much more than a backpack. How about we get out of here?"

I gesture down the ravine. "Home, James!"

His body stiffens. "James?"

"It's a joke."

"Hmm."

"Mush!" I give a little kick of my feet, trying to spur him forward.

He twists his neck and gives me a disparaging look.

"Giddy up?"

"Quiet, little backpack." Hooking his arms around my legs, he shifts me to a better position and tightens the ropes. I give a little screech as the rope digs into my butt. "That's better."

"Better? It's a little...um, tight."

"All the better to tie you to me, the tighter the better."

My heart about gives out.

"How about you tell me what happened," he says, "while I figure out how to get you to the medivac helicopter."

"The what?" His words sink in. "I don't need that."

"You were knocked out. Whether from a concussion, or smoke inhalation, or both, you need to be checked out by a doctor."

"I hate doctors."

"And I hate forest fires, but we do what we need to do."

With that, Asher is off.

He sets a grueling pace, half jogging, half walking, down the ravine. The light of his headlamp shows the way, and after a few minutes all I hear is the chugging of his breath.

The contraption he fit me in does a surprisingly great job of keeping me steady. Occasionally, he wraps his hands around my legs, but for the most part, he appears oblivious to the fact I'm on his back.

Despite the rugged terrain, I'm not concerned about falling, or whether the shifting of my body will off-balance him. The man is a machine, muscles powering through the climb out of the hills. For me, it would be a challenging hike. For him, it's effortless.

Every now and then, his radio squawks and he answers. Smokey, who I assume is his crew boss, gives updates on the fire. It's spilling downhill and growing. An orange glow lights up the night sky, but in the ravine, we're left in darkness and shadow.

When the ravine opens up, we travel faster. Asher lopes into a run, unaffected by the burden he carries.

I keep silent, not wanting to break his intense concentration. I'm fully aware he's running with a hundred and twenty pounds strapped to his back. The trees thin and we enter a clearing where a waiting helicopter sits on the ground.

A man with a flight helmet lifts his hand over his head and calls out. "Hey, Ace! Took your damn sweet time."

"Fuck off, Bradley." Asher comes to a stop and lowers himself to a knee. Without preamble, he works to free the knots. Looking over his shoulder, he speaks to me for the first time since we set off. "Steady yourself on my shoulder and put your good foot down. Bradley's team will help you from here."

"You're—not—coming?" I've done nothing but ride Asher, so why am I the one out of breath? As for Bradley's team, I don't know these people, and while I don't know Asher either, we share a connection. I know I'm not making that up.

"Sorry, little backpack, I need to get back to my crew."

"You're rejoining them?" I glance up the hill where the blaze is easy to see. We traveled so far. He's got at least a mile, or two, hike to get back up there. I feel guilty wanting to keep him with me. I understand he has a job to do, but I feel safer with him by my side.

The pilot saunters over with his team. They've broken out a gurney and set it next to the helicopter. Two of them come to me and help to steady me while Asher finishes untying me.

"Only you would go in to a fire and come out with a woman on your back." The pilot flashes a wide smile. The flight helmet covers most of his face, but I can tell he's arrestingly handsome as well. It makes me wonder what they have in the water around these parts. Are all the men insanely gorgeous?

"Watch it, Bradley," Asher says, a low warning tone in his voice, but it's not real. I sense these men are friends.

The pilot shifts his attention to me. "Name's Bradley Bingham and I'll be your ride from here on out, although my helicopter may not be as exciting as getting strapped to Ace's back here."

"I'm warning you." Asher finally releases me and quickly turns around to lift me to my good foot.

Bingham's team is on me, touching me, pulling me away from Asher. He seems unwilling to let me go, but Bingham's team takes over.

They bombard me with questions, shine lights in my eyes, and do a quick pat down of my body. One of them puts something on my index finger. It glows red.

All I want is to push them away and return to Asher, but I understand they have a job to do.

When one of them lifts my arm to sling around his shoulder, Asher gives a sharp shake of his head. The world tilts again, but this time, I'm cradled in his arms.

"Just a little further, my little backpack, and don't mind Bradley. He thinks he's a hotshot because he flies a helicopter. Just ignore him." Asher makes a point of bumping Bradley's shoulder as he walks past.

"Damn it, Ace, possessive much?" Bradley flashes Asher a megawatt smile and gives me a wink.

"Hands off." That sounds like a warning. "You do your job, and I'll do mine."

"I see." Bradley gives me a long hard look. "Seems like you're doing a damn good job of it too."

Asher deposits me on the waiting gurney while Bradley's team tell me to lay back. One of them straps me in while another wraps a blood pressure cuff around my arm. He glances at a display and his lips twist. Whatever it is, he doesn't like what he sees.

They ask questions about my injuries and I tell them what I can in between breaths. I mention the man who hit me with the rock, how I was unconscious for some time before waking up to the flames. One of them purses his lips and asks for an oxygen mask. While he puts it over my face, I watch Asher with his friend and can't help but hope they're talking about me.

Next I know, I'm being loaded inside the helicopter. Asher and Bradley thump each other on the back. That's when I realize Asher is going to leave without saying goodbye and for some reason that hurts more than it should.

I try to wipe away a tear, but it's hard with the way I'm strapped down. It seems I was nothing other than a backpack to him, a burden to be delivered and discarded.

I hate being helpless, and I hate that Prescott is right. It's not safe out here for a woman. I think that, more than anything else, is what makes the tears fall.

Something rough presses against my cheek.

"Don't cry, Ev-e-lyn."

I open my eyes and blink to clear the tears. Asher looks down on me, concern and something else, scrawled on his face.

"You're going to be okay." Somehow, with his promise, I believe I just might be.

"Thank you…for…rescuing me." It's challenging to speak, but I huff out the words.

He gives a cheeky grin. "Definitely, the best part of my day. Bradley is going to take real good care of you, and I'll come check in on you later, right now…"

"You have a job to do." I lift my hand and wrap my fingers around his powerful bicep. "I hope you find the asshole who started it."

"We will." Asher's brows pinch together and he wipes another tear from my cheek.

Those are the last words I hear before he jumps out of the helicopter and moves a safe distance away. The whine of the rotors spin up and the helicopter cants forward as it slowly rises out of the clearing. Asher stands below us and waves as the helicopter spins around and heads down into the valley.

When we bank into a turn, I gasp as the full enormity of the fire becomes apparent.

A living thing, it spills down the hills, pushed by the wind, eagerly consuming the dry brush. It's headed straight to the valley floor where the twinkling lights of hundreds of homes stave off the darkness.

Hundreds of homes which are now at risk.

8

EVELYN

There's a soft knock on the door of my hospital room.

"Yes?" My words are soft, cautious, maybe a little hopeful. The doctors and nurses don't knock.

Nobody in this town knows me, except for one person; a man I can't stop thinking about.

Thoughts of Asher La Rouge invade my dreams, fill nearly every waking thought, and storm around my body stirring up sensations I have no right to feel.

I don't know the man, yet I ache desperately for him.

It's unsettling, because I shouldn't be aching for anyone. Granted, it's been well over a year, yet I still feel like I should be mourning Justin's death.

Ah, but Asher?

He makes me want to stop running and soak in the feelings I thought I'd have again.

That knock is probably Prescott. He has the resources to discover what's going on, and he wouldn't think twice about flying across the continent to be with me where he can smother me and assume the role my father left vacant, or the role he would have assumed if life didn't have other plans.

My stomach twists as grief rips apart wounds which never seem to heal.

"Ev-e-lyn?"

The low, throaty way my name is enunciated sends shivers down my spine. The fine hairs of my arms lift.

"May I come in?" That voice belongs to a man I never thought I'd see again, but hoped I would.

"Asher?"

My boring hospital room seems to shrink as he steps inside. There's simply too much of him to take in.

Damn, the man cleans up fine. If I had any doubts about his looks, they disappear the moment Asher La Rouge, decked out in a pair of denim jeans hugging him in all the right places, enters into my lonely hospital room.

His poor tee-shirt is losing the struggle to contain his muscles. Scrawled across the front is a graphic of a grape leaf and a cask of wine which displays La Rouge Vineyards in flowing script. My mouth dries up when he spreads his arms wide, like he's happy to see me.

"How's my little backpack doing?"

"Getting better every day." I speak the truth. "I passed out in the helicopter. They said I had smoke inhalation. I guess it did a number on my lungs."

"Smoke can do that." He gives a solemn nod. "I'm glad you're doing better. You had a rough go the first couple of days."

"Really?"

"Yeah, you were in intensive care." He lowers his voice. "I tried to visit, but they wouldn't let me see you."

"You visited me?"

"Tried too. I wanted to see how you were doing."

"Wow, that's really sweet." But did he try to visit me because he wanted to see me, or was he simply checking up on his little rescue? I hate to think I'm a charity case.

"You were kind of in and out of it, and a combative little freak. You gave your nurses a run for their money."

He leans against the wall and his gaze sweeps me from head to toe. Something simmers in his eyes, but I'm not sure I want to assign any importance to it. I don't think I'm brave enough to hope it means what I want it to mean.

There's heat burning in that gaze, a hunger ravenous to be fed. I've never had a man look at me like that before. It makes me wriggle a little in the bed.

Asher is a man who challenges me. That excites me more than it scares me. The challenge lies in those eyes and the message they're sending. It's in the casual way he occupies my room as if he belongs there, as if I want him there.

Which I do.

Except, I'm not supposed to be interested in getting close to anyone, or at least that's the lie I hang on to. My grief runs too deep. It's still raw, ugly, and a tragic mess, but hell if my animal brain doesn't ignore all of that.

The rational side of my brain tries to feed caution to the animalistic part and it's not liking it one bit. In fact, it's spitting all that caution back out at me, telling me to ignore all the reasons for turning Asher away, and simply accept the inevitable.

The inevitable?

What exactly do I think is going to happen here?

I scoot up in bed and straighten the sheets after doing a quick check of my hospital gown. His lusty gaze sees right through the mess of my clothes, or lack thereof. I'm ashamed of my makeup-less face, but it's like he doesn't care. His simmering look promises to fulfill all the fantasies I've let run wild while trying not to go crazy in this hospital bed.

I take stock of my attire. Everything's covered by a hospital gown. The fabric is thin and my body is primed and reacting to his presence. My nipples practically poke through the see-through fabric.

"My memory is a bit foggy." I hate admitting it, but it's the truth. He mentioned intensive care but I have no memory of that. "How bad was I?"

"What do you remember?" He sounds concerned.

"Not much actually. You rescued me, strapped me to your back like a backpack, carried me out. There was a helicopter, then nothing. I woke up with a mask covering my face."

"It's called bi-pap."

"Bi-what?"

"It's a form of assisted breathing. Fortunately, you didn't require intubation and a ventilator. I was concerned when I found you. You couldn't finish sentences and were out of breath. Not to mention you were unconscious in your little hidey-hole. How much do you remember from that night?"

More than I should, like how insanely hot my rescuer was.

How my body responded to his touch like a feral house cat in heat and desperate for attention.

How I wanted to climb his towering frame and rub myself up against him.

Then there were his eyes and the way they stole my breath.

Most importantly, and most damaging, was how I didn't feel guilty about any of it.

"I guess the smoke did a number on my lungs," I say. "I didn't realize I was in that much trouble."

"Smoke and other gases in a fire can be very dangerous, but I'm told you'll make a full recovery."

I give a nervous laugh. "Thank goodness for adrenaline, right? It's amazing what it does for a body."

I'm not really sure why I say this, except I'm dumbstruck by the man standing before me and I'll spit anything out to keep from staring at him with my mouth open, drool spilling out, and looking like a damn fool.

"And of course, I have you to thank for my rescue."

"Well, it's a part of my job." His deep tenor vibrates the air and does strange things to my body.

I still can't believe he's here. Asher leans against the wall of my hospital room, arms casually crossed over the expanse of his chest, biceps bulging, and that charismatic smirk lifting the corners of his lips.

He came to check on me.

This makes me ridiculously happy.

I feel like giving a little shout, or pump my fist in victory.

When that helicopter took off, I didn't think I'd ever see him again, but here he is, all six-foot-sexy of his imposing self. I bet he makes girls stupid and their panties drop with one well-placed smile. He definitely has that effect on me.

I'm a little uncomfortable in the thin hospital gown and very aware I'm naked underneath it. My clothes are shoved in a plastic bag and sit in the bottom of the tiny cupboard the staff gave me to store my things. As for the rest of my worldly possessions? They went up in smoke.

I literally am down to only the burnt clothes on my back, or rather, shoved into a plastic bag.

"Does it hurt?" His attention focuses on the bandages covering my forearms, reminding me of the burns. I didn't make it out of the fire completely unscathed.

"Nothing major." Bandages cover my arms where the flames licked a little too close. "It's not as bad as it looks. Second degree burns, but they should heal without scaring." I point to my ankle. "Even my ankle is getting better."

I parrot back what my doctors told me. The wound care nurse who came around knows what she's doing and I trust her knowledge. She said the same thing as the doctors. My injuries aren't extensive enough to land me in a burn unit, which I'm thankful for. Things could be much worse.

"That's good to hear." His attention shifts from my arms back to my face, but not before sweeping across the expanse of my chest. I give a little look down, then hunch my shoulders inward. My nipples stand loud and proud, practically announcing the dirty thoughts swirling in my head.

"I'm hoping they'll release me soon." I focus on the mundane. Not that it matters. He knows.

I see it in his eyes.

"What then?" He glances out the window and squints like he doesn't care about my answer, but the tension thrumming in his body says otherwise. He's hanging on my every word.

I give a little shrug. "I'm not sure."

"You're off the bi-pap, but still on the cannula. You sure they'll be releasing you soon?" His brows pinch with concern.

My hand lifts to the plastic tubing which wraps around my head and sits along my upper lip. Two tiny prongs fit inside my nostrils. I forgot it was there until he brought it up.

Now, I feel incredibly self-conscious, and it's not because my nipples are peaked and aroused.

"I must look like such a mess."

It's been days since I've showered and I'm not winning any beauty pageants in a threadbare hospital gown and bare face. We're not even going to mention the rat's nest of my hair.

"A beautiful mess, little backpack." He gives a shake of his head and kicks off the wall. Two steps bring him close and he sits on the side of the bed near my knees. "Women worry too much about how they look."

"Appearances matter." I run my fingers through my hair, pulling the tangles free.

"Looks don't mean much to me."

"If your next words are to tell me I have a great personality, I'm going to punch you."

"Is that so?" His eyes twinkle, twin flashes of green which melt my heart. "Do you have a great personality?"

He's teasing and it relaxes me.

I forget to be self-conscious about how I look.

"You're insufferable," I say, but damn if I don't love the way he looks at me, like I'm the only thing worth looking at. I feel beautiful in his eyes, and that's saying something considering I haven't had a shower in nearly a week.

"I aim to please, but let me set the record straight. Even in the most hideous patient gown, you are one of the most stunningly beautiful, heart-stoppingly gorgeous women I've ever had the pleasure of carrying on my back out of a forest fire. As for your personality? Jury's still out on that."

I laugh. "That's so much worse."

"How is that worse?"

"How many women have you carried out of a fire before?"

"You're my first."

"So…I'm also the least beautiful woman you've carried out of a forest fire."

"You can twist that any way you want, but you're far from ugly. If I said you were fine on the eye you'd probably be ripping me a new asshole for being focused only on your looks. If I tell you you're sweet, or have a nice personality, you'll say I called you ugly. It's a no win situation for me."

"For the record, I'm not one of those."

"One of those, what?"

"Militant feminists."

"Your words." He held up his hands. "Not mine."

"Well, how about this? Thank you for the compliment. I appreciate it very much, even as I sit here in the world's most unappealing hospital gown and haven't showered or washed my hair in days. I don't mind compliments and, for what it's worth, my brand of feminism is a bit old-fashioned."

"So, you admit you're a feminist?"

"You say that like it's a bad word, but I am. I believe men should be gentlemen and women should be ladies. If you've got height and muscles, I expect you to lift the heavy things and get stuff off the tall shelves for me. I like when a man opens a door, holds out a chair, and scoots me close to the table. I even like the tiny, possessive hand to the small of my back, or the way a confident man will guide me through a room. I'm an old-fashioned feminist because I like men with manners who respect women and aren't afraid to treat them like women."

"Good to know."

I give a sharp shake of my head, not really sure where that little speech came from.

Why the hell did I tell him all of that?

Because you want him to do all those things for you.

"And Asher…"

"Yes?"

"Thank you for helping me. I really appreciate everything you did for me, and the risks you take to keep us regular people safe. I'll never be able to repay you."

"Ah, you're so sweet. Look at that personality shine."

"Ass! I'm trying to compliment you and say thanks."

He gives a little chuckle, then fixes me with an intense stare. "Honestly, it was my pleasure. I'm happy I was able to help."

"What happened with the fire? Is it out? Still burning?"

"It burned for a few days, but we were able to get it under control. They're investigating now."

"Investigating?"

"Standard procedure. Nothing to worry about."

"I'm not worried, but no one's talked to me about the man who hit me upside the head. I took pictures of him, although my phone is probably an unsalvageable wreck. I lost everything in that fire."

He glances away and picks at the sheet over my knee. "I'm really glad you're doing better, Evelyn. Do you prefer Evelyn or Evie?"

"Either one. Evie is what I was called as a kid."

"Well, you're not a kid anymore."

"No, I'm not. What about you? Do you prefer Asher or Ace?"

"Everyone around here calls me Ace. It's a nickname I can't escape. I like it when you call me Asher. You're the only one who does and that makes it special, like kind of our thing."

Our thing?

There's an us.

He just admitted it.

I'm not really sure what to say about that. I didn't realize we had a thing, but I'm giving myself a mental fist bump. He's been thinking about me, which means it's not just me.

I point to his shirt. "I'm a little confused. Are you a firefighter or a wine maker?"

"Both, and a bit of a rancher, I guess. Although that makes me think of cattle and I don't have those. I have a herd of plodding mares."

"So you're a fire fighting, cowboy, vintner?"

"I suppose so." He shrugs. "How about a man of many talents?"

My brows pinch together because I'm not sure if he's teasing me. "So, firefighter, wine-maker, and rancher? How does all that work?"

"Volunteer firefighter. It's not my main job. The family business is the winery. I run it with my brothers, and we operate a trail riding business on the side. I have twenty mares who love walking the forest trails behind our vineyard, but only at their slow, plodding pace, which is perfect for the tourists."

"How do you find time to do all of that and pull people from burning buildings?"

"I'm not that kind of firefighter. I'm on a helitack crew."

"Hell-a-what? What's that?"

"Helitack. We're first responders to wildfires. That's what I do. Forest fires, brush fires. Wildland fires are my specialty. I'm not one of those firemen with a pole, a shiny red truck, and a Dalmatian called Spot."

"Explain helitack. I've never heard of that, and is 'wildland' a real word?"

"Yeah, it's a real word, and a helitack crew are kind of like hotshots, everyone's heard of those, but instead of parachuting into remote wilderness areas to put out forest fires, we rappel out of helicopters. Similar but different, and the focus is on forest fires not civilian fires. Does that make sense?"

"It sounds intense. I guess every profession has its specialists."

"I suppose we do. One of my best friends is a firefighter. He's the one who got me started in volunteering. You met his brother."

"I did?"

"Yeah, Bradley's the medivac pilot who brought you here."

"Wow, a pilot and firefighter in one family. Their mom must be proud."

"Yeah, Mrs. Bingham is something special." He gives a soft laugh. "Their older brother is a cop, so yeah. They're a family of everyday heroes. I'm good friends with Brandon. He's the youngest and the firefighter. His brothers are a bit older. They're good guys, solid, you know."

"I bet your mom is proud of you." I'm not as interested in his friends as I am in what makes Asher tick.

"I'm her favorite." He gives a wink.

"You said you have brothers. Any sisters?"

"No sisters. Two brothers, both younger, and they're a pain in my ass." He places a strange emphasis on the word 'younger'. "What about you?"

My stomach seizes with the question I should've seen coming. I deflect. I'm getting too damn good at it.

"I really can't thank you enough for what you did for me. If you hadn't—"

"But I did, so we don't need to go into what might, or might not, have happened."

"Fair enough." I give him a soft smile. "Thanks."

If he hadn't found me, I would be dead and Prescott would be beside himself with the mess I would've left behind.

Shit. I need to give him a call. He and Gracie are probably worried sick I haven't checked in.

"I'm glad you're doing better." He shifts a little closer and reaches for my hand, but then he draws back at the bandages.

Which sucks.

I want to see if that electric shock is still there, or if my oxygen-starved brain imagined that sizzling connection.

"I appreciate it."

"And, I wanted to see if there was anything you needed? Anyone you need to call? A husband?" He pauses and watches the hitch in my breath.

"No husband."

"Boyfriend?"

I'm careful with my words. "No, no boyfriend." There's no husband because my fiancé never made it to the alter.

"Good to know."

"Why?"

"They said there's nothing in your personal effects to identify you. I gave them your name, but I think you're officially listed as a Jane Doe. You're a bit of a mystery. Not sure how much help you want, but I can get a few things from your home. Since you've ridden me, I'm no longer a stranger, right?"

"Right." It's too easy to agree with him. No longer a stranger? "I'm not from around here."

"Oh." The corners of his mouth turn down. "Is there someone I can call?" He gives a long hard look at the hospital gown. "How about clothes? While you're rocking the hot patient look, it might not be the best thing to wear around town when I take you out." He's trying to lighten the mood, but it only reminds me of everything I've lost.

"Actually…" I need to call Prescott, sort out my life, and pay for this hospitalization. I'll need to buy new things. "I guess I need a little help."

Everything I had burned in the wildfire. I'm a little worried about my revolver. California gun laws are strict and I may have been skirting the spirit of the law carrying it, loaded, on my person. It's not in the bag of my stuff shoved in the cupboard, which means, it's still up there.

Did that man take it? I'm a little worried about how to handle that. Of course, my phone is somewhere up there with the selfies I took. Unlike my gun, which can survive a forest fire, I'm pretty sure my phone is a melted mess.

Well, this is one way to cut all ties to my previous life, burn it all to ash. Except—there's always an except—the whole heiress thing still needs to be dealt with.

"Can I borrow your phone?" I hate imposing on him, but he's offering.

He stands and fishes it out of his pocket, then hands it to me after taking off the screen lock. When I hold it to my chest and stare at him, he clears his throat.

"Oh, um, I'll just wait outside."

"Thanks. I really appreciate it."

After Asher leaves, I close my eyes and try to remember Prescott's number. Fortunately, it comes to me and I dial before the screen lock reactivates and I need to call Asher back in.

Prescott picks up on the first ring. .

"Hey there."

"Evie! What number is this? I don't recognize it. We've been worried about you."

"You have?" Prescott will never stop worrying about me.

"We heard there were fires in wine country."

"Um, yeah."

"Gracie was checking the news and saw reports about a major forest fire near Napa. Isn't that where you're hiking?"

More like ground zero.

"Um yeah, about that." I don't want to tell him all his fears turned out to be true, so I hedge.

"What about it?" His voice deepens. "How close were you?"

"It's kind of a long story, and I need a little help." It's not like me to ask for help. Of course, he jumps all over it.

"Help? What kind of help?" He's anxious, and overly eager.

All Prescott wants is to help his best friend's only daughter get back on her feet. While I appreciate his enthusiasm, Prescott will never see me as anything but a little kid. He doesn't understand I'm a grown-ass woman who can take care of herself.

Look what a great job I'm doing. A man attacked me, set fire to the forest, and left me for dead.

I deserve a good chewing out, but I'm still running from my past and I'm in deep denial about pretty much everything. Too bad for me, I'm not the kind of person to lie.

It's time to come clean.

"I was kind of in that fire." I pull my shoulders to my ears, expecting him to blow up, but there's only silence on the other end of the line. "Did you hear me?"

"Hang on, Evie."

Deep sighs come from his end of the call and muffled voices which I barely make out.

Gracie is in some kind of hysterics. I guess she's listening in. Prescott's trying to calm her down. He's got the phone covered with his hand rather than placing it on mute like a sane person, but he's old school like that.

"Prescott? Did you hear what I said?"

"I did." Strain fills his voice and I can tell he's holding back a choice string of expletives and unsolicited fatherly advice.

He's not my father.

We both know this, even if he keeps trying to fill those shoes.

"I'm safe. I'm in a hospital." I try to reassure him.

A hospital! Gracie's shriek rings through the speakers. She's in a hospital. Give me the phone. If you're not going to talk some sense into that girl, then I will.

Calm down, Gracie. I'll handle this.

His sharp tone makes me cringe. I've never heard him speak to Gracie that way.

"Where are you?"

I rattle off the name of the hospital. "But you don't need to come, I just need—"

"I'm booking a plane now."

He wants to help, and I'd love to let him, but I need my space. Prescott reminds me of everything I lost.

"I appreciate it. I really do, and I know you care about me, but I'm good. I just need…" Everything. "If you could just get my credit cards reissued. I'll figure out my IDs."

"Evie, I wish you'd let us help. You don't have to go through this alone."

But I am alone.

"I know, and I'm incredibly grateful for all your help."

His sigh is deafening, full of all the things he wants to say, but won't. Or can't. He wants to tell me it's not my fault. That there was nothing I could've done. That I shouldn't feel guilty for surviving the unthinkable when everyone else died. I hear it in the deep pull of his breath, but we've had this conversation a hundred times and it doesn't help.

"Fine. I'll make the calls. Where do you want me to send them?"

Well, shit. I didn't think that through. I can't send them to the hospital.

"Hang on." Unlike Prescott, I hit the mute button. "Asher?"

He pokes his head inside my room. "You called?" The way his eyes spark shouldn't be legal, but they flicker and flash and steal my breath.

"I kind of need a favor."

"Real-ly?" He drags out the syllables and saunters into my room. "Are you asking for help?"

"Are you going to make me beg?"

"Depends. What kind of begging are we talking about? Because something fun comes to mind."

I want to smile, but I'm trying to be serious. His innuendoes are harmless enough, kind of, but what would he do if I bit and gave a little nibble?

"You're smiling and I want to know why?"

"It's nothing." No way in hell am I telling him what I was thinking about nibbling.

"Didn't look like nothing." He crosses his arms and stares down at me.

The man is simply too much to take in. I'm back to thinking about climbing his body and going for that ride he promised, the one that may, or may not, involve rope, and most definitely doesn't involve clothes.

"Well, it was." It totally wasn't, but I'm keeping Prescott on hold. "I need to send replacement copies of my credit cards, insurance cards, you know all the things which burned?"

"Yes?"

"And, I don't have a place to send them to." I'm very aware I barely know this man, but he did save my life, and he did take time away from wine and horses to visit me. I give a little nibble of my lower lip and look up at him. "So, what do you say? Wanna help a girl out? Pretty please?"

He said he wanted me to beg. I'm batting my lashes, nibbling on my lip, and staring up at him with what I hope is my best innocent, doe-eyed expression.

"Damn but you're good at that." He turns around and rubs his hand through his hair. "What's it worth to you?"

"You want me to pay?" I'm not sure if I'm supposed to be offended or if we're still playing a game. If we're playing a game, I have no idea what the rules might be.

"With your time." His attention shifts to my lips and I can't help but press them together.

All that's going through my head is how much I want his lips on mine and how they would feel running all over me. I bet he'd take his time.

If he kisses with the same intensity with which he stares, it will be exquisite torture. He looks up in the sudden silence filling the room which leaves me to wonder what is going through his head. Did he just fantasy kiss me?

"Um…"

"Relax." His smile is true, genuine, and warm. "You're not making this easy me on me."

"Huh?"

"Come on, Evelyn, I'm asking you out on a date."

"A date?" Damn, but all I can think about is how the scruff of his beard will feel between my thighs when he kisses me down there.

"Yeah, you know. Boy rescues girl. Boy asks girl on a date. Girl kisses boy." He wiggles his eye brows. "Boy kisses girl back. You know, date stuff, fun stuff."

Now I know we're definitely on the same wavelength.

"That kind of date?" The smile on my face is huge. "The fun kind?"

"Those are the best kind. What do you say? Send your stuff to my house. When you get out of here, I'll take you out."

It's an offer I can't refuse, but am I ready to jump back into those waters? I honestly don't know. If I'm going to jump, why not do it with this amazing man who makes the ache between my legs burn?

Only, I'm a chicken and dodge his blatant proposition.

"You know I'm not from around here."

"Yeah. So?"

"So—I'll be taking off."

"Yeah, but I still want to take you out. I like you, and I'd like to get to know you better." The way he says it speaks volumes and his eyes practically undress me.

"Get to know me better?"

"Yeah, it's what people do when they go out on a date."

"No strings?" If we get to know each other better there will come a time when I need to walk away.

"If that's what you want. No strings. We have a little fun while you're here, work out some of this energy between us and get to know each other. Have a little fun while we're at it."

"Fun?"

He arches a brow. "Yeah, fun, but I have questions."

"Like what?"

"Like what's a nice girl like you doing in a place like this? What you'll taste like when I kiss you. How you'll feel wrapped around my hips. You know, important questions. As for strings, that depends on whether you're interested in my rope work."

No need to ask what he means by that. I'm seriously considering it.

Maybe this is what I need to put my past firmly behind me?

A little innocent fling?

Asher seems willing. Not that I'm erasing Justin's memory, but it's been over a year.

"Sounds intriguing."

"So strings? Or no strings?"

"How about a little of both? A clean break at the end?"

Are we negotiating sex? I think we are and I give a sharp shake of my head. I've never done something like this before.

I unmute the phone. "Prescott?"

"Yes, Evie?"

"I'm going to give you to a friend and he'll give you an address to send everything to."

"Okay. We're not done talking about this." Prescott isn't amused, but he knows better than to push when I get like this.

"I know." Not wanting to continue that conversation, I hand the phone to Asher, but pull it back and give him a hard stare. "This is an old family friend, behave!"

"Of course." He takes the phone and puts it to his ear. "Hello?"

9

EVELYN

It's another five days before the doctors are comfortable enough with my progress to release me. In that time period, I've pushed Prescott off from flying out to rescue me no less than twenty times. The number of times I've thought about kissing Asher numbers in the thousands.

I cannot get that man out of my head.

Prescott sent my new phone via courier direct to the hospital along with a wallet full of fresh credit cards, a duplicate driver's license, and the insurance cards I'll need to break free of this joint.

Asher gave Prescott his home address, but Prescott must have felt uncomfortable sending my things to a stranger. My promise to hold off on that trip to the high Sierras is the only thing keeping Prescott on the East Coast. He threatens to fuel up the jet and whisk me away, but can't due to my continued hospitalization.

I'm not telling him they're breaking me out today, and I blocked him from getting updates on my status from the hospital staff three days ago.

Boundaries are necessary, because he'll steamroll right over my wishes under the guise of doing what's best for me.

For me, that means not heading back to the place where memories drag me under. I can't explain this feeling I have, but I'm lighter and happier here.

There's something about wine country which is helping me move on from the tragedy. Those feelings may, or may not, have something to do with the man sitting at the foot of my bed.

Asher sits cross-legged and looks funny as shit, because he's a big man and it's a small bed. A rickety hospital tray table sits between us; a barrier I'm happy to have, because there's nothing that ties me to the bed, the wall, or the IV poles any longer. I'm free to launch across the bed and claim the kiss I've been dreaming about every night and every day for the past two weeks. Instead, I stare at my cards, nibble my lower lip, and push my fantasies to the back of my mind.

Asher is too much of a gentleman to take advantage of me. I'm a little peeved about that. He visits every day, and brought me clothes to wear instead of the hideous hospital gown I've been trapped in for two weeks.

He says he came to check on me that first day, and he's here every day after work to keep me company. Skittish about touching me, his eyes wander to the bandages on my arms and linger on my lips.

I know exactly what he's thinking. I'm thinking it too, wondering how he'll taste when he finally kisses me.

As for the bandages on my arms, they're less bulky now. According to the wound nurse, I shouldn't need them much longer. The burns are minimal and healing nicely.

"It's your turn, little backpack." The low rumble of his voice never fails to send a shiver down my spine. The man won't touch me, but he loves to call me little backpack. There's a simmering intimacy building between us.

Between two people who don't touch, but I feel his eyes on me. They leave a blistering trail of heat behind them.

Smoldering.

Incinerating.

A firestorm ready to erupt.

I glance at the deck. "I'm tired of playing cards."

We've run the gamut of Gin Rummy, War, Go Fish, Spades, Hearts, and more. I'm ready to breathe a little fresh air.

"How can it take so long to kick me out of this place?"

It's a little before noon. Asher took off work early to break me out of this joint.

I'm hungry and cranky, because I don't want another hospital meal tray.

"They have procedures they have to follow." He says it with far more patience than I feel.

"Well, their procedures are slow as shit." I use air quotes for emphasis.

"You, my dear, are impatient. Don't worry, they'll release you, and when they do, I have the perfect place to take you."

I'm hoping that's his house and it has a massive bed where I can strip him out of his clothes and finally discover if his body looks as amazing as I imagine. If he kisses as good as in my fantasies. And finally, if he fucks like I hope he does, wild and unrestrained.

I need something earth-shattering if I'm going to move on.

"Sorry." I curl my lower lip between my teeth. "I don't like not having control, and I'm really tired of these four walls. I'm cranky and grouchy."

"Well, I have a solution for that."

"Go on?" I'm curious what kinds of plans he's made. It's Friday and he's alluded to taking me out on the town and introducing me to his friends. He hasn't mentioned taking me home.

He curls his finger in a come hither gesture and I lean forward. He leans close and lowers his voice to a whisper, making a show of looking out toward the hall.

"Closer, little backpack."

I've never had a nickname before, well other than Evie, but that's just a kid's name. It doesn't mean anything. When Asher calls me little backpack, my insides turn to mush and my fantasies kick into high gear.

"What?" I lower my voice and play along. I feel like we're two kids trying to get away with something.

We lean over the rickety hospital tray, our faces inches apart. My attention is glued to the door, following the direction of his gaze, which is why I miss it when he grabs my face, cups my cheeks, and presses his lips to mine.

An electric jolt shoots through my body and my muscles tense, but that means nothing to me. I'm lost to the sensation as he pushes his tongue gently between my lips. His hands slide around to cup my nape, making it impossible to pull away.

But that's the thing, I don't want to pull away. In fact, I have a little something in store for him, a tease to make him twitch, but first…this kiss.

Sparks rush through me and I sink into the way he holds me, like he's never letting me go. Like he owns this kiss and is taking what he wants. I'm more than inclined to give it to him.

His tongue teases mine, chasing, exploring, meeting me in a fervent dance as desire rushes through us. A groan slips from his throat.

Low, guttural, needy.

It's so damn sexy and sends a rush of sensation between my thighs. My panties dampen as my fingers curl in the sheets. Turned on doesn't begin to describe my wanton state. I'm ready to crawl onto his lap and ride him like I've done in my dreams.

Which brings me to how I intend to make him squirm.

I inch my fingers forward, well aware of how he's sitting and I aim to have some fun at his expense. I want to see how he'll react when I touch him.

My fingers brush his knee and another low groan escapes him. He lets go all pretense and curls his fingers in my hair where he can control me.

Like I'm going to let him control our kiss.

The thing is, I love it.

I love his take charge attitude.

His body tenses when my fingers slide up his thigh, I lean forward and beg for him to deepen the kiss. The man doesn't disappoint.

There's nothing soft or gentle in what comes next. He's hungry, ravenous even, as he bites and licks and nips at my lips. His tongue lashes against mine as I surrender to the kiss and slip my fingers right over the hard, rigid length of his cock which tents the fabric of his pants.

My expectation is he'll jump. As for me, my heart thuds in time with each stroke of his tongue against mine, each nip of his teeth on my lips. My breaths flutter and still, only to pick up again as I pant against him. My heart beats faster as his lips lock to mine, deepening the kiss.

Holy hell, the man can kiss.

Asher is kissing me and it's way better than what my poor mind imagined.

It's mind-blowing, pulse-pounding, and breathtakingly insane.

This is happening and he's rock hard. The turgid length of him stiffens in my hand and gives a little jerk. He clamps his fingers around my wrist and holds my hand tight against his groin.

"You get one warning. Don't tease the beast. Once you open those floodgates, I won't stop until I've had every piece of you, owned every inch of your hot little body, and buried myself so deep inside your warm, wet pussy that you'll never forget my name. I've spent every night with my fist right where your hand is, jerking off as I think about fucking you. About how it's going to feel when I finally slip inside of you." He draws back, hovering a breath away, but it's enough. "So be very careful. If you're not intending to take this to that level, hands off my dick. This is your one chance to take a step back, but it's the only chance you'll have. I want you."

I hear him.

I hear every filthy word and he steals my breath with his honesty, the freedom with which he talks about, not just sex, but wanting it with me.

Taking me.

I wrap my free arm around his shoulder and run my fingers through his hair. I don't move. I'm barely breathing, and I close my eyes as time comes to a screeching halt.

I can stay like this forever, wrapped in the potency of his desire, my fingers curved around the evidence of his arousal. I'm not taking this back.

Justin never made me feel this alive. Sex was something we shared, but didn't talk about, not openly like this. Instead, it was a dirty secret that needed to be locked away.

Asher doesn't lock anything away. He claims what he wants, expressing his desires head on, upfront, eager, open, and demanding. I believe him too. I can let go of his dick and he won't push things between us, or I can live recklessly. I can take from him, claim this moment as mine and pray it eases the unbearable pain within me.

Would that be so bad?

Asher knows I don't live around here. Anything we do is temporary. It comes with an expiration date. If he's going to use me, why can't I use him back?

My heart lodges in my throat and I consider pulling my hand away. My entire body trembles because this is a huge step for me.

"Evelyn…" His hot breath whispers across my skin, desperate, wanting, but waiting for me to continue. "For the love of God, don't let go." Tilting his head back, he stares at the ceiling tiles overhead. "Fuck, I've thought about you every second of every day. Your hand feels so damn good."

It's enough that I feel a visceral punch to my gut knowing he thinks about me the same way I think about him. That he not only fantasizes about me, but touches himself while he thinks of fucking me. It's erotic as hell.

Exciting.

And so far out of my comfort zone.

Am I brave enough to take what I want?

The color of his eyes deepens to the darkest emerald. They're unrelenting as they bore into me, begging me to choose him—to choose us.

He digs deep, uncovering my secrets, and making them his. I'm well aware I'm gripping his cock. The thin fabric of his pants is merely an inconvenience for what we want to pursue.

His grip on my wrist is firm, confident, and completely without shame. This is a man who's not afraid to fuck, not afraid to take what he wants, and is so much more confident about his body than I am.

"Feel how you affect me, how hard I get for you." He begins to move his hand, making mine move beneath him. He shows me how to stroke him, and it's not soft and gentle.

A throat clears behind us and we jerk apart. My hand however is still clamped around his dick. He refuses to release me there, although he no longer has his fingers threaded through my hair. He twists in the bed and glances over at the doctor, like it's nothing having him walk in on us mid-kiss and with my hand wrapped around Asher's dick.

"Miss Thornton?"

My chin dips and my hair falls over my face. Heat radiates off my cheeks. Talk about getting caught with your hand in the cookie jar. Or should I say pickle jar. Shit, Asher is packing. My fingers barely curl around his girth and I'm pretty sure I'll be walking bowlegged for a week after he finally takes me. Sadly, that won't be here. Or now.

"Yes, Dr. Allen?"

"I have your discharge papers."

"Well." Asher's voice is raspy, low, utterly addictive, and sexy as hell. "It's about damn time."

He releases me and cups his hands over his lap. Not that Dr. Allen is an idiot. I'm wondering how many times he's walked in on a patient with her hand on a man's dick and his tongue shoved down her throat. I scoot back on the bed, trying to look like I didn't have my hand exactly where it looked like I had it.

"That's great," I say.

Dr. Allen glances at Asher, but I give a little wave. "It's okay, you can say what you need to in front of him." I have little to hide, besides I came out of everything unscathed. Except for a few burns, I'm making a full recovery.

With me blocking Prescott from getting updates about my medical status, the hospital staff is hesitant about leaking anything they shouldn't. I appreciate this more than they know, and feel intensely guilty about it.

Prescott isn't my enemy. He only wants the best for me, but I'm incapable of accepting the help he offers, or the care, consideration, and yes, maybe even love he might feel for me.

I am, after all, the only thing left of his best friend. As for his son, I'm the daughter-in-law he almost had, until tragedy tore apart our world.

We're connected through my father and his son. I don't want to take that away, but he's not my father. He can't fill that void, and he can't make the tragedy I endured go away.

Nobody can.

Fortunately, Dr. Allen doesn't take much of my time. A few minutes later, the discharge coordinator comes in to give me last minute instructions.

"Where can we send your appointment reminders?" The nurse can't keep her greedy eyes off Asher. She barely looks at me.

I rattle off my email address fully aware she's barely listening to me. Her eyes are all over Asher and I want to dig her eyeballs out with my nails.

Go away bitch, he's mine.

But is he?

I have no intention of sticking around.

My plans for hiking the John Muir trail are derailed, but fresh plastic is burning a hole in my wallet. All I need is to get outfitted with the best of the best and set off...which means leaving Asher behind.

So, why am I hesitating?

Because I want to wake up beside a man like Asher. I want to feel his arms wrapped around me. I don't want to live lonely and alone, or waste any more days, or nights, running away from a past I can't change.

I bite my lower lip because jealousy is not my thing. Except, I see green.

His lips were on me. His tongue was inside my mouth, thrusting like he wants to fuck me. His entire body jerked the moment I put my hand on his dick. The man is mine, and this bitch had better take ten steps back before I rip her head off.

I clear my throat and pull her attention back to me.

"You can send everything to my email, or text me on my phone. I don't have an address—"

"You don't?" She looks at me as if I've grown two heads.

"Just give your home address. It doesn't have to be local." Asher places a hand on my leg and his fingers stroke my inner thigh. He's teasing me, seeing how close I'll let him get before pulling away.

"But I don't have a home address." I'm not ready to discuss this.

"What do you mean?"

He knows I don't live around here, but he doesn't know the truth. He doesn't know I walked away from my life.

"Um, okay," the nurse says. "We can use an email if you prefer." My discharge nurse does the bare minimum in getting me checked out. While, she shoves papers in my face, her attention zeroes in on Asher.

"I haven't seen you around much, Ace. How're you doing?"

"I'm good, Maggie."

Fuck, he knows her name. And Ace?

That's his nickname.

This woman knows Asher. Like, she know knows him on a level I don't; a level which involves history, familiarity, and maybe more. My eyes pinch as I clutch my discharge paperwork to my chest.

"I missed your party. Maybe we can get together sometime?"

Did she ask him out? In front of me? This bitch has balls.

Why do I feel so damn possessive?

Asher shifts on the bed and takes my hand in his. His eyes are on Maggie as he lifts my hand to his mouth and kisses the backs of my knuckles.

"Maybe another time."

Her gaze darts to our hands and she gives a little pout. "You always know where to find me, if you change your mind." With those words, she pivots and marches out of the room.

I can't help but clench my teeth.

A man like Asher, with his overbearing confidence and that smug smirk on his face, must have tons of women at his beck and call. I'm not his first, and I won't be his last.

But, will I be his right now?

The way my mind is spiraling out of control, I feel a bit off kilter, and I'm angry. Fury floods my veins and it has nothing to do with flouncy Nurse Maggie. A deep-seated anger has been brewing in my gut for over a year and it's about ready to explode.

I lost the man I loved.

Justin was supposed to be my forever.

Yet, the universe took him from me. All our love, hope, and dreams meant nothing. In the blink of an eye, I went from having it all to having nothing.

My heart pinches. Pain stabs through me. I remember why I walked away and rub my breastbone. It does nothing to ease the pain.

Live in the present. I need to remember my motto.

There are appointments with plastic surgery I need to keep, appointments with neurology for the concussion, and of course my primary care doctor needs to see me. Only he, or she, doesn't exist.

I have no home of record.

The medications I need to get filled will get filled, but not by my pharmacist. I have no pharmacist. The things I need to watch out for are a long list of symptoms I'm going to ignore. They should prompt me to seek immediate medical attention but I don't care. My doctors do. They're concerned about the holes in my memory. Frankly, I'm happy for the holes. If they could somehow figure out a way to erase all my memories I'd be a much happier person.

I'd be happier because I wouldn't remember that gut-wrenching sensation when I knew we were all going to die. I wouldn't remember the pain, the smells, and the screams which were replaced by the worst silence I'd ever experienced. I wouldn't remember the moment when they died and I lived.

"Evelyn? Are you okay?"

"I'm good." I shake off the heavy feelings and plaster a fake smile on my face.

"You sure?"

"Yeah." I glance at the door. "Can we get out of here?"

He stands and offers his hand to help me out of the bed. When my feet hit the floor, sudden panic overwhelms me, because I'm not sure of my next step.

If I had my gear, I'd be on a trail, looking for the next campsite. But I have none of that, and I have no idea where I'm going to spend the night.

A throat clears at the door. "Excuse me, Evelyn Thornton?"

"That's me."

Why is a police detective asking about me?

"Hey, Benjamin, what's up?" Asher's smile is big. He takes a step forward and thrusts out his hand. The cop's badge reads Benjamin Bingham and he clears his throat as he shakes Asher's hand.

Asher glances over his shoulder. His brows pinch together and his head swivels back to Benjamin. He takes a step to the side and places himself between me and Detective Bingham.

"Sorry, Ace, but will you please stand aside." Detective Bingham's tone is formal and devoid of emotion.

"Stand aside for what reason?" Asher's entire body tenses.

The detective pins me with his hard gaze. "Miss Thornton, you're under arrest—"

"Under arrest?" I reach for Asher. "Why am I under arrest?"

I've literally done nothing, unless this is about my revolver. California gun laws are a bit extreme, but I can't imagine carrying a weapon without a permit is grounds for arrest.

"What's this about, Benjamin?" Asher isn't moving except to step in front of me to block me from the detective.

"Step aside, Ace. You don't want to do this."

"I'm doing nothing but asking a question. Why are you arresting her?"

"Miss Thornton is under arrest for arson."

"Arson!" My screech makes the officer flinch. "I didn't set that fire. There was a man…"

"Ace mentioned your account—"

"Yes, that's damn straight, I mentioned it." Asher continues to block Detective Bingham. "She was assaulted and nearly died in that fire."

"Ace, I'm going to have to ask you to step aside."

"Not until you tell me what's going on."

Benjamin Bingham shakes his head and sighs. "Look, Ace, forensics just came in. The accelerant is all over her stuff, fingerprints on the lighter fuel—"

"My fingerprints?" My heart speeds up and I look frantically between the two men. "Asher, I swear I didn't touch any of that stuff. That man wrapped rags around the bases of the bushes. He doused them with lighter fluid. It wasn't me."

"I'm sorry, Miss, but I need to remind you anything you say can be used against you in a court of law." He pulls out a small card from his breast pocket and proceeds to read me my Miranda rights while I stare back, mouth agape and heart lodged in my throat.

This can't be happening.

I glance at Asher as Detective Bingham pulls out a set of cuffs.

"I need to call Prescott." My voice shakes and my hands tremble.

"You'll have a chance to make a call at the precinct." The officer cuffs me, being exceptionally gentle considering the bandages which still cover most of my arms.

"Asher," I say, "call Prescott. Tell him what's going on."

"Why Prescott?" He looks confused.

"It's the only number on my phone." I give him my four-digit passcode. There's nothing on that phone I need to worry about. I'm only concerned about the conversation Asher is going to have with Prescott.

"Do you really have to cuff her, Benjamin?" Asher takes a step forward, but one look from the detective and he retreats. I can tell he's unsure, but this is something we'll get sorted out.

"It's okay, Asher. Please just call Prescott. He will help me."

"Sorry, Ace, it's standard procedure." Benjamin Bingham glances around the room. "Are there any personal belongings you need to take?"

There's nothing in my hospital room except for the bag of ruined clothes. I give a sharp shake of my head. "No."

The detective presses his lips into a thin line. "See you around, Ace."

"You can damn well bet on that." Asher blocks Benjamin Bingham and pulls me tight to his chest. "We'll figure this out. I'm going to find out what the fuck is happening, then I'll meet you at the station. Okay?"

"Call Prescott." My words are terse, strained, and I'm barely keeping it together. Prescott will know what to do. He'll bring the full force of his protective fatherly instincts and impeccable skill as a trial attorney to help me out.

For the first time, in a very long time, I not only need his help, I want it.

"I will." He cups my chin. "Be brave, little backpack."

I'm overloaded and tears spill down my cheeks. The brave face I put on for Asher is a facade; I'm scared.

How do I prove my innocence?

What evidence do they have against me?

My fingerprints were found on the bottle of accelerant? How?

Nothing makes sense.

"Okay." I nod because it's all I can think to do, but what if it's not okay?

10

ASHER

More than a little pissed off, I follow Benjamin to the station in my truck. He has my girl on trumped up charges for arson. Whatever evidence they found, they didn't see the terror in Evelyn's eyes when she told me what happened.

A man assaulted her, and I don't see anyone looking for him.

Benjamin gives a sharp shake of his head when he sees I followed him. He leaves Evelyn in the car and approaches my truck. "You need to go."

"Why? Am I under arrest?"

Benjamin pushes his fingers through his hair and does an amazing job maintaining his cool. He senses I want to pop him in the face, kick his legs out from under him, and take him to the ground. That does no one any good, so I keep my shit locked down tight.

"You have no right arresting her, and shit, Benjamin…" It's my turn to pause. "Did you have to do it at the hospital?"

"When would you have had me do it, Ace?" He glances at the car. "Look, I'm just doing my job."

"A piss poor job from the looks of it. She didn't start that fire." I feel the truth in my gut.

"The investigation concluded yesterday. It's pretty cut and dry."

"I was there. Fuck, you didn't see the look in her eyes, the fear, the terror…"

"I would think those could be explained by getting caught starting the fire."

"She wasn't scared she'd been caught, she was trying to survive."

"Anything you have to add is nothing more than hearsay, and you know that won't hold up. Now, please…" Benjamin places his hand on the butt of his weapon. It's not a threat, but the message is clear.

I'm pushing him. It places him in a difficult position. Benjamin is my friend, but more through association. His brother, Brandon, is my real friend, Benjamin is simply Brandon's older brother, the one we all looked up to.

"Who headed the investigation?" A thousand questions spill through my head, ways I can help Evelyn clear her name.

"Pete Sims."

"You're fucking kidding me. He's a joke. Come on, you know how he works."

"I also know what they found. Her fingerprints are on the bottle of accelerant, and they found receipts for it in the remains of her things."

I give a sharp shake of my head. "I don't care. You're wrong. He's wrong. He never visited her in the hospital, never took her account. He never spoke to me. It's circumstantial at best."

"Look, if you want to help her, get her a good lawyer, but don't get in my way." As the oldest of the Bingham brothers, the trifecta of public service heroes, I grew up respecting Benjamin Bingham. He's the man who could do no wrong, the kid I wanted to be growing up. "If you need help finding her someone, come by the house later today and I'll give you a few names."

He doesn't have to offer that. My respect increases tenfold. It's his way of throwing me a bone, helping me when his hands are tied.

"Thanks. I might take you up on that."

"Sorry about this, Ace, but are you sure you want to stand by her side? How well do you know her?"

He knows our story, how I pulled her from the fire. His brother, Bradley flew her to the hospital. I have no doubt they've talked about her, and nothing happens in Sequoia Springs without the whole town knowing about it, meaning my daily visits to her in the hospital are a matter of public record.

I don't understand the strange pull Evelyn has on me, except it's profound and all encompassing. I want to help her. I need to defend her. I'm the only one who seems to be on her side.

"I know she didn't do it." I stand my ground.

"Then find something to prove it." Benjamin isn't backing down.

His convictions are as strong as mine, except this one time, we find ourselves on opposite sides of a confrontation. It's a tough place to be. I'm not used to being at odds with him.

My brothers and I followed in the Bingham brothers' shadows. The Bingham's are men I respect and admire. I call each of them friend. Their father was the chief of police and his sons followed in his footsteps, choosing to serve their community in police, fire, and rescue.

Benjamin is on the police force, making a name for himself as an upstanding man. When the time comes, I have no doubt he'll become the chief of police.

Brandon saves lives, fighting the fires which threaten our homes and our lives. And then there's Bradley, a medivac pilot who flies the wounded where they need to go, sometimes at great personal risk to himself.

These are not men I want to be at odds with. I respect them and I don't want to change any of that.

But I will.

I'll jeopardize all of that for Evelyn and I don't understand why. Or rather, I'm too chickenshit to face a sobering truth. I'm falling for my little backpack and my need to defend her is unwavering.

"I pulled her from that fire. You can't fake that kind of fear. She thought I was him, coming to finish her off. I feel it in here." I point over my heart and thump my chest. "You know Open-and-Shut Pete. No way did he do due diligence."

"Then how? How did her prints get on the bottle of lighter fluid? Why is there a charred receipt buried in the bottom of her backpack for the purchase of the accelerant? I'm going to be honest here, it doesn't look good." Benjamin purses his lips and I sense his frustration. I also sense something else. He's not happy with the investigative report either.

"Pete Sims?" I give a shake of my head. "He's a bureaucratic waste of space, more concerned with closing cases than solving them."

Benjamin's brother, Brandon, never says anything good about Pete and I have a mind to take this all the way up the chain if need be.

"Doesn't matter. The evidence—"

"Is rigged." I'm acutely aware she's still sitting in the back of Benjamin's police cruiser. "When can I see her?"

What's going through her head? How is she holding up? Does she know I have her back and will do whatever it takes to see her through this?

"Later, Ace. Come back in the morning."

My stomach seizes thinking about Evelyn spending the night in jail. Our town is small. The holding cells are generally empty, but still. It's jail.

"How long will it take to post bail?"

"I don't know." He scratches his head. "Considering it's Friday, probably not until Monday."

"You're not helping me out here." My frustration builds.

"I'm not trying to be difficult. Look, I have to book her, but I'll call the judge and see if he can expedite the posting of her bond. I'll let you know as soon as I know anything. Until then, be patient."

"Would you be patient if this was Haley?" Haley is his wife, and it may be a low blow to bring her into this conversation. He's insanely protective of her.

"Fair enough. Look, I'll let you know as soon as I can, but it probably won't be until morning. Sorry, but that's the best I can do."

I run a hand through my hair, feeling helpless. "Thanks, Benjamin."

He gives a slight nod. "I promise. I'll let you know."

Without another word, he leaves me to collect Evelyn. My entire body itches with the need to go to her, hold her, and tell her everything is going to be all right, but I stand there helpless as Benjamin takes her inside.

She glances over her shoulder and gives me a strained smile. She's trying to be brave, but there's fear in her eyes.

If I can't get her out tonight, there's one thing I can do. My hand slips into my pocket where I hold her phone. She asked me to call Prescott.

I lift the phone and tap the security code to open it up. She seems to think he can help and right now, I can use all the help I can get.

The phone picks up on the first ring. "Evie? Hunny, what's up?"

The voice on the other end is older, mature, and I'm envisioning what my father might have sounded like if he were still alive. It's been years since his passing. My grief has lost its raw edge, but I never know when that sharp ache is going to hit. This man's voice is like a punch in the gut and it takes a moment before I recover.

"Evie?"

"This is Asher La Rouge. Is this Prescott?"

"Asher?" He plays it off like he's confused, but we've spoken before and this man blew me off, choosing to send Evelyn's things via courier to the hospital rather than entrust them to me. "I'm sorry, who are you?"

I grit my teeth and remind myself to be the better man. "Evelyn asked me to call you. There have been some—developments."

"Developments?" He makes a disparaging sound. "I'd like to speak with Evie, please."

"That won't be possible."

"Excuse me?" My reply finally gets his attention. I can tell by the tick in his voice. "What have you done to Evie?"

What have I done?

The man says it like an accusation, as if I hurt her rather than saved her life. He damn well knows exactly who I am. As for what I've done to Evelyn? It's not nearly enough.

I'm not stupid enough to say that out loud. I still don't know who this man is to her, or why I'm supposed to call him.

"Sir, Evelyn asked me to call you, but before I do, who exactly are you to her?" I don't mind lobbing a volley of my own. If this man is going to challenge me and my place with Evelyn, I'm going to do exactly the same.

Evelyn is mine.

It's a truth I accept whole-heartedly and the fact it makes no sense at all, considering how we're still virtual strangers to each other, is exactly why it feels so damn right.

I'll defend her, because I believe she's not at fault for that fire. I feel it in my bones and I've seen it in her eyes. She's not capable of such blatant disregard for life. Her heart is too pure.

"Who am I?" Shock fills his words and his indignation spills through the line. "Who are you?"

"I'm the one looking out for her and I'm not interested in getting into a pissing contest. Evelyn asked me to call you. I gave my word I would, but I need to know who you are to her before I tell you what's going on."

"Son." His tone is disparaging, but full of protective male instincts. More than anything, that tells me all I need to know to trust this man, "I don't know who you are, or what your relationship is with our Evie, but if she asked you to call me, I can only assume she needs my help. Evie never calls, she's too damn independent. That she asked a stranger tells me something is terribly wrong. As far as who I am, Gracie and I are old family friends. Now, how about we get down to business?"

There's silence on his end while I absorb what he says. I sense a deep connection between him and Evelyn, one steeped in the weight of years, something I'd be wise to acknowledge and respect. He calls her Evie and she said it was a childhood nickname. If I want Evelyn in my life, and I'm pretty damn sure that's what I want, this man will be a part of that future.

"Evelyn has been arrested for arson. The preliminary investigation implicates her in starting the fire."

"Arrested!" The protective growl which follows silences any doubts I have about who this man is to Evelyn. He wants to protect her too. This makes us allies. "And what are your thoughts on this?"

"She didn't do it." The words tumble out with zero hesitation. "I believe her innocence and I'll prove it."

"Good. She needs someone on her side." He says something to someone else, covering the mic so I can't hear anything but muffled sounds. A few seconds later, he's back. "Tell Evie, we'll be there in the morning."

"She needs an attorney."

"I'll take care of it."

"No." My response is as immediate as it is visceral. "I'll take care of her."

My reply silences him for a moment, but then he's back to business. "Who's holding her?"

I give him the name of our local sheriff's department.

"I'll call the judge. Gracie and I'll be there first thing in the morning."

Call the judge?

Like anyone can pick up the phone and make that call.

"Sequoia Springs is a small town. I can recommend a few places."

"Thank you, but that won't be necessary. Please tell Evie we'll be there in the morning."

"I have her phone. Until they let her out, she won't be able to contact you."

"That won't be a problem, son."

My shoulders bunch when he calls me son. It borders on being derogatory, as if he's an old dog letting a young pup know his place. I'm cool with that, because I know exactly where my place is in all of this.

"As soon as her bond is posted, we'll sort this out. In the meantime, please let her know Gracie and I are on our way."

"I will."

Our call ends and I stand in the parking lot unsure about what to do. I should leave.

Benjamin told me he'd do what he could, but the thought of leaving Evelyn all alone is too much.

Then an idea hits me. Prescott mentioned calling the judge, like it's nothing, but what if I visited the judge?

I'll need an introduction, and I know exactly who to call. If Benjamin can't help, maybe his father, our ex-chief of police, can. I hop in my truck and head to the Bingham's. I spent a fair amount of my childhood in their house.

When I knock, Mrs. Bingham answers. "Why, Ace, how are you doing?"

"I'm good, ma'am." I give her my best smile. "I was wondering if Chief is home?"

I'm certain the man has a first name, but all the kids called him 'Chief' growing up, and Mr. Bingham just sounds plain wrong.

"He's out back by the grill." She doesn't ask why I want to speak to her husband, but there's curiosity in her soft gaze. "Come on in. We're making hamburgers and hotdogs. Do you want to stay for dinner?"

Mrs. Bingham never fails to welcome anyone. With three sons, her house was always filled with kids when we were growing up. I'm sure most of that has changed, although Bradley has a kid and Benjamin just got hitched. I guess her home will be filled with grandkids.

I don't want to impose, but my stomach decides to rumble. She waves me inside.

"Come in, Ace. Do you want a beer?"

It's weird, her offering me a beer. It was always juice or soda growing up, but with the day I'm having, I could use a beer.

"That would be great."

"Go on out back. Chief is out there and I'll bring you something to drink."

"Thank you."

I make my way through her home without help. I don't need it. Many of my fondest memories were made in this house. Brandon and I are the best of friends. Brody and Cage hung out here too, but not nearly as much as I did.

My brothers and I are tight, always were, but we started keeping our own friends once we reached high school. I think that separation was something we needed as we separated our identities.

Chief Bingham looks up as I step on the porch. "Ace?" His face breaks into a huge smile. "Haven't seen you around in a while. How are things going at La Rouge Vineyards? I heard you lost some vines to the fire."

My shoulders bunch a little. Evelyn asked if the fire was out, and it is, but not before it caused significant damage.

"We did."

"I'm sorry to hear that. Not too bad I hope?"

Most of the fire damage was contained to La Rouge property, but there were a few adjacent structures which burned to the ground. My team, along with Brandon's firefighters, were able to get it under control, but the blaze burned for days.

This is why I'm concerned about the arson charges against Evelyn.

She may be facing stiff fines and prison if they decide she deliberately set the fire, which from everything Benjamin mentioned seems to be the case. And we're talking up to thirty years. It's a big deal, especially since the fire had the potential to harm people in addition to buildings.

"We lost ten acres before containing the fire."

"And your mom?"

"Mom's cottage was right in the path of the blaze, but it survived without damage. The fire charged down the hills, split in two, separated, and moved around her home as it continued onward to destroy our vineyard."

"That had to be tough to see."

"Watching ten acres of La Rouge profits go up in flames is going to hit our bottom line. It'll be a rough season and I'm worried." Our survival is at risk.

"You need anything, just ask."

"Thanks." I left that bit out when Evelyn asked about the fires.

We'll pull through, barely, but only because Brody will be floating the family business cash until we can rebuild. "Regrowing the vines will take years."

Chief Bingham grimaces at the news. "I'm sorry to hear that. Brandon mentioned your mom's home."

"Brandon and his crew helped put out the fire around her cottage."

"And she's okay?"

"My brothers evacuated her. Nothing inside burned although she complains about losing her she-shack." Sitting on the edge of the fire break, our mother's prized artist's retreat is now a pile of ash.

"He mentioned your brothers are in town. How are Brody and Cage?"

"Cage got back from his Everest ascent and has some awesome shots for the magazine. He's hanging around for a few weeks until his next assignment."

"What about Brody?" Chief Bingham knows my brothers well. He's one of the few people we were never able to fool when we switched identities growing up.

"He came to spend the weekend, but with the fire damage, he's extending his visit."

I'm thankful for my brothers' help. Brody has to take time off from work, but he didn't hesitate. Cage has a few weeks before he heads off on an expedition to Alaska to photograph polar bears. We have a lot of work ahead of us to clear the burned fields and begin the task of reconditioning the soil.

"Your mom must be happy having you all under one roof again."

"She's very happy to have all her boys home. It's been years since she could properly smother us."

"Now, that's something I understand." He glances toward the porch where the door opens.

"Who wants a beer?" Mrs. Bingham lifts two bottles in the air.

I take mine and she gives the other to her husband. I say thank you while Chief Bingham pulls her in for a kiss. They've always been an affectionate couple and their passion for each other is as strong today as it was when I first met them at the tender age of eight.

Back then, I thought the kissing and hugging was gross. Now, I'm envious of what they share.

I thought I had that with Erin until I caught her fucking Felix.

"What're you boys talking about?" Mrs. Bingham takes a sip from her beer and checks on the progress of the burgers Chief Bingham is cooking. There's more than the two of them can eat. "Did you decide to stick around for dinner? The boys are coming over."

Chief Bingham follows her gaze to the grill and his mouth twists. "All of them?"

"You never know." She flashes a smile.

He puts his beer down. "Better grab a few more burgers for the grill."

"Oh, I can do that. You two sit and talk." She gives me a pointed look, knowing we haven't gotten beyond the pleasantries.

Chief Bingham picks up on her subtext and gets straight to the point. "So, what brings you around, son?" When he calls me son it isn't grating on my nerves like when Prescott does it.

"I was wondering if you wouldn't mind calling Judge Simon."

"Really? Why is that?"

I explain to him about the fire, Evelyn's rescue, her recovery, and Benjamin arresting her earlier.

"So you see, I was hoping I could speak with him about setting her bail. I don't want her in jail overnight." Or through the weekend. It's Friday, if I don't get her out today, she'll sit in there until Monday.

"And you believe she's innocent?"

"I know it." Again, my conviction rings with truth. "She's a victim in this."

"Let me see what I can do." He says nothing about my interaction with his son, Benjamin.

What can he say? Benjamin is doing what the law demands, but

Chief Bingham is smart. He knows some situations require a little thinking outside the box.

He speaks to Judge Simon on the phone. I catch most of the conversation and I'm shocked by how hard he pushes to get the judge to set bail tonight. He's going on nothing other than my word. His faith means the world to me.

With a glance to his watch, he looks up at me. "He's setting bail now. If you really believe in her, he'll see that she's released."

"I do." Actually, it's more than that. The feeling inside of me is indescribable.

He gives a nod and reaches for my hand. "Go get your girl, son."

"Yes, sir."

I don't finish my beer, and there's nothing else to say. I make my excuses with Mrs. Bingham and head to the courthouse. I've got less than an hour before five and I'll be damned if Prescott is the one who rescues my Evelyn from jail.

The amount of bail Judge Simon sets seems incredibly high. I beg and plead, knowing finances will be tight with the damage to my vineyards, and he agrees to reduce the bond on one condition. I hope it's palatable to Evelyn.

Twenty minutes later, I'm waiting to take her home.

11

ASHER

ASHER

Evelyn races into my outspread arms. The minute her tight body presses against mine I swear I've died and gone to heaven. As cliché as that sounds, this is what my body tells me.

Not because I'm aroused—I'm getting there—but because holding her makes me feel like that piece inside of me which is missing is finally home.

"Oh, Asher, that was horrible. Did you get a hold of Prescott? Did he get me out?" Her words rush out in quick succession. I hold her tight, giving her the reassurance she desperately needs.

However, I hate she thinks Prescott had anything to do with getting her out and bite my lower lip to keep from saying something I'll regret. Until I better understand her relationship with Prescott, I need to tread carefully, but I'll correct her assumptions.

"He's on a plane and will be here soon, but I spoke to Judge Simon and convinced him to post your bail today."

Our conversation was far more involved than that, but she doesn't need to know all the details, or the promises I made.

"You did?" Her wide eyes stare up at me and she lifts up on

tiptoe to press her lips chastely against mine. "You didn't have to do that."

That kiss gets my attention.

"I didn't want you spending the night in jail." More than likely, it would've been the whole weekend.

"I'm glad you were able to get a hold of Prescott and he was able to bail me out."

She still thinks her release is because of him? I'm losing ground.

"I bailed you out."

"You did? Oh, you didn't need to do that."

I pull her tight against me. "Of course, like I said, there was no way you were spending the night in jail, but there's a condition."

"Oh lord. Thank you. I'll pay you back. Just as soon as Prescott gets here, I'll have him wire the funds. How much do I owe you?"

More money than I can afford.

"Let's figure that out tomorrow. As for tonight——"

She cuts me off, placing her finger over my lips. "Right now, I need a stiff drink, a shower, and bed. Is there any place in this town where a girl can drown her sorrows?"

"I'll take you to my favorite place. It's really the only bar in town that's any good."

"Thanks, and I'm buying." She lifts her forefinger to emphasize her point.

"Right." No way in hell is that happening. I'm acutely aware of our previous conversation about her brand of feminism. I plan on living up to all her expectations and more.

Which is why, after opening the door for her, I place my hand in the small of her back and gently escort her into the bar. It's Friday night and the place is hopping. People are getting off for the day and are ready for the weekend.

Evelyn's enthusiasm about getting a drink wanes a bit. She's quiet and unsure as all eyes turn toward us.

These are all people I know. I grew up with half of them, which includes Bradley and Brandon who hog the far corner of the bar. It's the best place to catch the bartender's eye and score some drinks.

Brandon notices us and waves me over. "Hey, Ace!" He turns to the bartender and lifts three fingers. "Another round." His astute gaze zeroes in on Evelyn. "What's she drinking?"

I bend down to ask and barely hear Evelyn's response.

"Gin and tonic." I cup a hand over my mouth and raise my voice to be heard over the hopping crowd.

Things are in full swing. Nearly every table is occupied. Music blares over the crowd, pumping up the energy, and making us all raise our voices to be heard. It's loud as people shake off the work week and unwind as they get ready for the weekend.

I wish I could unwind. My work is only beginning.

The bartender plops four drinks down on the counter. Bradley grabs a beer. Brandon hands me mine and gives the Gin and tonic to Evelyn.

"You must be Evelyn." The smile on his face comes easily and I let out my breath.

I'm a little nervous hanging with them considering Benjamin arrested Evelyn a few short hours earlier. Until I know where they stand on her innocence, or guilt, I won't be able to relax.

Evelyn dips her head and takes the drink. She's quiet around people and this comes as a surprise because she's not shy or quiet around me.

"You look much better than when I saw you last." Bradley lifts his beer for a toast. "To surviving a firestorm."

It's a cavalier toast which carries a lot of subtext. For the police, firefighters, and Bradley's medivac crew, it means a whole lot more. It's about staring down the gates of hell and refusing to let the devil win. It's about fighting, surviving, and living to do it all again another day.

We toast and Brandon climbs off his stool, offering it to Evelyn.

"Do you remember Bradley?" I ask.

Her brows pinch together.

"I doubt she remembers me at all considering you're the one who carried her out on your back." Bradley extends his hand. "Bradley Bingham, I flew you out of that fire to the hospital. You gave us all a scare."

Evelyn dips her head. "I don't remember much. Um, thank you."

Not a man who enjoys the spotlight, Bradley deflects. "I'm not the one who deserves the thanks." He tilts the neck of his bottle toward me. "Ace carried you out. I was just the taxi driver."

"You were more than a taxi driver," she says. "I'm really thankful for what you did."

"Well, I'm feeling a bit left out. I've heard all about Ace's little backpack, but haven't had the pleasure." Brandon's hand shoots out to shake hers. "Brandon Bingham, nice to meet you. Ace hasn't stopped talking about you. I was beginning to think he was making it all up, but seeing you in the flesh…" He takes a moment to check out my girl and I lean forward a little until he flashes a cheeky grin. The bastard is testing me and I fell for it. "Anyway, it's clear why he can't stop talking about you."

"Um, thanks I guess." I help her onto the stool and settle myself protectively around her.

Locking eyes with the two Bingham brothers, I try to read them. They have to know their brother arrested Evelyn, but they're in good spirits and rib me like they usually do.

Evelyn gives a little tug on my shirt and I lean down to hear her soft voice.

"Where's the restroom?"

I point to the far corner of the bar. "Here, I'll take you."

She places a hand on my arm. "I'm perfectly capable of walking across the room. Stay and order me another drink."

I look down and see she's downed her entire drink. My girl is more than nervous.

Getting a hold of the bartender is easy and I order another round for us all. Evelyn scoots off the stool and I watch her tight and toned body sashay across the room. She pivots around crowded tables, moving lightly, and disappears down the hall leading to the restrooms.

"Ace got bit by the love bug." Bradley elbows me in the ribs.

"He got bit real good." Brandon responds in a sing-song voice.

They both gyrate their hips and pump their arms. It's a dumb thing we did growing up when any of us got soft on a girl. I punch Brandon in the shoulder.

"Stop it."

"He's got it real good. Uh-huh, Uh-huh."

I hit him again. "Ha-ha, not funny."

"Have you kissed her yet?" Bradley turns his back to me and wraps his arms around himself as he makes kissie noises. He's a bit overly suggestive with the groping. I'm about ready to pop him too. The two of them are teaming up on me.

"I mean it." I practically growl out the words, which only proves their point.

Brandon points at me and laughs. "You have, haven't you?"

"The real question is whether you've fucked her yet. That woman is fine, fine, fine, and oh so easy on the eyes. You picked a good one." Bradley turns back around, huge, sheepish grin plastered all over his face. He takes a swig of his beer, as if I'm going to answer.

"That's my girl you're talking about."

"Well, there you have it." Brandon gives me a one-two punch in the gut. "He's soft on the girl."

I lock Brandon in an arm bar and give a jab to his gut. We're playing—almost. I'm not keen on them talking about Evelyn like this. He twists out of my grip and gives a shake of his head.

"Dad said you came for a visit." Bradley's tone changes. He's digging, but I'm pretty sure he already knows what I talked to his dad about. He wants a reaction, something to confirm how far I've fallen, but I give him nothing and wait him out. "Considering she's here, I'm assuming things went well with the judge?"

"She's out of jail if that's what you're getting at."

Bradley's eyes pinch. "Look, you know we love you like a brother, and we respect the hell out of you…"

"Yeah?" What's he getting at?

"If you really believe her story, we'll back you up." Bradley gives a sharp nod.

"Will you?"

"I've never heard Benjamin so pissed. He told us all about

arresting her. Said it left a bad taste in his mouth." Brandon joins in, telling me something I already suspected.

"Because I questioned him?"

"Because it's the first time you ever stood up to him. He thought he was going to have to take you in as well. If it's any consolation, he trusts your instincts, but the investigation..." Brandon's words trail off.

"Pete's investigations are a joke. He goes for the easy close and doesn't take the time to really look."

"She made first page news in the Gazette." Bradley piles on bad news.

"Fuck." But I should expect it. In this town, any news is juicy gossip and quick to spread. It's faster than a wildfire. "How bad is it?"

"Considering she's an out of towner, and the extent of the burn, people are calling for blood. What did you do to get Judge Simon to let her out?" A scowl fixes on Bradley's face. He's not happy about this either.

I rub at the back of my neck. "I gave him my word I'd watch out for her."

"Watch out?" Brandon gives me a look. "As in how, exactly?"

"As in not letting her out of my sight."

That's not exactly the conversation I had with the judge, but it's pretty damn close. I gave him my word I wouldn't let her leave town. I don't know how much control I have over that, but she's my responsibility. The kicker is she doesn't even know it, yet.

"What can we do?" Brandon places his hand on my shoulder.

"Help me find the man who knocked her out." I shrug. It seems hopeless, but how else will I prove her innocence? There's little they can do, but I appreciate the offer.

Bradley gives a chin bump toward the front door. "Look who's back. Did you know Felix was back in town?"

I glance over my shoulder to see my high school nemesis walk through the entrance like he owns the place. Rivals in high school, we became enemies after his family lodged a land dispute against La Rouge Vineyards.

With our father's death, my brothers and I were left to fight that battle. We were young, green, and gullible. Felix's dirty tactics nearly shut my family's operation down.

"Felix fucked Erin at Cage's welcome home party." Neither of them have mentioned one word about Erin, but they must be curious.

"No shit," Brandon says. "Is that why she's no longer around?"

"To say there's bad blood between us is an understatement."

"So, where's that bastard been hiding the past eight years?" Brandon shifts to stand beside me.

"He cleaned himself up." Bradley bolsters my other side as Felix locks eyes with me.

My shoulders bunch and my fingers curl. I'm ready for a fight, but his oily gaze slides to the side and he takes a table as far from us as possible.

"Guess he's not interested in a reunion." My words are clipped. It's hard not to launch myself at the man who tried to destroy everything my family built. Now that he's back in town, I'll be watching my back.

At least I'll have the Bingham's watching it with me, as well as Brody and Cage.

12

EVELYN

It takes me longer than normal in the women's restroom, but that's because my mind won't stop. Overanalyzing, overthinking, I'm pretty much overwhelmed.

There was a time when I was the belle of the ball, society's up and coming socialite, primed to lead the next generation of New York's social elite.

I played the game. Looked the part. Fulfilled the role I was born to lead.

I did it seamlessly, effortlessly, at least on the outside.

Inside?

It was exhausting and draining and suffocating and I don't miss it.

Not one bit.

The constant pressure to be perfect, polite, and gracious wore me down, but I excel at imperfect perfection. I'm good with people.

This bar crowd?

I should be able to work them without a thought. Instead, they drain my energy and leave me a buzzing jangle of nerves.

All the smiling and pretending I'm having a good time? I don't know why I thought going to a bar was a good idea.

I officially suck at life right now and I'd give anything to return to the solitude of my mountain trails where I don't have to pretend or put on a show that everything is fine.

The bar is hopping, full of locals who stare at me, the newcomer, like I don't belong, which I don't, but I don't understand the dirty looks. What happened to small-town-friendly?

My imagination is hard at work it seems. Nobody here knows me and they have no reason to dislike me, but a palpable hostility vibrates in the air.

I'm certifiably crazy because my mind is making up stupid shit.

In my defense, it's been months since I've been around this many people. My solitary wilderness existence evidently has had some profound effect on me. Quiet is soul-soothing. Raucous bars are not. People who stare make me wary.

My hackles raise.

I'm in defensive mode.

This terrible unease manifests with an itch between my shoulder blades, one of those you can't quite reach. It feels as if nobody wants me around. Maybe, it's all in my head?

I'm a stranger in a strange town, out of my element and it shows. I used to be so good at this social shit. This was my zone, a socialite flitting about a crowd, working it to my advantage. All those social skills are stunted now, leaving me to hide out in the bathroom and overthink.

My comfort zone is out in the wilderness, hiking the trails, camping under the stars, and letting the world continue on without me.

People never used to make me nervous.

I sprinkle water on my makeup-less face and ignore how tired I look in the mirror. While I'd love to disappear, Asher is waiting on me. I can only hide in the bathroom for so long before it become too obvious. With a sigh, I force my feet to move.

Time to face the masses.

I toss my paper towel in the trash bin, and a crumpled newspaper catches my eye. It's the Daily Gazette. The headline screams: 'Arsonist Implicated in Local Fires.' My picture is plastered all over the front page, and it's not pretty. Who the hell took that, and when?

Maybe I didn't imagine all that hostility and anger. If my face is on the front page, everyone out there knows who I am. Which means I'm not some forgettable nobody. I'm front-fucking page news. My hand flies to cover my belly, where a troupe of butterflies takes flight. I feel like I'm going to be sick.

Fucking shit.

This isn't good.

I'm ready to find a rock and hide under it until this all blows over.

But will it?

There's the matter of proving my innocence, but how?

I suck in a breath and brace myself to face the people in the bar. It's pretty clear those scowls and pinched expressions aren't the result of an overly active imagination.

Shit!

What about Asher? If he associates with me, he's going to take the brunt of that fury, which means I need to place as much distance between us as possible. My stomach twists at the thought of leaving him.

But what else can I do?

My head is down as I turn the corner to head back to the bar.

I run right into a man.

"Whoa there. You okay?" He grips my arms to steady me. His voice sounds familiar, but one glance at his face and I know I've never met him before. He's clean-shaven with a rugged jawline. Tall with a stocky build. Sandy blond hair, cropped military short, his warm copper-colored eyes peer deep into mine. He's handsome, in the-guy-next-door kind of way, but nothing compared to Asher.

It feels as if he's looking for something out of me, a reaction, but I'm too out of sorts for idle chit-chat.

"I'm sorry. I didn't see you." I dip my head and mumble, hoping that's sufficient enough to end this engagement.

"Ah, it was my fault but, darling, you can run into me any day." His voice is warm and sociable, looking to draw me into conversation. I glance up, ready to make my excuses and get the hell out of here.

The way he looks at me, eyes boring, pupils dilating, makes me uncomfortable. His expression is expectant, searching, but I'm not sure what he's hoping for. I'm not interested in getting picked up.

I'm with Asher.

The man's hands remain on my arms. Isn't there a rule about how long casual contact should last? If so, we're far beyond that.

After seeing that headline, I'm skittish and afraid to lift my face to the room. I'm not sure if him holding me is the gesture of a kind individual, a horny looking-for-a-good-time kind of guy, or what comes right before a lynching.

Everyone's eyes are on me.

I'm ready to leave. Flee is more like it.

"You're not from around here, are you?" He continues to try to pull me into a conversation.

"No. Just passing through."

His sharp gaze never leaves me. He's easy on the eye and I bet the man is a ladykiller, but I'm not interested.

He's still holding my arms. His fingers wrap around my elbows and he doesn't let go when I give a little tug. Instead, he pulls me closer.

"You look familiar. Are you sure we haven't met?"

"I don't think so." I'd remember a man as handsome as him. He smells nice, almost too good. His cologne floods my senses with woodsy warmth and cinnamon spice, but I find it a little off-putting rather than sexy.

"Let me buy you a drink." The man is persistent, I give him a gold star for effort.

"Thank you, but—"

"She's with me, Felix." Asher's tone brooks no nonsense. He's staking his claim, and that claim happens to be me. Felix releases me as if bitten by a snake.

"You sure about that?" he snaps at Asher, full of male bravado, the kind when men mark their turf. I sense true hostility between the two men; a simmering hatred.

"Pretty damn sure." The way Asher speaks implies a whole lot of something. I'm not sure if the growl in his voice is because Felix had his hands on me or if there's something else between these men. One thing is certain. Asher staked his claim.

I'm his.

It's enough to make me sway on my feet. I'm used to men desiring me, but I've never been in a situation where they fought over me. As exciting as it sounds, in practice it's terrifying. I'm afraid they'll come to blows. This whole situation needs to be diffused.

But all I can think about is how much I enjoy Asher's hands on me. I sink into the comfort of his touch. He makes me feel not only safe, but protected.

Which is dangerous all on its own.

Whenever he's near, I want things I shouldn't.

Felix stands a little straighter, puffs his chest out, and breaches Asher's personal space. They're seconds from going toe-to-toe with each other. Fists curl. Muscles bunch.

I'm caught in the middle.

"Asher…" I press my hand against the flex of his bicep. "I'm thirsty."

Lame. I know, but it's all I can think of to distract the two men from initiating an all-out war.

I hold my breath, but Asher wraps his hand around my waist and spins me around.

"Yeah, let's get you a drink."

I need something much stronger than a drink.

Felix stands down, but his angry glare is hot on my back the whole way back to the bar. His intensity unnerves me, and he doesn't like the way Asher took me away from him.

Brandon and Bradley sit right where I left them, perched on barstools, fresh beers in hand. Their camaraderie is difficult to watch, because I miss that easy banter with my brother.

Brandon jumps off his stool. "And she's back!"

I lift on tiptoe and whisper into Asher's ear. "I want to go."

"Go?" His brows draw together.

"Yeah, it's too much."

Asher doesn't hesitate. He's comfortable here, surrounded by friends, and I can tell he's eager to hang out, but he doesn't try to convince me to stay.

"Sorry guys, we're taking off."

"Taking off?" Brandon places a hand to his chest, like he's wounded. "But we've barely begun. Come on, stay. The night is young, the beer is flowing, and the chicks…" He stops mid-sentence and gives me a wink. "Well, you know."

All I can think of is whoever finally lands one of the Bingham brothers is going to have her hands full. They're incorrigible, hot as sin, and evidently practiced at playing the field, but as attractive as they are, I'm happy with Asher by my side.

His hand hasn't left the small of my back and he leans down so that he doesn't have to yell over the crowd. "You sure you want to go?"

My nod is forceful.

"The lady has spoken. I'll catch you guys later." He steers me out of the bar and onto the quiet of the street.

13

EVELYN

Dusk fell hours ago and a smattering of stars dust the sky. A light breeze blows my hair against my cheek and I tuck the loose strands behind my ear enjoying the quiet. It's beautiful and I can't help but breathe it all in. How long has it been since I've been outside? It feels like forever. I miss my tent, my campfire, and the solitude of an empty trail.

My stomach gives a little rumble and Asher's soft laugh pulls me up short.

"What's so funny?" I ask.

"I should have taken you to dinner instead of a bar. You must be ravenous."

"I am." I missed lunch in my eagerness to get out of the hospital and, with the arrest, found myself cooling my heels in a holding cell. "What's good around here?"

"You like greasy diner food?"

"The greasier the better." There's nothing better than a greasy burger to take all my worries away. I've been living on trail food for months. "A burger sounds perfect."

"Ah, my kind of girl. Come on. I know just the place."

He takes me to a small diner and we snuggle into a corner

booth. It's quaint and empty. We're the only customers, just what I need. Our waitress fills our drinks, takes in an eyeful of Asher, and pretty much ignores me. Good thing I told Asher what I wanted. He orders for us and the starry-eyed waitress finally leaves.

"Sorry." He bites his lower lip.

"Does that happen to you a lot? Women falling over themselves when you're around?"

"Is there a safe answer to that question?"

"It's not a trick question. You can be honest." It's not like we're dating. All we've done is kiss, and there's the whole me grabbing his dick thing.

"Well, yeah. I'm sure you get it too. You're a fucking knockout. I bet men trip all over themselves trying to get to you."

"Me?"

"You don't see it, do you?"

I'm aware of my looks. My parents blessed me with their genetics. My looks let me get away with things I shouldn't, but I never flaunt them, and men don't trip over themselves trying to get to me. I've been taken nearly my entire life and only ever had eyes for one man.

Justin and I grew up together. We were pals in grade school. Best friends in those early, awkward tween years, and dated all through high school. We were never apart and shared all our firsts. High school sweethearts, we graduated and attended the same university. After getting my father's blessing, Justin proposed. Our union was inevitable.

He went to work for his father, while I planned our wedding with my mother and future mother-in-law, Gracie. I thought of nothing but the family Justin and I would raise, the grandkids my parents, and his, would enjoy and spoil. I was living my happily-ever-after. Other men were never on my radar.

Then life happened.

"How well do you know our waitress?" I need to change the conversation. Not to mention our waitress seems overly familiar with Asher. That doesn't sit well with me.

"I grew up in this town, so I pretty much know everyone."

"Meaning you've played the field?" Why does that pop out of my mouth? I sound like a jealous bitch. I have no claim on this man.

"In a small town, it's hard not to kind of get around."

"So, you're a self-proclaimed man-whore?"

"I wouldn't call it that, but I've dated my fair share of eligible bachelorettes." He rubs at the back of his neck, a gesture I'm beginning to associate with him being uneasy.

He says bachelorettes like he's looking for a wife.

Not girls.

Not women.

Not chicks-I-like-to-bang.

Bachelorettes.

His word choice does not go unnoticed.

"I bet every eligible bachelorette has fallen for you and they're probably plotting to figure out how to land a catch like you."

"I wouldn't say every bachelorette." He gives a devilish, satisfied grin and puffs out his chest like a preening bird.

It shouldn't be sexy, but damn he's broad shouldered and that poor shirt of his struggles to contain the bulk of his muscles. Subconsciously, I rub at my chin because I swear I'm drooling.

"You think I'm a catch." His smirk says everything. I just gave him all the ammunition he needs to use against me.

"I didn't say that. You're putting words in my mouth."

"I'd rather put something else in that pretty little mouth." Heat fills his gaze.

The air between us goes from a banked simmer to a full-on inferno in zero-seconds flat. And damn if his hooded gaze doesn't work magic on me.

I'm hot and bothered and resist the urge to fan myself in front of him. Instead, I place my hands between my thighs and squeeze against the unbearable ache. The corner of his mouth tics up when I squirm in my seat.

Yeah, he knows exactly what kind of effect he has on me.

"You have nothing to worry about." He announces it as a fact.

"Is that so?"

"Were you not there during that kiss? Fuck, Ev-e-lyn, that was nuclear explosive hot. You felt what you do to me, or did you forget where you had your hand?"

I glance around the diner, worried we can be overheard.

He gives a soft laugh and puts his hand over mine.

"You jump like a scared little mouse."

"Maybe this isn't the best place to be talking about where my hand may, or may not, have been."

"Your hand most definitely was on my dick, my hard, rigid cock." His voice drops to a lower register and there's a throaty growl to it which melts my insides.

I turn into a liquid puddle, a needy mess who wants everything he promises.

"My lips were on your mouth, and all I could think about was how my dick would feel with your lips wrapped around it. Or better yet, what you'll taste like when I finally get to bury my face between your legs."

"Asher!"

"What?" It's his turn to look around. "There's nobody in here besides us. Tell me you aren't wondering the same thing?"

"What about the waitress?"

"I don't want her mouth on my dick."

"I meant that she can hear us."

"Oh, Katy might be watching us, but she can't hear what we're saying. She's trying to figure out who you are, and is probably plotting your murder."

"My murder?"

"I'm kidding. She's probably just hoping you're a one and done kind of fling so she can get back in line. Unfortunately, that's not happening."

What part wasn't happening? The one and done bit or her getting back in line?

Katy? I don't remember seeing a name tag, which reminds me how small this town must be for him to know her name.

"Have you lived anywhere but here?"

"We moved here when I was eight," he says.

"What brought you here?"

"The La Rouge Vineyards passed to my father. He came to take over the family business when his uncle grew sick."

"Really? How long have the vineyards been in your family?"

"My great-grandfather established the vineyards."

"That's cool. And when your father passes? Does it go to you?"

"It did." He uses the past tense.

"Oh, I'm sorry."

"Thanks, it was some time ago, a couple years after graduation. Technically, it belongs to me and my brothers. We co-manage it."

"That's cool."

"How's that cool?"

"It's a family legacy." A sharp stabbing pain rips through me. I'm all that's left of the Thornton name and what am I doing to our legacy?

You're running away from it. You're letting it die.

All of Prescott's concerns slam into me and it's difficult to catch my breath. He's right. The bastard has been right all this time. I might be able to run from my past, but I can't deny my birthright.

"You got real quiet, little backpack. Is everything okay?"

His silly nickname brings a smile to my face.

"Sorry. Just a bit overwhelmed. It's been a long day."

I'm saved from explaining anything further because Katy returns with my greasy cheeseburger and Asher's chicken wings.

"Mm, looks great," Asher says.

"Thanks, Ace. You need anything?" Her eyes stick to Asher. Her hand slides over his shoulder and her fingers rub at the side of his neck.

I've ceased to exist.

Hello, bitch! He was kissing me just a few short hours ago and his dick got hard for me!

My lips remained sealed and I stew in my seat while shooting daggers at Katy with my eyes. She's oblivious, too wrapped up in Asher to notice me.

However, he's not giving her two cents of his time. Without breaking stride, he removes her hand from his neck and lets it drop.

"We're good, Katy. Just need a little privacy for our date."

Katy's eyes widen. Her lips press together, but she says nothing.

That thrills me, more than it should. I'm a greedy, jealous bitch which is totally not like me. I've never been like this with anyone.

Not even the man I was going to marry.

With a chicken wing in his mouth, Asher dismisses our overly eager waitress. He stops gnawing on the wing and glances at me. Putting the bones on his plate, he slowly licks his fingers. Why is that so damn sexy?

Because you're wondering what it will feel like when he licks you…down there. My cheeks heat from the visual. That's exactly what I'm thinking.

I'm not sure why, but it's easily the most erotic thing I've ever seen. Probably because I imagine how his lips and that talented tongue might feel licking me instead. A low ache builds in my core. I press my legs together and squirm in my seat.

"Katy can be a little over the top, but she's harmless. We went to high school together. Hung out a little. Fooled around once or twice, but that's way in the past."

"Oh." I want to ask so much more—Like, did you sleep with her?—but I hold my tongue. We both have pasts. I haven't told him mine. No reason to expect him to spill his dirty secrets.

He reaches across the table and grips my hand. "Relax. You're wound up pretty tight. And for the record, there's only one woman I want to sleep with, sleep definitely not being the operative word." The wink he gives me is enough to set my heart racing.

Holy hellfire he gets directly to the point. I find it insanely hot. I can make all kinds of bad decisions with Asher La Rouge.

But where's the harm in a little fun?

Because you don't do casual. Never have.

I really hate when that little voice in my head starts hammering at me with truths I want to ignore.

But it is the truth.

I don't do casual. I've never had a fling. No one-night stands. No sex with strangers. Nothing adventurous or wild like that.

I've always been a good girl, with a good reputation, a boyfriend who respected me, and who begged for years before I finally spread my legs for him. Not that I ever intended to save myself for marriage.

Cautious and content is my life. I'm so damn boring.

Maybe, in escaping my past, stepping things up a notch isn't such a bad idea. If I really want to take charge of my life, I should let my wild side out and live a little. Experience what a little reckless-ness might feel like. It does seem as if a willing participant sits directly across from me.

Asher La Rouge are you the man to pull me out from this suffo-cating shell?

"Do I wear my emotions on my sleeve?"

"Yeah, a little. Want to tell me what happened in the bar? You sounded like you needed to let off a little steam, but then I couldn't get you out of there fast enough. What changed?"

"I saw the headline in the Gazette." My shoulders slumped.

It hurts saying it out loud. I feel victimized, tried and found guilty without a chance to defend myself. All the dirty looks from the bar make sense now. It wasn't my imagination and that makes me want to hightail it out of this damn town. I'm not sure if that's allowed with this damn arson thing hanging over my head.

The only thing keeping me here is the man sitting across from me. Leaving him, before I have a chance of exploring what's happening between us, simply isn't a consideration. For the first time, in a very long time, I want to stay in one place for more than a day.

"Yeah, right," he says.

"You knew about it?" If so, he should have warned me.

"I didn't know you made front page news until after you left to use the restroom. Brandon mentioned it."

"So, the whole town knows?"

"Most likely." The affirmation in his voice scares me.

"And that doesn't bother you?"

"Why should it?"

"I've been tried and convicted in the court of public opinion, which means you're associating with an arsonist."

"But you're not an arsonist." He gives a shake of his head. "Besides, I don't care what they think."

"You're not worried that hanging out with me might blow back on you?"

This is his town. I'm an interloper, here and gone, but he'll stay behind and deal with the fallout after I leave.

"No one has the guts to say anything to me. They might be watching and gossiping, but don't worry. We're going to sort this out."

"You're really not concerned?" He should put as much distance between us as possible. He has a business to run, two businesses, and the whole volunteer firefighting gig on the side.

"I'm one hundred percent not worried. The Gazette is a gossip magazine. Once we figure everything out, everyone will move on to the next juicy bit of news. Don't let it bother you. And as for being seen with you, I don't give a shit what anyone thinks."

"Not even your friends?"

"Brandon and Bradley trust me. They even offered to help."

Frustration spills through me. "Honestly, I have no idea what to do. It's my word against hundreds of acres of scorched earth."

And no one seems to care about the man who knocked me out. He's a ghost in the wind, or rather a ghost in the ash.

"We'll figure it out." Asher sounds assured of the outcome.

How is he so certain? I know I didn't do it, but all he has is his faith in me.

I'm scared.

I'm really scared.

14

EVELYN

A YAWN ESCAPES ME. IT'S LATE AND MY LACK OF LODGING accommodations is going to be problematic sooner rather than later. A quick internet search reveals very few local hotels. None which come close to anything I consider safe.

Prescott thinks I'm not concerned enough about my safety, but I am. Two motels on the edge of town are quick discards. Their online photos look seedy, more of the rent for an hour kind of place than where I want to spend the night. There's one hotel near the center of town, but they don't seem to have internet booking. I'll have to call them once Asher and I leave the diner.

We finish dinner in relative quiet. An easy silence flows between us with no need to fill it with random words or aimless discussion. As the evening wears on, my curiosity about Asher increases and I dig for information with soft probing questions.

He's easy to talk to, like an old friend, and forthcoming about La Rouge Vineyards. His animated stories about some of the tourists he's taken on trail rides leaves me in stitches. His stallion, Knight, who loves to test him, is a character. I love horses. People often underestimate them, but they're full of personality.

He speaks fondly of George, his foreman, who helps him

keep everything working smoothly at the vineyard, and there's something else I learn. He loves his workers, often working beside them during the harvest, and joining their families for barbecues, birthdays, weddings, and the rare funeral. He's easy going, fast to smile, and an expressive talker. We laugh more than we talk.

And I let down my guard.

I breathe easier and imagine what such a life might feel like. It sounds wonderful.

Katy fills our empty glasses for the fifth time with an audible sigh. She plops a check on the table and spins around without a word.

"I guess we've been told it's time to go," I say.

Asher laughs. "I suppose so."

My lack of sleeping accommodations—my lack of everything actually, weighs heavily on me. All I have is a phone, the clothes on my back, and a wallet full of fresh credit cards. In a small town like this, however, I don't anticipate many late-night shopping opportunities.

Asher pays the bill, leaves a generous tip, and wraps his arm around my shoulders as we leave. Every chance he gets, he touches me. Whether it's his hand on my back, an arm draped over my shoulder, or his fingers entwined with mine, we're in constant physical contact.

He's completely absorbed in me.

I'm not used to the attention, but I love it. The degree with which I love it makes me question some of my previous choices.

I've known Asher less than two weeks, yet feel closer to him than I ever did with Justin. Sure, Justin had a comfortable familiarity about him. Our history bound us together. We were good in bed, nothing earth-shattering, and I was happy.

Content.

But I wasn't head over heels in love.

It never occurred to me how much of a spark Justin and I never shared.

It makes me sad. Sad for me. Sad for him. Sad that we were

ready to commit our lives to each other without ever really being in love which each other.

Things are different with Asher, if I decide to head down that path. It's not as if I'm head over heels in love with Asher. The spark igniting between us is too new, too incendiary. It's combustible which makes it unreliable. We're more likely to burn and crash than sustain whatever this is that's happening between us.

The thing is, Asher appears more than eager to lead me into the inferno of what we can become. It's written in the smoldering looks and the soft touches which linger longer than they should. The way his touch sets off a storm of electrical sparks shooting through my body, tells me I'm happy to follow. Yet, Asher doesn't push.

The one kiss is all we've had, yet it reverberates inside of me with echoes of what might be.

The heat.

The passion.

The promise for more.

All it'll take is one spark to kindle an awakening inside of me. The only question is will it burn through me like a firestorm, leaving nothing but destruction in its path? Or is it sustainable, a low simmering heat which can last a lifetime?

But as that fire burns, what price will it claim? This is what worries me the most. Will my memories of Justin fade away? Will my love for him be obliterated in the sizzling heat promised in the lusty gazes Asher so easily tosses my way?

Is that something I want?

Is it something I can live with?

When we head out to his truck, I pause.

"What's wrong?" He spins me until I face him, placing both of his hands on my hips.

He towers over me and I brace against his overwhelming presence. There's too much of him to take in.

"I've been so caught up in everything I haven't really thought about where I'll stay for the night. Not to mention I have no toothbrush and nothing but the clothes on my back. What are the chances there's a store open this time of night?"

"There's always the mother of all superstores. They're open 24-7. It's about a half-hour drive. Does that fit the bill?"

I cringe. I'm a bit more discerning in my tastes, but then I can generally afford to be. This is not the case right now, however.

"It'll have to do. I should probably find a hotel first."

"Hotel?" His brows pinch together and he rubs at the back of his neck. "I figured you'd stay with me."

"You?"

"Sure." He gives a shrug, like it's a foregone conclusion. "I just assumed."

That I would stay with him, or sleep with him?

Okay, I may be assuming the exact same thing, but I'm a little concerned. This is moving too fast. Can I handle a relationship that's only about sex? Is that even considered a relationship? What does it mean when I want more? And I do want more. I don't want to be a notch on Asher's bedpost. The wild and free me simply doesn't exist. My brain, and heart, are hard-wired for commitment. That may be a problem.

But if I'm going to throw caution to the wind, Asher's just the guy. I can do this, and it'll be fun. My hope is I won't wake up regretting it when I walk away.

And I hope I'm the one who does walk away.

I can't argue with myself. And as far as being safe, Asher's more than proven he's trustworthy. He's already done so much for me and hasn't asked for anything in return, but I'm not ready to jump into the deep end.

Why not?

My head spins, considering all the options, weighing the best course of action, and deciding if the risk is worth the reward.

I could go on all night, but the truth is I'm tired. This whole ordeal finds me overwhelmed; my confidence is undermined. I second guess every decision I've made and those I'm considering.

I thought I could take on the world and thought nothing about heading out into the wilderness alone, hiking and camping in an attempt to find myself and escape my past. Now the idea terrifies me. Some might call it PTSD from getting whacked on the head. I call it discouraging.

"I don't know. I'd hate to impose."

"Impose? Shit, I'd count myself lucky if you say yes." He wraps his arms around me and kisses the top of my head. "Look, it's away from town, prying eyes, and gossiping townies. It's the perfect place to relax. If it makes you feel any better, I offered your friend to stay there too."

"My friend?"

"Prescott."

"Oh." No way would Prescott stay with a stranger. "What did he say?"

"It was a polite, yet firm, hell no."

"That sounds just like him."

"Well, he'll be here in the morning, and I'm sure you'll have tons to talk about. But in the meantime, you'll stay with me." He says it as if it's a foregone conclusion.

"I appreciate it. I really do, but that's a big ask, and you've already done so much for me."

He bites his lower lip. "This might sound a bit weird, but I kind of need you to stay with me."

"Come again?"

"Well, other than the obvious…" The crooked grin he gives is easily becoming one of my favorite features. "I kind of promised the judge I'd keep an eye on you until your arraignment."

"What?"

He releases my hips and takes a step back. "I gave my word that I'd watch over you until the arraignment. If you want to stay in a hotel, we can do that, but my place is much more comfortable. You'll have your own room, of course, unless…" He's quick to add that last bit, but I'm pretty sure that's not where he wants me to sleep.

"Who did you give your word to?"

"The judge. I had to convince him to set your bail."

"Wow, I thought Prescott sorted that out. I'm really in your debt. I can't believe you did that for me."

It's not possible, but I'm falling for Asher's heroics. I've never had someone go to such great lengths on my behalf.

"Perks of knowing pretty much everyone in town. Besides, Judge Simon loves La Rouge wines."

"You really do know everyone, don't you?"

"Well, he's actually kind of sweet on my mom. I may, or may not, have promised to arrange something to help get them together."

"You did what?"

"I pimped my mom to get my girl out of jail." He winks, and I swear my heart skips a beat. "It was either that or leave you in a holding cell through the weekend. I'm sure your friend, Prescott, could've gotten you out tomorrow, but I couldn't bear thinking of you staying there all night. It's the least I could do."

"The least?" I place my hand on his arm. "You've done more for me than anyone. Thank you." I wrap my arms around him. "Of course, I'd love to stay at your place."

"Where I can keep my eye on you." Another one of his devilish smirks makes an appearance. "And do very bad things to you." The rasp in his voice sends chills down my spine.

"Bad things?" I play coy, like I have no idea what he's thinking.

"Very bad things."

"Like what?" How deliciously deviant can he be? I lift up on tiptoe and kiss the tip of his chin.

"You really want to know?" His arm wraps around me and he pulls me tight against him where the evidence of his arousal jabs into my hip.

"That depends."

"Hmm... You stretched out on my bed comes to mind. I'm thinking a little rope to keep you right where I want you. And then I intend on taking my time getting to explore every inch of your body."

Holy shit, but he doesn't mince words.

"Rope?"

"It's a particular skillset I'm good at. You might remember how efficiently I tied you up the first time."

"Oh, I remember." Being a living backpack and riding Asher away from that fire is not something I'll ever forget.

"I plan on getting lost inside of you. How's that for what I want?"

"Pretty damn clear."

"I can be a saint. The guest room is yours, if that's what you need, but damn if the devil in me doesn't want to come out and play. There are so many sinful things I want to do to you."

His words heat me up from the inside and I bite my lip thinking about some of the things I want him to do.

"Hmm, I'm not sure." I shouldn't tease him, but I can't help myself.

Spending the night with him doesn't feel like relaxing. It sounds like taking all this sexual energy swirling around us, bottling it up, and shaking it until it explodes.

It sounds a whole lot like a bad idea.

Which is why I'm fully on board.

"I want to kiss you until your lips are imprinted on my soul. Devour you until your taste lingers on my tongue. Your cries of pleasure will be the only thing I hear for weeks to come. I want to bury myself inside you, feel your pussy milk my cock and spend all night inside of you. But, if you prefer the guest room, you can sleep alone."

"I guess we'll just have to see. How about we stop and get a few things?" Like clothes I probably won't wear if Asher gets his way.

The entire weekend stretches before us and I plan on spending that time in Asher's bed letting him do all the devious things he wants.

He takes a deep breath and leans into me. Every molecule of oxygen in the air disappears because I'm suddenly breathless and panting. His lips hover, kissably close.

"I hope I'm not scaring you, my little backpack, but I haven't felt this way in a very long time."

I've never felt this way.

The distance between our lips vanishes as he brushes his over mine. Unlike our previous kiss, this one is slow, determined, and utterly breathtaking. There's a power he holds over me. It's mesmerizing and there's a very real chance I'm falling for him.

It's as if he's captured my breath and is holding it hostage until he decides to release me. Surrender is my only option and I freely let myself go as he nibbles and licks, soft at first then a little more insistent.

"I want you." The words are possessive and reverberate within every molecule inside of me.

My body comes alive pressed against his, lips locked to his, his arms wrapped around my waist. The soft, gentle, but insistent kiss, morphs into something needier, hungrier. Desperation fuels my breaths because I want to give him everything he wants. The deep groan spilling from him elicits an answering murmur from me.

"Fuck, Evelyn, what you do to me is criminal."

"Asher..." His name slips from my lips in a drawn-out moan, full of desire and unrequited need. I'm inpatient and needy. I grab at his shirt, needing to pull it off, but he grips my wrist and tugs it free.

A low chuckle escapes him. "Fuck. I need you, but if we don't cool this down right now, we'll both be arrested for indecent exposure."

"Take me home."

"The best words I ever heard, but what about that shopping trip?"

"Fuck shopping." I'll deal with my lack of clothing and toiletries later.

Still gripping my wrist, he lowers my hand to his groin where he places it over the hard ridge of his erection. "Do you feel what you do to me?"

My fingers stretch against his arousal. Denim separates me from what I want.

"We need to stop for condoms." His low chuckle vibrates the air.

I'm not sure what it is about his voice. Either it's the low rasp, the deep rumble, or something else, but it's like throwing gasoline on a smoldering flame. Every groan, each rumble, ignites an inferno within me. Flames licks along my skin, scorching hot, it sears a path to my heart where it burns its way inside and settles in, warming me up from the inside out.

"We need to go," I say.

He walks me to my door, holds it open while I climb in, and I stifle a little cry when he releases me to get in the driver's seat. Nothing is said between us as he drives through the dark streets and makes a stop at a small gas station. We both head in. Me to buy a toothbrush and other sundry goods. Him to purchase the condoms we plan on using tonight.

We're back on the road, silence descending between us. Unlike the comfortable quiet we shared in the diner, this one fills with anticipation for what's to come.

Vineyards are all around us, marching off in ordered roads. He pulls off the main road and down a tree-lined drive, where the branches arc up and over us, forming a living tunnel. It's beyond gorgeous. The long drive takes us to a stone manor, wrapped all around by a massive covered porch. That's all I see before he drags me inside.

I'm not sure which one of us starts what happens next, but there's a brief moment of eye contact. A nod from me, then we stagger down a hall like a bunch of drunk and horny teenagers, careening off the walls as we head to his room.

My back bumps against the wall as his hands find their way beneath my shirt. He grips the edge and pulls it over my head where he releases it. My shirt falls to the floor as we trip over the long rug running down the hall. I laugh. He joins me. Then our bodies collide once again with grabbing hands and desperate lips.

He slams me against the wall and I tug at his shirt while he kisses me senseless. We're a frenzied mess, divesting each other of the clothing which keeps us apart.

We greedily remove the barriers keeping us from feeling the heat surging between us. There's a brief moment when he hops on one foot, trying to get his jeans off over his shoe. He finally stops and braces an arm against the wall to bend down and free first one shoe and then the other. Then he kicks off his jeans.

The entire time I feast my hungry gaze on the ripped expanse of his shoulders, his back, and the well-defined six pack he's sporting. One article of clothing separates us and I reach for the waistband of his briefs.

"Uh-uh." He points to my pants. "You're falling behind."

I bite my lower lip as he prowls toward me and flicks free the button of my pants. I'm panting, breathless, and Asher stares at me with heat simmering in his eyes. "Last chance. The guest room is right there." He gestures somewhere back the way we came.

"I don't want the guest room."

He smiles in victory then goes to his knees before me. Slowly, inexorably, he tugs my pants over the flare of my hips, around the globes of my ass, and draws it down the length of my legs. I step out of each leg as his face is eye-level with the apex of my thighs. My girly bits tingle in anticipation.

"God, you smell fucking phenomenal." He buries his nose between my legs and breathes me in.

It's a little uncomfortable. I don't know what to do with my hands or where I should look, but when he pulls aside the fabric of my panties and licks right there, I no longer care. I rise on my toes and dig my fingers into his hair.

He laughs at my reaction and teases me with the sweet torture of his tongue. Then he draws down my panties, baring me to him. He knocks gently at my knees, encouraging my legs to part to give him unrestricted access.

I'm wet and ready. He slides his finger inside of me and my breath hitches. When he sucks on my clit, gently biting down, my hips buck as I beg for more.

15

ASHER

ASHER

Sensory fucking overload.

I found heaven and I'm in no hurry to leave.

Evelyn is a fucking minx, responsive to my touch like no one ever before. Bare to me, her pussy begs for attention and I intend giving her exactly that. My dick hardens and aches, but I'm not ready to slip inside her.

Not yet.

But soon.

My fingers flutter over her folds, discovering her secrets. I pay attention to her breaths, those low, sultry moans spilling from her lips, and how she yanks on my hair. God, it's fucking sexy as hell with her fingers digging into my scalp. I could make her come with a well-placed flick of my tongue, but where's the fun in that?

With deliberate intent, I slip my fingers inside her pussy, barely entering as I use the pad of my thumb to rub and press against her clit.

I'm learning what turns her on, and right now, that's about everything.

"Fuck…" My low growl reveals the beast I barely contain.

"Asher…" The way she moans my name is indecent. "I need you to…"

Oh, I know exactly what she needs, but we're not rushing through our first time.

"Hold on, luv."

She squirms and writhes while my fingers slide in and out of her wet heat. I find and claim her g-spot as my own. She lifts on tiptoe the moment I find it and yanks on my hair again.

Her climax builds. I read it in the fine tremors of her body, the way her legs shake, and by how hard she yanks on my hair. My roots are taking a beating, but I don't fucking care. Her breathy moans, and her cries for more, are the road signs leading me down the path of her pleasure.

I slide my fingers up and down her slit, dipping two at a time inside, and lick her clit, giving tiny flicks of my tongue as I devour her sweet essence. Her hips buck, begging for more. Her breaths turn rapid and shallow as my fingers pump in and out, then her legs tense and one wave after another rushes through her. Back arching, legs tensing, she comes all over my hand and face.

Fucking-amazing. The taste of her on my lips. Her arousal glistening between her legs. It's all I can do to lick and finger her through her orgasm rather than take her right then.

My dick is hard. Needy. And no longer willing to wait its turn.

"Fuck, luv, but you're so damn gorgeous when you come."

She releases my hair and her head tilts back against the wall. "Holy fuck that was intense, but if you don't fuck me right now, I'm going to scream." Her gaze is needy, hot, and far from done. "I need you inside of me. Now."

More than willing to follow that command, I tear open a condom wrapper and roll it quickly on. I stagger to my feet, drunk on everything Evelyn, and more than a little concerned I'm not going to last. I'm ready to fucking explode as it is. Her eyes are on me, teeth biting into her lower lip, eyes hooded, breaths lifting her fucking amazing tits with each inhale.

My hands go to those, drawn irresistibly to cup her soft curves and run my fingers over the hardened nubs of her nipples.

"I'm not kidding, Asher. I need you now, and don't you dare take things slow."

Who needs more encouragement than that?

My room is at the far end of the hall, but I'm not wasting any more time. I grip her legs and lift them around my hips. "You ready for a ride, little backpack?"

Her eyes flare, opening wide, when she realizes I intend to take her here, right up against the wall. I'm more than strong enough and far too eager to take those final steps down the hall.

Her legs wrap around me and her ankles dig into my back. Her eyes flash and our eyes lock.

She gives a little nod and it's time for my breaths to go shallow.

Fuck taking things slow.

We'll have all the time in the world to get lost in each other later. Right now, I need to move.

I position her over the flare of my cock. My thick head teases her entrance and I lower her just enough for her to feel the size of my cock. I'm not a small man and I don't want to hurt her, but damn if I'm going to be able to go slow.

Her knees tighten around my hips and squeeze. I'm not sure if she's putting a stop to this or bracing for what's to come.

"Evelyn?"

"Don't stop." Her words are clipped short, but are all I need to hear.

She said not to go slow, but this first little bit I want to savor. The heat of her body promises intense pleasure to come. With her back braced against the wall and my hands holding the globes of her ass, I don't lower her down on my length so much as lift up and thrust.

She cries out, not in pain, but with pleasure, as I slide inside of her.

"You like that, luv?"

"Yes. God, yes." Her knees tighten around my hips and I realize she's trying to impale herself on my dick rather than brace against the intrusion. I, however, don't fucking care. Her wet heat encircles my dick and I feel every inch as I bury myself inside of her wet heat. I take my time, enjoying the wicked, delicious torture of taking it slow. This is the only chance I'll have to really feel her wrapped around me and I aim to enjoy every damn second of it.

Before I know it, I'm buried fully inside of her. She said not to take things slow, but I know she needs time for her body to accommodate to the slow burn my invasion causes. When I can't handle standing still any longer, the muscles of my arms flex in time with my hips. I draw out and slide back in, loving the exquisite sensation of sinking inside of her.

A few more times in and out and she's panting again, climbing toward another orgasm. Her fingers claw my shoulders and dig into my back. I draw out and then, in one dizzying thrust, I slam my hips up, thrusting hard until I'm sheathed root to tip. A moan escapes her.

"Fuck, you feel amazing."

"More, Asher. Please."

With my restraint pushed to the breaking point, there's no more taking this slow.

Our eyes meet. Her fingers dig into my shoulders. Her legs wrap around my hips. And I move. Not slow. I clench my muscles and pick up the pace, thrusting into her as deeply as I can, slamming her hard against the wall.

I love how her eyes close and her mouth parts. I lean forward and claim that mouth as my assault continues. Kissing her, my tongue moves in synch with the thrusting of my hips. My biceps are getting a workout, lifting and lowering her as I thrust, but what do I care. I can do this all day.

She writhes and bucks as I chase every ounce of pleasure from our coupling. One bruising thrust after another, I pound into her as every nerve in my body stands up and takes notice. My dick is greedy, insatiable, and mindless with its need.

Pleasure hums in my blood and races around in my veins, as she grinds down on me. There's no thought, only action, as our climax bears down without mercy.

She's close. I feel it.

Time stands still. It rushes forward. It slows the fuck down. I don't know if I've been fucking her for seconds, minutes, or hours, all I know is the pleasure building within me is bearing down on me with all the tenacity of a freight train.

And I'm holding out for her second orgasm before I finally allow myself to fulfill my desperate need to come.

The sound of our bodies connecting, her soft cries of pleasure, my deep breaths, the slapping of flesh on flesh, it's intoxicating. She returns my kisses eagerly. Then lets go, arching her back as I drive her against the wall.

The smell of sex floods my senses. The taste of her coats my mouth. The feel of her sliding up and down my cock is enough to drive me insane. Her breasts bounce between us, and I'm torn between grabbing them and supporting her as I fuck her senseless. Those breasts have been painfully neglected.

I'm aware of everything about her, unsure how I got to be this lucky, but knowing one thing for certain. I'll never get enough of this amazing woman.

With every part of my body attuned to her, the moment she peaks is not one I'll ever forget. She cries out as she comes, her pussy pulses around my cock, and she buries her head against my neck. That's all I need.

With every nerve ready to fire, my dick explodes in a tidal wave of sensation reaching all the way to my groin where it shoots up the base of my spine. I drown in pleasure as she milks my release, drawing me under, pushing me sideways, stealing my breath, until I can't take it anymore. My hips still. My arms ache. Blissful satisfaction courses through my body and flashes of ecstasy randomly fire as I slowly come down from that blissful high.

She wraps her arms around my neck and murmurs in my ear.

"Fucking amazing. I've never come that hard. And that's my first time getting fucked against a wall. Fucking fantastic."

While I preen under her praise, I'm nowhere near to being done. That was fast and reckless. It's time for slow and purposeful. Our clothes are strewn down the hall, and my brothers will likely rib me about that later. I have no idea if they're home or out banging random chicks. Frankly, I don't give a fuck.

My dick is spent, and as I carry her to my bedroom, our connection is momentarily severed. Not that I'm worried. We have all night in each other's arms and it won't be too long until I'm buried deep inside of her again.

I walk to the foot of my bed and slowly lower her down on the mattress. Turning my back, I take care of the condom, pulling it off and tying it closed. It goes in the trash as I spin around where I can finally feast upon Evelyn's gloriously naked body.

She stretches and yawns. Her toes curl tight and her tits jut forward as her arms lift over her head.

"Don't think for a minute you're going to sleep. We've barely started."

"Is that so?"

A quick glance at my twitching dick tells me this is so. I need a little more time to recover, but I know exactly how to pass the time.

Those amazing tits are calling my name.

16

EVELYN

THE NIGHT PASSES IN A BLUR OF SENSATION. WE GO FROM FRENZIED fucking to more leisurely lovemaking. I ride the ebb and flow of Asher's hunger until we both finally give in to the sweet embrace of sleep.

Morning comes far too soon and, when I wake, the intoxicating smell of bacon fills the air. Light streams through a gap in the curtains and dust motes dance in the sunbeams spilling into the room. The comforter lies in a crumpled mess on the floor and the sheets are a knotted mess. Wrapped in Asher's arms all night, I found myself blissfully content, but he's not here.

The bed is empty.

Asher must have awakened early, which explains the mouthwatering smells coming from down the hall. It tickles me that he's making breakfast for us. I'm finding Asher exceptionally attentive and I'm not ashamed to say I'm loving every second of it. My life has been easy, but nobody's ever pampered me the way this man does. No one's ever made love to me the way he did last night.

Rising from bed, my quick scan of the room reveals my clothing propped on the overstuffed corner chair in a neat little stack.

A blush rises in my cheeks. Asher bent me over the arm of that chair and fucked me from behind, bringing me to my third epic climax. The memory of everything we did makes me smile.

My heart fills with the tender display of the neatly stacked pile of my clothes. We left a mess of discarded clothing strewn down that hall. His consideration for my comfort means more than he'll ever know. Not many men would pick up a woman's clothes, let alone fold them.

My clothes aren't clean, but they're far from dirty. Not that dirt bothers me. I'm a hiker and a camper. I've worn my hiking gear for days before considering it in need of a fresh wash. Not knowing how long Asher has been up, I make use of the adjoining master bathroom to freshen up. Then I pull on my clothing from the day before, minus the panties, and head out of his room in search of those mouthwatering smells.

In our sexual frenzy, we skipped the obligatory house tour, but I find my way without difficultly by following my nose. Music blares through what appears to be house-wide speakers because the pulse-pounding invigorating rock music pours into every room. It's throaty, deep and powerful with its unapologetic lyrics and demanding bass lines.

And it's loud.

The mouthwatering smell of bacon frying on the stove lures me down the hall, through a massive living area, into a study, and finally to what must be a gourmet chef's dream kitchen.

The house is gorgeous with stone walls, wooden floors, and massive wood beams holding up a towering ceiling. Neutral tones predominate; from the brown leather couches to the light taupe widow dressings.

Yet there are pops of color here and there. Nothing feminine. A flash of cornflower blue in a pillow, ruby red in the floral display on the coffee table. A dash of yellow on the built-in bookcases which are crammed full of well-loved books.

The weight of history hangs over the place and I envision generations of La Rouge children running through these rooms. Family portraits decorate the walls, La Rouge families gathering with stern-faced fathers, stoic mothers, and kids with lots of smiling and goofing off. The place feels like home and I can't help but wrap my arms around myself.

When I make my way to the kitchen, I stop dead in my tracks. I'm not particularly inclined in the cooking department, but Asher appears to be fully at home in front of the stove.

But that's not what pulls me to a dead halt.

All night, I had Asher naked in bed, but that's nothing compared to a shirtless Asher filling out a pair of denim jeans which hug him in all the right places. That ass is fine and I'm not against ogling it for a few seconds. Not to mention the broad expanse of his back. The way it tapers down to a trim waist is enough to make any girl drool. And those biceps, perhaps my favorite feature, the way they flex and bunch makes me squirm.

He's a powerful man, a gentle lover, and a raging beast all rolled into one. I told him not to take things easy last night and he put me through my paces, deliciously so, exposing me to his feral nature in what I can only describe as the most intense sexual experience of my life.

The straps of muscles across his back flex as he dances to the music. He rocks the beat, moving his hips in a seductive dance. If I were wearing panties, this is the moment they would burst into flames and land me flat on my back ready for an encore of last night. Actually, that countertop looks a bit underutilized.

We christened every available surface in his bedroom. Why not do the same in his kitchen? Hell yeah, I'm ready to go another few rounds.

His back is to me, and he doesn't hear me enter. He can't because the music is too loud.

Damn, the man can move. He's good enough to star in one of those all-male dance reviews. Thunder from down under? Hell, I'm ready for a little more thunder down there right now, courtesy of one Asher La Rouge, and I know the man can bring it.

Biting my lower lip, I decide to take advantage of the opportunity and sneak up behind him. I bite my lip as I debate my options. Completely oblivious to my presence, his hips gyrate and thrust forward.

I slide my hands up his back then drag my nails back down over his hard muscles. His entire body stills and I take the opportunity to wrap my arms around his waist where I trace the expanse of his chest with my fingertips.

After last night, I'm officially an expert in every rise and dip of his sculpted perfection, but that doesn't mean I don't want more.

"Good morning, handsome." I use my most seductive voice. "Wanna go for a ride? I'm not wearing panties." It's not my fault, I'm needy and horny.

The direction of my exploratory fingers change course, dipping down the hard ridges of his well-defined six-pack where I allow them to sink below the waistband of his jeans. My fingers flitter across the tip of his cock encouraging a response.

"Whoa!" His entire body jerks. He grips my wrist and spins around, holding me out and away from his body. "Good morning to you too sweetheart, but how about a 'Hello nice to meet you' before you go shoving your hand down my pants and grabbing my junk."

"Huh?"

Asher's grip is firm on my wrist and he looks at me as if it's the first time he's ever seen me.

"Well, aren't you a pretty thing?" He cocks his head as his gaze takes a leisurely stroll down my body. He unabashedly stares at my tits. Since I'm not wearing a bra, my nipples are tight little nubs which practically poke a hole through the soft cotton.

"Damn, you're fine." He gives me a long, hard look. "And as much as I'd love to have your hands on me, especially down there, I think my brother will have something to say about that."

"Huh?"

"I didn't know Ace had company." He keeps talking while my head spins. "I'm guessing he's been keeping you hidden in his room, which explains the noises last night."

I gulp and stare.

"This isn't funny." I'm thoroughly confused.

The same forest-green eyes stare at me. That same smirk tilts the corners of his mouth. He's got the same dark hair, identical build, identical height.

Identical everything.

But this is not Asher.

The realization hits me like a ton of bricks.

"Oh my God." I jerk my hand out of his grip. "What the hell?"

He gives a low, throaty laugh, the same one Asher uses when he's amused. "I guess he didn't tell you about me?"

"He mentioned brothers, but not that you're identical." I swear Asher said he was the oldest brother. He never mentioned being a twin.

"In every way." The bastard is having far too much fun with me.

"You're his brother?"

He holds out his hand. "Name's Brody. I'm number two, the middle, wild child. Nice to meet you…" He pauses to let me fill in the gap.

"I'm sorry." I take a step back, then replay the last few moments, especially the part where I shoved my hand down the front of his pants and flicked the tip of his dick. "Dear God, I'm so sorry."

"Don't be. Any guy would be lucky to have a sexy vixen like you around. Ace is a very lucky man. You're definitely not shy about grabbing a man's junk."

"I can't believe I—I thought you were him. I mean—I didn't mean to…"

"Grope me? Cop a feel? Flick my dick?"

"Oh my God, you have to stop talking, right now!" Heat radiates off my cheeks.

"I wish I was Ace." He gives me another head to toe look. "He's fucking lucky. I'd love to have a chick grab my junk like that. Just dig in and go for it. Damn, that's fucking hot."

"I didn't know who you were. I thought you were—"

"Yeah, yeah. I get that a lot. Unfortunately for me, I'm not him, otherwise…" He glances at the countertop and I know exactly what he's thinking.

Holy fuck, this is mortifying.

From the blood rushing to my face and the heat radiating off of it, I'm fully capable of setting off my own damn forest fire. I cover my cheeks and take a step back, putting as much distance between myself and Brody as possible.

I had my hands down his pants. I touched the tip of his dick. I just can't…

This isn't something I'm going to walk away from.

"I'm so embarrassed right now." I cup my face and cover my eyes, but there's nowhere to hide. It's not like I can go back and erase time.

"Don't be. It could happen to anyone."

"Not me."

"But it did happen to you, and to me. We were both here for that little bit of grope-age."

"I can't believe I did that. I really thought you were him."

"Well, I'm not. And you know my name, but I still don't know yours. It's been some time since my brother brought a girl home. You must be special, which means I need to know your name. I gotta do the mandatory background checks and make sure you're not some random groper."

"Oh my God, will you please stop? And, please don't tell him that I…" Holy hell. My fingers brushed the tip of Brody's cock. "Mortified doesn't begin to touch on how I feel right now."

"You're the first chick to say she's mortified after touching my dick." His chuckle sounds exactly like Asher's. "I usually get a far more positive reaction, but then you kind of know what it all looks like below my belt, considering Ace and I are identical—"

"You seriously need to stop right now."

It's hard to tease apart the fact that the man standing before me, who looks exactly like Asher, sounds exactly like Asher, feels just like Asher, and smells exactly like Asher, is not in fact the man I spent the night with.

I don't know whether to feel turned on or sick to my stomach. If there's an ick factor to this, my mind and body isn't connecting with it. Brody is just as handsome as his brother, which is fucking confusing as hell.

"Where is Asher?"

"Yeah, you better tell him first. He's likely to punch me in the face for letting you grope me."

"Can you please stop saying that word?"

"You mean grope?"

"Yes."

"Okay, if you tell Ace you copped a feel, then I won't have to explain how you were flicking my dick with your finger. Since it's unlikely he'll punch you, I'd appreciate you calming him down a bit."

"That's not any better."

"Sorry, sis. I am what I am. And you are? I still don't have a name."

"It's Evelyn. Now do you know where he is?"

"Hmm, that's a pretty name." He's cocksure, just like his brother. Brody glances out the kitchen window and I follow the path of his gaze. The corner of his mouth tics up. "You know, I think I remember him heading to the barn. Why don't you try out there? He'll be the one wearing a yellow shirt."

"Thank you, and again, I'm so sorry."

"Hun, this has definitely been the best part of my day."

"Well, that makes one of us."

"Chin up, hun. It happens more often than you know. I barely register it anymore."

"Well, it's a first for me."

"And now you know."

Yes, Asher has an identical twin running around. That would've been nice to know before I tickled the tip of his twin's dick.

I head out to the barn to give Asher a piece of my mind. He doesn't deserve my anger, but I'm fuming and need an outlet.

My senses are assaulted by the smell of sweaty leather, fresh pine shavings, and the aromatic smells of horse, manure, and hay. My nose tickles at all the pungent aromas flooding my senses. There's a munching sound as the horses chew away at their hay. One horse is eating something crunchy. I'm imagining apples or carrots, or pellets of grain.

I love the smell of horses and am privileged enough to have

grown up around them. There's a spot behind their ears that's really soft and feels almost like fur. When I was little, I discovered each horse, like people, had its own unique scent. And it isn't unpleasant. To me, it's a natural perfume, not that I advocate bottling it up and selling it to humans, but I associate the smell with some of my happiest childhood memories.

Now, as for adult memories, the man of my dreams and deliverer of adult fantasies, turns around at my entrance. Sexy, and a little rough around the edges, Asher with his sharp jawline, messy hair, and piercing eyes, looks terribly fine in his faded denims and yellow flannel shirt. He's dirty, with sweat dripping down his chest. Hay sticks to his muscles and mixes in his hair. He runs the back of his hand over his brow.

"Well, hello," he says. "Aren't you a fine-looking filly?"

"Are you really comparing me to a horse?"

"Not in the slightest, but damn don't you make a man take notice."

My anger from accidentally fiddling Brody's dick is wearing off, but the trauma remains. I close the distance between us and fold into his arms. I don't care that he's dirty or sweaty. He smells divine, a mixture of horses, hay, and manly Asher smell. I'm in heaven.

"Whoa, what's this?" He doesn't wrap his arms around me like I expect. Instead, he holds his arms up and out as I bury my face in the crook of his neck and nuzzle in.

"You should have told me about your brother."

"My brother? Um, which brother would that be?"

"Brody, and you won't believe what happened."

"What happened?"

Asher smells good. I bury my nose in his neck and resist the urge to lick his skin. He feels good in my arms, solid, muscular, and safe. My fingers grow restless pressed against the hard planes of his back. I hug him a little tighter and let my hands drift down where there are two dimples right above the rise of his jeans.

"It was horrible. He was cooking, and I thought he was you. I went up to him, and…"

He brings his hand down to the small of my back. It's a hesitant touch, like maybe he doesn't want me pressing too tight against him because of the sweat. Frankly, I don't care about that. Asher smells wonderful, even if his hug is a bit half-hearted as he holds me.

"And what did you do?"

I can't help myself. Asher's too hard to resist. I reach down and squeeze his ass. "You know, you promised some rope action." I give his ass another squeeze and grind against him.

He lifts up on the balls of his feet. "Whoa there! That's awfully friendly forward, even for me."

"Considering where your dick was last night, I'd say we're far beyond the friend stage." I reach my hand around to cup his groin and I'm surprised to find him long and soft instead of long and hard.

"Um..." His voice cracks. "I don't think that's the dick you want."

"Cage, you've got half a second to get your hands off my girl."

My entire body tenses.

That voice?

I know that voice, and holy fuck but my hand is full of yet another man's dick.

Fuck. Fuck. Fuck!

"What the hell!" My screech echoes through the barn and brings irritated whinnies from the horses and snickers from the man I practically vault away from.

I spin around only to see Asher in faded denims and a red and black plaid shirt that hangs open to display all the magnificence of his stunning physique.

He leads the most gorgeous black stallion I've ever seen into the barn. The horse huffs, shakes its head, and stamps at the ground. It yanks on its reins and nudges Asher's pocket. Soft horse lips give a little nibble to the edge of his pocket.

Cage lifts his hands up, palms out and takes two steps back. "Hey, bro. She fondled me. I didn't do nothing."

"Like shit you did nothing. You very well know what you didn't do."

I spin between the two of them, doing a double, triple-take. I must look like a goddamn fool. "How many of you are there?"

Exasperation fills my tone and I lift my hands in the air in frustrated defeat. I've just successfully groped both of Asher's twin brothers. Correction, identical triplet brothers.

Cage gives a low chuckle. "I take it Ace didn't tell you there are three of us?"

"He most certainly did not." I spin back to Asher wanting to be pissed, but unable to muster any anger from him when he's dressed like a girl's wet dream.

"Now, I know what all the noise was coming from his room last night. Nice to meet you." Cage flashes me a devastating wink. "Not sure how they do it where you're from, but around here we settle for shaking hands instead of grabbing dick."

I cover my face and put my back to both men.

Asher comes to me and puts a hand on my shoulder, but I'm not having it. I turn on him and jab him in the chest. "First off, you could have told me you had two identical brothers. Are there any others running around? Quads? Quints? Sextuplets?"

He releases his breath, long and slow. "Just the three of us."

"Well fuck. You might have warned me they were here. It would have saved me a whole lot of embarrassment."

"Evelyn…" His voice is raw, rough, and hungry. The sexual charge between us builds. It's an undeniable force.

I shake my head. "Don't even try. I can't believe you didn't tell me." With the tattered remnants of what is left of my dignity, I storm out of the barn. Asher's horse snorts as I pass. "It's not funny, fuzzball."

Asher may have forgotten to tell me about his brothers, but at least he has the sense to remain silent as I make my dramatic exit. Except, the moment I'm out of the barn, laughter fills the air.

And it's coming from two men.

"You fucked up, Ace." Cage's laughter is deep, booming, and sounds exactly like Asher. "But damn isn't she sexy."

17

ASHER

ASHER

I'm going to kill my fucking brothers. Cage is doubled over, laughing his ass off, while Evelyn stalks out of the barn. I'd go to her, but a very insistent Knight demands his treats.

It was a risk getting up early and leaving Evelyn in bed. Her gorgeous hair spilled over the pillow and her naked body begged to be touched, but the work doesn't stop around here because I want to stay in bed with my woman.

I thought I'd have an hour or two before she woke to check on the fire damage and the work of my crews pulling up the stumps we can't salvage. We lost several acres and I was ready to write the whole thing off until George texted about surviving roots.

We may be able to salvage something out of this mess and I made the decision to check it out, knowing I was leaving Evelyn behind. Never in my wildest dreams did I think my brothers would prank Evelyn.

And they definitely took advantage.

They should have introduced themselves. Instead, they toyed with my girl, letting her get close, put her hands on them, and... Okay, I can't help but snicker here.

She's one wild minx and not at all shy about going after what she wants. I wish I'd been in the barn instead of Cage. Listening to him tell me what happened, brings all kinds of dirty thoughts to mind.

She mentioned rope.

I kept things chill last night. Edging into more adventurous sex on the first date isn't recommended. I usually take a few dates to feel a girl out. Now I know she's thinking about it.

But so is Cage.

The fucker knows I like my sex dirty, but it's not something I want to discuss with him.

"When exactly did you think it was appropriate to tell her you weren't me?" I kind of want to pop him in the face. "Was it before or after she had a hand down your pants."

Cage lifts his hands and takes two steps back. "First off, her hand wasn't in my pants. She copped a feel, and it's not like she gave me a lot of time to stop her."

"I'm pretty certain Evelyn didn't walk up and grab your junk." Bastard should have said something. "I bet she hugged you first. You should have said something." The way he won't meet my eye tells me all I need to know.

"Fucker." I take a swing at him, but he dances out of reach.

"Hey, she copped a feel of Brody, too. Don't take out all your aggression on me."

"You could've told her when she hugged you."

"But she smelled so good. And it's not like I hugged her back. Next I knew, she was squeezing my ass and copping a feel."

"Asshole."

"Sticks and stones may break my bones…"

"Shut the fuck up." I jab my finger toward him. "And keep your hands off my girl."

"Tell your girl to keep her hands off my junk and we'll be good."

I take another swing at Cage, but my heart's not really in it. I need to find Evelyn and apologize. Not that I've done anything wrong, but apologizing up front tends to work best with women.

I dig out the carrot I've been hiding in my pocket and use that to lure Knight into his stall. Despite my desire to smooth things over with Evelyn, I don't rush through taking care of my horse. Ten minutes later, I find her sitting on the front porch with her cellphone to her ear.

She lifts a finger telling me she'll be right with me and continues speaking to whomever is on the other end of that phone.

"Yes, I'm at La Rouge Vineyards... No, you don't have to do that... Okay, if you insist, but it's not necessary... Do you need the address? You can Google it... Oh, okay, your driver has it? How long before you get here?" She leans back and tucks a strand of hair behind her ear.

My fingers itch to touch and smooth away what I can of what happened this morning.

Brody comes out. "Breakfast is ready." He looks between me and Evelyn and huffs a low laugh.

"Met your girl earlier. She's quite handsy."

"That's it." I'm up in a flash.

My fist connects with his smug face before he can raise his guard. I get one or two hits in, before he fights back. We stumble back, off the porch, trading blows, while Evelyn pulls her feet up and tucks her legs beneath her on the lounger.

Her grip on the phone tightens, but she makes no move to intervene. That comes in the form of our mother who arrives in her little, red corvette stingray. It's the car she and our father dated in back in the early seventies and she holds onto it, diligently maintaining it even as my brothers and I urge her to buy something more practical.

The engine cuts out and her crystal-clear voice pierces the air. "That'll be enough, boys." Her tone promises punishment and we snap apart.

Brody spits on the ground while I dust the dirt off my hands. We're a mess, dirty from head to toe. Cage trots out from the barn and gives mother a peck on the cheek.

"Hey, mom," he says.

"Don't you mom me. Why are they fighting?" Her head swivels

and her eagle eyes land on Evelyn who's desperately trying to hide out on the porch.

Just what I don't need.

"We have a guest for breakfast?" Her tiny fists go to her hips as she stares us down. "Brody, why didn't you tell me? And the two of you are fighting?"

"Wrestling." I stretch out my fingers and rub at my knuckles. I got a couple good hits in.

"Wrestling?" She looks between the two of us and I give Brody the eye. Our mother doesn't tolerate fighting, and while we may be pushing thirty, we respect the hell out of our mother. "Is that true, Brody?"

"Yes, ma'am. Just a little fun." He returns my look, letting me know we're good.

My brothers and I settle most of our disputes with our fists. We're well matched, literally, and it gets all our aggression out in the open where we can deal with it and move on. I slap Brody on the back and give mom a hug.

"Good morning." I place a kiss on her cheek. Brody does the same.

She turns toward the porch. "And who is our guest?"

I take my mother's hand in mine and lead her up the porch. "Mother, may I introduce Evelyn Thornton. Evelyn, my mother, Abbie La Rouge."

"It's nice to meet you, Mrs. La Rouge." Evelyn stands and shifts awkwardly on her feet.

My mother wastes no time in pulling Evelyn into a hug. "Please, call me Abbie, unless you want me to call you Miss Thornton." As my mother takes in Evelyn her eyes twinkle. "Now tell me, what were my boys fighting about?"

Before I can intervene, mom drags Evelyn into the house. She calls out over her shoulder. "You boys get cleaned up in the barn while Evelyn and I get to know each other."

Well, fuck.

Brody laughs beside me. "Damn that was quick. She got her

claws in your girl in two-seconds flat. You're so fucking screwed. She'll have you married with five kids before breakfast begins."

"Asshole," I say.

"Asswipe," he replies.

"Come on, fuckers," Cage says. "You know she's not letting us inside until we're cleaned up."

We're three grown-ass men trudging out to the barn to wash our hands before our mother allows us back inside my house. The irony is not lost on me.

I'm more reluctant than my brothers because Cage is one hundred percent correct. Our mother is a meddler and I need to get to Evelyn as fast as I can.

It's too late.

By the time we return, my mother's sharp gaze sweeps the three of us. I feel like I'm five again, caught with my hand in the cookie jar. Brody and Cage bow their heads. They know we're all about to get dressed down by our mother in front of a guest.

"I know I taught you better than this." She draws me into a hug.

My eyes grow wide because this is not a dressing down. She hands me off to the table, pointing to the spot next to where Evelyn sits. I'm silent as shit as she gets toe to toe with first Brody and then Cage. Her finger shakes inches from their noses.

"Now you two will apologize to Evelyn." She gives a shake of her head and makes a tut-tut-tutting sound. "Teasing her like that." Her attention swings to Evelyn. "I swear my boys have been taught better than this."

I don't know how my mother does it, but she never fails to draw out the truth from someone. She had Evelyn alone for how long? Five minutes? How did 'Hello, nice to meet you', turn into your sons pranked me and I accidentally fondled them?

Does my mother know what Brody and Cage did to Evelyn?

From the look in my mother's eye I have no doubt Evelyn either told her, or she figured it out other own.

I reach over and grip Evelyn's hand. "I'm sorry. I should have told you. In my defense, I was otherwise preoccupied." This is the truth. We'd been going at each other like two horny teenagers. The last thing on my mind was my brothers.

"I suppose we're still learning about each other. I'm sorry I got mad at you. It wasn't your fault."

"Well, I should have mentioned my brothers were staying here. They're usually out of town. It honestly didn't occur to me. In hindsight, I can see how it would've been very confusing, not to mention embarrassing, although…"

"Although, what?"

I lower my voice. My mother's dressing down of my brothers continues not ten feet away.

"I kind of like where your head—and hand—was at."

The first smile of the morning lights up her face. "I guess no morning special is on the menu."

"Maybe a nooner?" I'm hopeful.

"Probably not."

"Why not? We could head to the barn, try out a little rope work."

Her flush is enough to melt my heart. "As much fun as that sounds, that was Prescott on the phone. They're on their way from the airport and should be here soon."

"Damn, that sucks."

"Yeah, in light of this morning's events, there's something you need to know about Prescott."

I'm all ears, but my mother's dressing down is winding down. I thread my fingers with Evelyn's and pull her hand up where I can kiss the backs of her knuckles.

"Tell me after breakfast."

"Okay."

Brody and Cage take their seats opposite us and my mother pulls platters off the stove and out of the oven. She didn't cook the meal, but she's going to serve it. That's our mom, smothering every chance she gets.

"So, you live with your mom?" Evelyn says teasingly.

"Not at all, hun." My mother answers for me. "It's just temporary until we can get my cottage fixed up after the fire damage."

Ah shit. Talk about a failure to communicate. I've yet to tell Evelyn about the damage La Rouge Vineyards sustained after that fire. It, along with the farms next to us, are what will take her arson arrest and make it a felony charge if she's convicted.

Fuck.

"What fire damage?" Evelyn's voice is soft, but cautious. She pulls her hand out of mine and clasps her fingers together in her lap. The whites of her knuckles show and I place my hand over hers in silent support.

"The fire burned for five days. It destroyed a lot of land and spilled into the valley. My mother's cottage survived, but there's damage we need to fix."

"Is that all?"

"No. We lost several acres in the fire before we could put it out."

"Oh, I'm so sorry. I didn't know. Why didn't you tell me?"

"I was more concerned about you, to be honest." She needs to know what's important. Land and buildings mean nothing in the grand scheme of things. I'm not ready to express everything I'm feeling just yet. We're still getting to know each other. Case in point, my failure to mention my brothers and the subsequent shenanigans they pulled on her this morning.

To them, it is all in good fun. How many times have we played that prank on the girls we've brought home growing up, or the times we switched mid-date. It's one of the reasons Mom is so pissed at Brody and Cage. We broke a lot of hearts in our youth and weren't exactly respectful of the girls we fucked.

And I do mean to say fucked. I'm the only one to ever have a steady girlfriend. All the others were nothing more than conquests, something to pass the time. I'm not proud of this, but it's the truth.

18

EVELYN

IF I THOUGHT THE BAR WAS OVERWHELMING, IT DOESN'T HOLD A candle to sitting down and having breakfast with Asher's family.

Our relationship is what I'd call a whirlwind. We've skipped a lot and covered impressive ground.

Abbie La Rouge is a blast. I mean that in the best of ways, but it's a bit too soon to lower my guard and relax. Yet, that's exactly what happens.

She sent her boys to wash and drew the most embarrassing moment of my life from my lips, commiserated with me, then smoothed all the jagged edges as if they never existed. All before Asher, Brody, and Cage could dry their hands.

The woman is amazing.

We're beyond all of that now and gather around, passing bacon, pancakes, and eggs down the table.

Like this is a normal occurrence.

But it's not. I pass the bacon. Share the syrup. They treat me as one of their own, but I'm an outsider. Abbie refuses to allow me to feel that way. She's already welcomed me into the fold, but she has no reason to do so. I'm a stranger, but to look at her, it's as if I'm the long-lost daughter she's always wanted.

Talk about big shoes to fill.

I'm drowning.

Asher piles his plate full with a stack of pancakes then sandwiches bacon slices between them.

"What are you doing?" My brows pinch together as I watch the carb overload and artery clogging event.

His cocky grin is back. "It's more efficient."

"More efficient how?" Healthy how?

"All the good bites in one." He looks at my plate where I've barely touched the one piece of bacon and the small scoop of scrambled eggs I placed there. "Not hungry?"

I place a hand over my belly. Whether it's nerves or something else, the thought of food is unappealing.

"Maybe later." The food looks amazing, but there's no way I'm getting any of it to stay down. Not only am I sitting across the table from his brothers, each of whom I've felt up, but his mother sits at the head of the table.

This is so far out of my comfort zone, I want to scream.

"You should eat, Evelyn." His mother looks at my plate and shakes her head. "You're practically skin and bones."

I'm skin and bones because I watch what I eat.

"Yes, ma'am."

Brody snickers across the table and Cage rolls his eyes. Asher places a hand on my leg as his mother gives me a look.

"Evelyn, and I mean this in the nicest way, please call me Mom or Abbie, but I prefer we stay away from ma'am. I'm not that formal and I hope you understand why that may be."

Shit. Way to put my foot in my mouth. "I'm sorry, Abbie." She smiles as I relent. "It's just how I was raised. I mean no disrespect."

"None taken, my dear. I appreciate the lessons your parents taught you, and I don't mean to overstep, or diminish them, but I prefer to keep things more casual."

"Abbie it is." I give her a soft smile, letting her know her lesson has been received and acknowledged.

Somehow, being dressed down by Asher's mom, rather than

making me feel more distant, makes me feel closer to her than before. It's as if we've crossed a line together.

As for the food, I consider myself to be athletic, although I do feel like I've lost weight. Under her admonishment, I finish off the eggs and force down the bacon. I should have a pancake with some of that amazing syrup they keep passing around, but my phone flashes with an incoming text.

I look up, apologetic. "I'm sorry, but that's my lawyer."

"Your lawyer?" Asher asks.

"Yes Prescott." Didn't I explain this to Asher? "He says they just turned down the lane." I look between Asher's brothers sitting opposite me, not entirely sure which one is Brody. I pick the one on the left and hope for the best. "Um, thanks for making breakfast. It was really good."

Cage points to Brody. "You mean him."

Shit. Wrong triplet. God, they're nearly indistinguishable.

Brody chuckles. Abbie covers her mouth. And Asher's body stiffens.

"Um, sorry. It's pretty incredible how much the three of you look alike." I turn to their mother. "Did you ever mix them up when they were little?"

I imagine a stressed and scatterbrained mother trying to keep track of three identical triplets. Put them all on a changing table, shuffle them around. How improbable is it to think she got them mixed up?

I would've confused them multiple times. How she kept them straight is beyond me.

Her laughter is soft, like the fluttering of butterfly wings. "Oh, so many times. I'm almost certain I got them sorted out though." She lowers her voice and whispers. "I think. It's all in how they're circumcised." She winks at me. "You know, one is clipped too short, one a little generous on the left, the other one…."

"Mom!" Brody rolls his eyes.

Cage gives a shake of his head. "Don't listen to Mom. She never mixed us up. Especially me, since I'm her favorite."

Asher and Brody exchange exaggerated moans.

"You're not her favorite." Brody punches Cage in the arm. "She just lets you think that because you're too dumb to know the truth."

"Right," Asher jumps in. "I'm her favorite. That's why I came out first. She wanted alone time with me before the two of you crashed our party."

"What?" I look between the three of them. A smile fills Abbie's face as she looks at her boys.

Asher explains. "I'm the eldest."

"Like a minute or two really matters," I say.

"More like two weeks." Asher is quick to correct me.

"Is that even possible?" I've never heard of such a thing.

"Yeah, I was born two weeks before those two slackers. Like I've always said, Mom wanted time alone with her favorite son before the lesser sons arrived." Asher puffs out his chest.

"Bullshit. She was eager to get rid of you and pop your ass out. She loves us more." Brody is quick to engage. "That's why she hung onto us."

My phone flashes and I hop to my feet. "Sorry. Prescott is pulling up outside." I turn to Brody, who I hope is the correct triplet. "Again, thank you very much for breakfast. It was wonderful."

"No problem." Brody inclines his head, accepting my compliment.

"Here, I'll go with you." Asher rises to his feet.

I never told Asher about Prescott. After the whole triplet fiasco, the last thing I want is for Asher to discover my little secret.

Not that it's a secret. I simply prefer not to open old wounds. I want my past to stay in the past. Asher and I are too new to go ruining things with bad memories. I don't want him to feel sorry for me. As a result, we haven't had those heart-to-heart talks couples usually have.

The secrets I hold are big enough to blow us apart.

Asher walks with me to the front of the house. Behind us, his mother tells the boys to clean up. I love their tight familial bond. My hand flies to my chest. The knot which suddenly forms, all the pain and agony, it's too much. I pull to a stop and Asher nearly runs me down.

"You okay?" He grips my arm. His warm eyes simmer with concern.

"Yeah, it's just, I wanted to explain Prescott to you before you meet."

"Okay." He releases my arm and shoves his hands in his pockets. "I'm all ears." Asher looks suddenly vulnerable.

"It's a long story, and this isn't the best time, but Prescott is special to me."

"As in how special?" He shifts foot to foot.

"Not special like that." God, not like that. "It's just…" God, how do I begin?

I suppose the beginning is the best place.

"I grew up with his son. We dated." I did far more than that.

"Okay? I hear past tense, so you're not getting ready to tell me you're seeing someone else." Asher keeps his tone light, but there's an edge of concern laced through his words. "After what we did last night, that wouldn't be cool."

Yes, about last night.

God, last night was wonderful.

Anything I had with Justin doesn't hold a candle to what happened between Asher and I.

There is no comparison. With Justin, I felt comfortable. With Asher, I feel as if I'm hanging on a precipice. One wrong move and everything will come crashing down.

But.

If I can hold on.

If I can hang on, all my dreams will come true.

I know it's corny. It's corny as hell.

I could say Asher and I are like oil and water. Except, we're not. We're more like a match and gasoline, a combustible event ready to set off a firestorm.

Simply put, Asher and I make sense.

Not that I'm minimizing Justin's life, or his death.

For over half my life, Justin was my everything, but that was only because I never knew what everything could be. I didn't know I'd been living a lie.

I dip my head, unwilling to look Asher in the eye. "I'm not taken, but I failed to tell you something pretty important."

"I'm all ears." Asher's expression is intense. Open, unapologetic, he's ready for whatever I throw at him. I don't deserve this level of trust. I'm going to destroy him with the next words out of my mouth. He deserves more, but we don't have much time.

"This isn't how I wanted to tell you, but I don't want you to hear it from Prescott instead of me." I'm stammering and I don't know how to stop. The words just flow out of me "There's a reason I was out hiking that day."

The day he found me.

The day he rescued me.

The day everything changed.

He's silent and waits for me to continue. It's hard to break it down and terribly complicated. Asher deserves a more thoughtful conversation.

"I…" Shit, there's no time for what I want to say. "Shit."

I'm firing on one cylinder here. Hell, I'm lucky if one cylinder is the best I can give him.

He pulls me to him, wrapping his arms around me. "It's okay, luv. You don't have to tell me, but if you need to know, it's not going to change how I feel about you, and I have a feeling it's not going to change how you feel about me. As long as that's the truth, you tell me when you're ready. Okay?"

His words are a pronouncement of truth. Only, I don't know if I can honor his truth.

"This will break us," I say.

"You certain about that?"

Yes.

"Where's your faith?" He says it like it's nothing; a foregone conclusion.

I have no faith. All I have is the universe's sick joke: find happiness and the universe will rip it from you in the most horrific way possible.

But I'm not inclined to get into a philosophical argument with Asher.

"My faith is stretched thin. It's stretched very thin." I drag my fingers through my hair. "This isn't fair, to you or to me, but it is what it is. If it means anything to you, it doesn't change how I feel about you."

"Then that's all that matters." He gives a chin bump. "It looks like they're here."

"Shit." I'm not ready for this. I grip his hand. "Please, don't judge me."

"Never." He says it as if it's gospel, but I'm a bit more hesitant. I'm giving him every opportunity to walk away.

Why isn't he taking it?

I don't get it. Any sane man would read the red flags I'm raising and take a step back.

Instead, Asher is right by my side.

How the hell do I process this?

Asher cups my chin and turns to face me. "If I can get past you groping my brothers, then we can handle whatever you're worried about. In the end, it's just life. As silly and foolish as that is…it's just life. And if not that, you need to know I'm not going anywhere. I'm here for you. Not for the short haul, not for the easy and fun times, but for the hard road and the difficult climbs. I'm committed to you, Evelyn. You're not ready to know how thoroughly I'm committed, but know that I'm not turning my back on you."

Holy hellfire, my ovaries may have just exploded. Not sure if I can fall anymore head over heels, I tumble into the oblivion Asher promises and give up all hope.

My darkest secrets? The most precious pieces of who I am? They all spill into the space between us. He will either stand with me or run.

Either choice is fine by me, but I'm hopeful he will stand firm.

It's been far too long since I've had an anchor which I can depend upon.

Prescott and Gracie—God I love them—but they aren't enough to see me through the gaping emptiness in my heart.

I can only bridge that distance by exposing my vulnerabilities. I do that now, hoping Asher will catch me, hold me, and carry me through to the other side. I'm well aware this is a crash and burn kind of moment.

But, I'm not afraid of the flames. Into this, I speak the truth Asher needs to know.

"I grew up with Justin. He's Prescott's son. We dated. He proposed. I said yes. Prescott is more than just my lawyer. He's an old family friend and was going to be my father-in-law." I blurt out the words in one rush of breath, because there's no way Prescott is going to be the one who tells Asher how we know each other.

Asher doesn't blink. "What happened with Justin?" His tone is level, controlled, but tight with emotion.

"He died." That knot in my chest tightens.

The love of my life died a tragic death, and I thought that was what would hurt the most. It isn't.

Far from it.

The worst part of Justin's death is the man standing in front of me.

Because I know.

Justin was nothing but the shadow of true love. He was a comfortable excuse, an easy lie I convinced myself was the truth. He was everything which shackled me to the perfect life.

He wasn't the breath of life, not like Asher. I would have suffocated in that version of my life.

It's a shame death taught me how to live. I never would have known this cosmic truth if Justin hadn't died and I hadn't met Asher.

"Shit, Evelyn. I'm so sorry." Asher sweeps the ground with his foot, looking guilty for something he has no control over.

"It's okay." I glance out the window.

Prescott and Gracie are out of the car and looking around. They expect me to meet them outside. "There's more."

So much more.

"It's okay, luv." He takes my hand in his. "I'm here for you."

But I'm not sure that he is. He's standing differently, stiffer. Tension girds his frame and the smile on his face feels strained and a little bit fake.

Not that I blame him. This is so much worse than me accidentally feeling up his brothers. I just unloaded what amounts to a nuclear bomb by telling him I was in love with another man. But that's the thing. I wasn't, but how do I explain that to Asher?

Asher opens the door as if none of this means anything. "Let's greet your guests."

Greet my guests?

That's all he's going to say?

He ushers me outside and hangs back on the covered porch while I approach Prescott alone.

I feel like a recalcitrant child caught in a web of lies. Which is totally not true. I've done nothing wrong. I'm the victim. An innocent bystander affected by a tragic accident.

"Gracie, it's so nice to see you." My wooden arms wrap around her.

Gracie kisses both my cheeks and hugs me tight to her bosom. "We've been so worried about you, love."

I clasp her tight then release her to face Prescott. We have other words to share.

"Evie…" His tone is solid, smooth, nonjudgmental, but he's not pleased with me.

"Hi." I don't hug Prescott. Instead, I turn to Asher. "I'd like to introduce my…"

How do I navigate this? Do I introduce him as a friend? A lover? I'm supposed to be married to their son. How do I insert another man into that equation?

Asher takes care of the problem for me. "Hi, I'm Asher La Rouge. I'm the one who brought Evelyn out of the fire."

"And continue to take care of her, it seems." Prescott shakes Asher's hand. "Thank you for looking out for our Evie." He's polite, but definitely asserting his dominance.

Asher lets it roll right over him. "Of course, it's been my pleasure."

"Well, we appreciate everything you've done. Now Evie, I've rented you a place to stay in town. I've arranged for a meeting with the judge, and I'm hopeful we can expedite your arraignment. I think we should take some time and discuss your case before I speak with him." My almost father-in-law doesn't waste time. He's a brilliant defense attorney. I'm incredibly fortunate to have him on my side, but I don't like how he's taking over.

"Evelyn is welcome to stay here," Asher says.

"That's incredibly considerate, but it's best if she keeps a place for herself. We need to manage her public image." Prescott dismisses Asher's offer.

I really want to say something, but I've seen Prescott work his cases. Image is everything. It shouldn't be, but it is. Cases should be decided by the preponderance of the evidence, but Prescott understands how juries work. He's not so subtlety telling me I need to keep my nose clean and project a pristine image. That's not going to happen if I'm seen shacking up with the firefighter that rescued me. Everything in my life needs to be beyond reproach.

For this reason only, I concede to Prescott's plans.

I grip Asher's hand. "Thanks for letting me stay last night."

"You're welcome to continue staying here. No need to rent a room in town. The guest room is yours." He says that for Prescott's benefit, but we both know I won't be staying in any guest room.

"I've already rented the house. We should get going. I have a meeting with Judge Simon at noon, and I don't want to keep him waiting. Evie, why don't you grab your things?"

"There's not much to grab. I lost everything in the fire."

"Oh, sweetie, that's horrible." Gracie grabs my hands. Her eyes light up with excitement. "That just means we get to go shopping. Now, while Prescott is talking with the judge, you and I can hit the stores. I've been itching for a shopping trip, and you can definitely use some retail therapy. We'll get you something nice. None of that wretched hiking gear," she continues on, pulling me toward the car.

Their driver stands by the passenger side door, tall, impassive, and unmoving until Gracie draws close. Before I know it, he opens the door and I'm staring inside the luxurious car. I pull to a stop and disengage myself from Gracie's overly eager grip.

"I need to go back inside, grab my purse, and say my goodbyes." There's no way I'm going to leave Asher without a proper goodbye.

In many ways, I feel as if Prescott is pulling me away from Asher. Which he is, but only for my own good.

I hate how that sounds.

But that's the thing with Prescott, he thinks he knows what's best for me. He thought so after the accident, but I went and did my own thing. It's my belief he's hanging on to me. I lost my fiancé in the accident, along with my entire family. He lost his son.

Holding on to me, I believe, is his way of holding onto his son. I was a day away from becoming his daughter-in-law and I don't think he's moved on.

That's how I got myself into my current situation. I needed space and he smothered me with paternalistic love. Why he did it is something I understand, intellectually, but emotionally it's too much. He tried stepping into my father's shoes too soon when my grief was too raw.

For now, I'll have to play along with his plans, at least a little, if only because he really is a fantastic criminal defense attorney. I'm not going to bite that gift horse in the mouth.

"I'll be right back." I pull away from Gracie and head back to the house.

"Would the two of you like to come inside?" Asher offers his hospitality. "We were just finishing breakfast, but there's plenty to share."

"We ate on the way over," Prescott says. "We'll wait here."

Asher grabs my hand and tugs me inside. The moment the door closes, he spins around. "He's a tough nut to crack."

"You have no idea."

"You really want to leave? You can stay here. You don't have to go."

"I know, but he's good at what he does. It may not make sense, but he knows what he's doing. I guess he wants to show me off as the girl next door, someone everyone loves, and who would never in a million years set a forest fire."

"Ah, I see, but you can still stay here. The thought of you all the way in town is killing me, especially when I want more time to savor you. We didn't exactly take our time last night."

"Hun, what's going on? Who is that outside?" Abbie joins us from the kitchen and peers outside.

"An old family friend," I say. "He's going to be helping me out."

"Her old family friend is a criminal defense attorney," Asher explains. "And he's stealing my girl."

She looks between us, her gaze zeroing in on our interlocked fingers. "I see. Did you invite them in? We have plenty to share."

"I did."

"Hmm." Her mouth gives a little disapproving twist.

"They already ate and I think they're working on a timeline." I try to explain, but the frown on her face deepens. "He wants to get me settled before he meets with the judge."

"Well, if that's the case, I suppose it makes sense. If you don't mind, while you help Evelyn get her things, I'll just go outside and introduce myself." Asher's mother gives him a wink and Asher groans beside me.

"Behave," he says.

"Honey, I always behave." With that, she leaves and marches across the porch, all smiles and hugs, as she greets Prescott and Gracie. Gracie returns her hug enthusiastically while Prescott returns Abbie's hug stiff as a board.

"Come on." I pull Asher down the hall. "I need to get my purse."

Our goodbye is heated as he presses me against the wall of his room. I'm reminded about what he did to me up in the hallway and find it difficult to head back outside with Prescott. Asher echoes my sentiments, but we don't have time for a hasty fuck. I leave Asher hard and needy, while I'm more than a little out of breath.

19

ASHER

Asher

I get the rationale behind Prescott's plan. He's grooming Evelyn's public image, but damn if I don't want to put my fist in his face for taking her away. I watch them leave, tires crunching over the drive, with my mother standing by my side, and a profound ache throbbing in my heart.

My mother takes my hand. "She's special, isn't she."

"She is—more than makes sense." I take a deep inhale and blow it out slow. It does nothing to ease the ache.

"Sometimes, that's the best kind of love."

"I didn't say I'm in love with her."

"Hun, you didn't have to." She regards me with a pensive expression. "It was like that with your father. When you know, you know, and there's jack shit you can do to stop it."

"Mom!"

"Oh, just because I'm old doesn't mean I can't swear."

"You yell at us when we do."

"Parental prerogative. Anyhow, if that girl is special, which I believe she is, do what you can to help her, give her space if she needs it. If she feels the same, there won't be anything the two of you can do to stop the firestorm from happening between you."

"Firestorm?"

"An all-consuming love. I see the spark of it in your eyes, and in hers when she looks at you."

I've heard my parents story my entire life, a whirlwind romance ending in marriage less than three weeks later. They were married for twenty-one years before a tragic accident took him from us. It's been nearly eight years since he passed and she's never looked at another man. Her love runs that deep.

I understand her grief, but my mother is a woman with a big heart. She deserves a second chance at love.

"Do you know Judge Simon?" I turn and take both her hands in mine.

Her eyes pinch as she looks up at the sky. "I've seen him at church. He's a nice-looking gentleman. Why?"

"There's something I need to tell you."

Her eyes grow wide as I explain my meeting with the judge and the promise I made to put in a good word on his behalf with her.

"You set me up?" She crosses her arms and gives me her stern mother look, but I see a faint flush in her cheeks.

When I asked if she knew him, she commented on his appearance which tells me she's taken notice. Perhaps my meddling isn't such a bad thing.

"I told him I'd put in a good word. So, what do you want to do about it? Want me to set something up?"

"Well, if it helps Evelyn."

Yeah, my mom is great, but she's not that much of a saint. She's definitely interested in Judge Simon, and I'm not above using that to my advantage.

As for Evelyn, I'm concerned. The arson findings are not in her favor. If I can't find some evidence of this other man, it's going to be hard proving her innocence. We head inside and help my brothers finish cleaning up after breakfast.

We work together, washing the dishes, as I lay out my concerns. Brody and Cage listen while Mom watches. She won't say it, but she's thrilled we're all back home. I get to see her every week, but Brody works in the city and Cage is often on assignment, gallivanting across the globe.

She worries about each of us. That we're not settling down. That none of us have ever had a steady girlfriend. I had Erin, but that blew up in my face when she fucked Felix. Mom's afraid we aren't going to find our soulmates and never know what true love feels like.

She had us before turning twenty-one. The desire for grandbabies stirs in her eyes, but we're not holding up our end of the deal, which frustrates her to no end.

"I don't see what you can do." Cage slaps the drying towel over his shoulder. "The arson report is going to be tough to beat."

"Yeah, but Pete Sims is a putz. He does the bare minimum. Besides it's all circumstantial."

"I hear you," Cage says. "You want to believe her, but her fingerprints are all over everything."

"Yeah, it's weird that they picked up prints." Brody drains the sink and watches the suds swirl down the drain. "I thought the fire would have burned everything up."

"You'd be surprised what survives a fire. Things you think shouldn't be affected are unrecognizable. Other things, like paper, are surprisingly resilient."

"And fingerprints?" Cage asks.

"In plastic, they're incredibly durable." My brothers have a point.

Everything points to Evelyn, but they weren't there. They didn't see the terror in her eyes. She wasn't concerned about the fire or its threat to her life. Her fear came from thinking I was the man who knocked her out.

"If we could find this man who assaulted her." I blow out my breath in frustration, "That would clear Evelyn of everything."

"And how do we do that?" Cage flips the towel in the air, folding it in half. He hangs it on a drawer handle. "There's no proof he was there. Other than footprints, but wasn't your crew working there? If you can identify the center of the fire, then you could try that, but it's been over two weeks. I'd think any prints would be gone by now. I think you're fighting a lost cause."

"Think about it." I persist in my defense. "After he knocked her out, he had the perfect opportunity to pin the whole thing on her. He could've shoved that receipt in the bottom of her bag. Who keeps receipts like that anymore? And he could've put the bottle of lighter fluid in her hand. There's plausible deniability."

"I think you mean reasonable doubt," Brody corrects.

"Whatever." I kick back and lean against the kitchen island. "She didn't do it, and if we had her cellphone, there would be proof."

"What do you mean?" Cage perks up, interested.

"She said she took some selfies and he's in the photos."

"What happened to her phone?"

I shrug. "She said it was lost with the rest of her stuff."

"But they found her backpack," Cage says. "Her phone could've survived."

Brody scratches his head. "I still don't see how her backpack survived that fire."

"She was in the epicenter. It burned outward from where she was."

"Ah, then we go up there and look for it." Brody says it like it's so damn easy.

"Wouldn't they have found it during the investigation?" Cage still isn't convinced.

"Only if they were looking for it, and Pete Sims found what he needed to string together his case and stopped."

"So, we saddle up and go look ourselves." Cage grabs the dishtowel, spins it real quick, then snaps it at me.

"Mother fucker!" He scores a direct hit on my hip and gives me a cocky grin, pleased with himself.

I snatch the towel out of Cage's grip and quickly twist the end.

"Game on!" I flick the towel at him.

Cage tries dancing away, but I score a direct hit on his ass.

"Fucker!" He spins around and snags one of the drying towels.

Mine's wetter, which means it snaps better and is more likely to leave a welt behind.

We used to prank each other all the time growing up, covering one another with welts over our wet bodies as we ran semi-naked through the house after a shower. Our father would sit in his over-stuffed chair and mutter 'Boys will be boys' while our mother scolded us to stop hitting one another.

We're almost thirty, but we're racing around the house, snapping each another with towels. Not to be left out, Brody grabs a towel and joins in on the chase. It's two on one during these things as we gang up on one another. That generally changes several times. With Mom telling us to stop, we race outside where she can't yell at us.

Brody and I gang up on Cage, landing several direct hits before he dips his towel in one of the rain barrels to get it wet.

Minutes later, we're covered in welts and laughing hard inside the barn. Mom leaves, driving off in her little red corvette when she realizes we aren't going to listen.

We collapse against the hay bales and Cage looks over at me. "So, when are we going up?"

"Up?"

"Yeah, to do our investigation." He makes air quotes with his fingers.

"You seriously want to help?" He didn't seem convinced earlier.

"Damn straight." Brody gives a nod. "Evelyn is amazing."

Cage cracks up. "Yeah, even if she's a little handsy."

"That's it!" I pile on top of Cage, punching and jabbing play-fully as he blocks my fists. Brody is no help. He holds his sides from the laughter spilling out of him.

I love my brothers, because no matter what they have my back, and I miss having them around. We stop goofing around and saddle our horses. After I go inside, to get my bag and water for the trail, we're off.

It's late summer and still hot. Broad green leaves flutter on the vines and heavy grapes hang from the stems. In a few weeks we'll begin harvesting, but for now the vineyards remain quiet. Scattered over the fields, footlong mylar streamers flutter in the wind. Their reflective coating scares off the birds who would otherwise decimate our crop.

"Vines look healthy." Brody gives an appreciative nod. "Looks like it's going to be a good year."

"It should be, or would've been. We lost a lot in the fire."

"We'll rebuild," Cage chimes in.

"We?" Not likely. Brody is busy in the city and Cage disappears for months at a time.

"I'll help out when I'm home." Cage reaches out from horseback and tries to snag a clutch of grapes. He's unsuccessful and we move on. He leaves in a couple of weeks for an expedition and who knows what will pull him away after that.

"Honestly, there's not much to do. George is examining the roots, seeing what we can salvage. We'll spend winter reconditioning the soil, but it may take a season or two before we can replant."

Then years before the vines mature and begin producing.

My brothers know all of this. We were raised learning everything about growing grapes and making wine. Our father put us to work on nearly every job involved in the whole process over the years. The wine business flows in our veins.

A bead of sweat forms on my brow and I swipe my forehead. There's not a cloud in the sky, which leaves the sun to bake the land as morning stretches into noon. Knight, Chesty, and Brody's Arabian, amble through the fields until we get to the burned part of our fields. On the surface, it looks like a deadman's land. Scorched dirt and the husks of vines stretch before us. Our carefree banter grows silent as we wander through the devastation.

On closer inspection, there are small signs of life. Grasses poke up through the charred ground. Those will give way to low scrub and small bushes if left alone. My decision will be whether to allow the land to lie fallow for a season or two before attempting to replant. It will come down to whether the roots of our vines survived.

If they start sprouting, we'll focus on the vines. If not, I'll let the land recover. It means decreased production and diminished profits for several years. I need to sit with Brody later to see if our business has the cash flow to survive.

As the horses begin the climb into forest lands we come upon what's left of the trees. The burnt husks of their trunks chill me. The fire stripped the trees of their beauty, leaving nothing but gaunt, skeletal remains clinging to barren soil. They reach up with gnarled and snapped limbs as if desperate to be whole again.

The canopy which once sheltered so many is gone. It's too quiet as if the land is trying to heal.

"It's horrible," Brody says. His horse gives a soft snicker as it picks its way along the path.

"It's been a hot summer with a savage sun. All that heat baked the ground and turned the underbrush to tinder."

"Looks like it all just went up. Is it always like this after a fire?"

"Not usually this bad, but all the deadwood dehydrated in the heat, providing the perfect fuel to feed the fires. It was incendiary." I rub Knight's neck, giving him a light pat. "As bad as it looks, as quiet as it feels, there are signs of life." I point out little shoots of green poking through the soot. "Fast growing grass come first. Birds and small mammals will follow. Seedlings will sprout and a new forest will emerge from the ashes."

"You spouting the circle of life crap," Cage says.

"It is what it is," I say.

We ride through the devastation, each of us caught up in our thoughts.

This is why I volunteer as a firefighter. To prevent horrific scenes such as this. But this is a part of life, devastation followed by life.

Everything works in a circle.

Hot and sweaty, the horses climb up the hills as the sun beats down on us and heats the air. The horses plod onward, putting their heads down and hearts into the effort. I listen to the steady clopping of hooves, the gentle switching of tails, and their soft snorts as they work.

It's a gorgeous day and the summer heat on my back is welcome. The leather reins rub between my fingers. I ride often and am protected from blisters by the rough callouses on my skin. Brody and Cage wear thick gloves. Their time away from La Rouge has softened their hands.

Knight's neck lathers in thick sweat which clings to the short, stiff hairs of his summer coat. Foam leaks from his mouth as he works the copper snaffle in his mouth.

Gently, I lean down and pat his neck. "Good boy."

He responds with a change in gait, trotting a few steps before settling back down to lead the way.

It takes a few hours, but we make it to the ridge a little after noon. We had a generous breakfast, but my stomach rumbles and I'm glad I had the foresight to pack snacks into my bag before setting out.

We come upon the primitive campsite, identifiable by the soot-covered ring around the fire pit. I hop off Knight and tie him to a nearby trunk which is covered in black soot. Normally, I would let him graze, but there's nothing alive. Brody climbs off his horse and Cage follows. They tie their horses and join me by the fire pit.

"Shit." Brody shades his eyes against the glare of the sun. "This place…it gives me chills."

I nod in agreement, although the last time I was here the entire place had been engulfed in ghastly red and raging orange as flames tore through the woodland. The unfettered flames hungrily devoured the vegetation and licked their way up the trunks of trees while they chewed through the underbrush.

"It smells." Cage walked toward the fire ring. He stops and sniffs the air. "That acrid scent is potent. I'm surprised it's still so thick."

"It'll last for a while, at least until the forest recovers," I explain.

"And you were here?" Brody turns in a circle, surveying the destruction.

I point toward the edge of the ridge. "We rappelled down over there and dug the trenches which prevented the fire from spreading deeper into the forest."

That was back-breaking work, but saved the main part of the forest. Denied that avenue, the fire poured down the hills where it destroyed not just forest, but several acres of our family's land and chewed through several homes where the homeowners had failed to maintain an adequate firebreak.

Brandon and his team from Station 13 fought those blazes, trying to get in front of the fire to cut what firebreaks they could to limit the damage and starve the fire.

I agree with Cage. An acrid scent lingers in the air. It's pungent and noxious.

My helitack team worked endlessly through that night, putting in a twenty-four hour shift before taking a break. Four hours later, we were back at it, trying to save as much as we could. Days later, the fire ended leaving behind death and destruction.

Brody walks around the campsite, surveying the damage. "This is surreal."

"Yeah." I join him and glance around the area. Any confidence I have in finding Evelyn's phone fades. We're looking for the impossible.

But my brothers give it their best. We stay up on the ridge for hours, kicking through the ash, turning over every stone, but as the sun begins to dip toward the horizon we decide to call it. I don't like walking the horses in the dark and we've got a long ride ahead of us.

By the time we make it back home, dusk deepens into night. We unsaddle the horses, rub them down, and make sure they have plenty to eat.

I reward Knight with an apple for a job well done. Then we're all back in the house, sitting on the couch. After a brief discussion about whether to binge watch TV or play a game, Brody and Cage opt to play a game.

"You guys start." I lift my phone. "I'm going to give Evelyn a call and see how she's doing."

I've been separated from her for the better part of the day and feel unsettled not having her by my side.

Before I can dial her number, my phone rings. It's Benjamin Bingham, and I can't for the life of me understand why he'd be calling me.

20

EVELYN

La Rouge works magic on me, leaving me oddly at peace, as if there's a little piece of me I never knew was missing that found its way home.

Whether that's the blooming romance with Asher, or the way his family makes me feel at home, despite all the inadvertent groping, is difficult to say. Whatever the reason, La Rouge Vineyards feels like a place I want to spend more time at.

Maybe tomorrow.

For today, my time is monopolized by Prescott and Gracie. I've been too hard on them when all they want is what's best for me. And Prescott is a veritable saint. He could say all manner of things to me, the top on that list being 'I told you so' but he keeps his own counsel. That shouldn't mean as much to me as it does.

Prescott has a lunch meeting with Judge Simon which leaves the morning for shopping. Gracie takes me to a string of boutique stores in Napa, while Prescott dutifully trails behind us.

We hit all the shops and rebuild an impressive wardrobe in a matter of hours. When lunchtime comes, our driver drops Prescott off at an establishment where he'll meet with the judge and get a sense of how bad things are for me.

Gracie and I consult our phones and pick a five-star restaurant to whittle away the afternoon. Lunch becomes a two-hour event, which we follow with more shopping.

Prescott texts that he'll join us at the house he rented for the duration and we meet up with him a little before five in the evening. It takes several trips to empty the trunk of my new purchases. Gracie and I definitely gave my new plastic a workout.

"With my black thumb, that's not going to last." I point to the ornate garden with its myriad of flowering plants. The small house Prescott rented perches up on the hills overlooking the valley. It's quaint with an English garden filling the front lawn.

Prescott chuckles. "Which is why you have a gardener to take care of it. Don't worry, all the amenities are taken care of." Knowing him, that means I have a gardener and housekeeping service already scheduled. He hands me the key to the front door. "I hope you like it."

I'm not used to carrying keys. In the past year, I've spent the majority of nights camping out on the trail. It's going to feel weird sleeping with a roof over my head. I'm thankful the house is at the end of the street. There's no traffic and we're far enough from any roads it's going to be very peaceful.

"Thank you so much for taking care of everything." He doesn't have to do this for me, but I sense taking care of me helps to ease some of his grief. I lost my fiancé, but he lost a son. I can't imagine what that must feel like, and to have me standing in front of him, instead of his son, must be incredibly difficult.

"You know we'd do anything for you." Gracie places her hand on my arm. She's sweet and cares deeply for me.

"I do." I take a deep breath and insert the key into the lock. "How long do I have to stay here?" My anxiety builds, feeling as if the world is closing in on me. I crave the open spaces of the outdoors where I'm most at peace.

Prescott waits on the small porch while I head inside. Gracie follows me in and he's right behind us. The door closes with a snick and I can't help but feel a little trapped.

"It's going to be awhile," he says. "I've asked for an expedited trial, but we have some work to do. I hope I don't need to explain that you won't be able to disappear."

Disappear.

He means head back to the trails; my version of escaping reality.

The house comes fully furnished. Prescott really did think of everything. The inside is country cute; not exactly my style. I'm more into clean lines, muted colors and understated elegance, not the vibrant splashes of color decorating every surface. The sofa looks like a florist vomited on it. The bright yellow arm chairs make me want to wear shades. At least the carpet is somewhat neutral, although whoever thought white was a good idea for carpet needs their head examined.

A bright red and blue afghan covers the back of the couch. Depending on how long I need to stay, I'm going to need to hire a designer and do a complete overhaul on the house. We walk through it together and I bite my tongue at the bright yellow and blue color scheme in the kitchen. It's going to take more than an interior designer to take care of that, and fire engine red appliances? My eyes need bleach.

"It's…" I turn in a circle and take in the riot of colors.

"Unique." Gracie gives a nod. "Very—unique."

"That's one word for it." I wrinkle my nose at the garish colors. "It's country cute mixed in with art deco disaster."

"It's the best I could do on such short notice." Prescott shoves his hands in his pockets and looks down. "We can find alternate accommodations if you want."

There's no way I can do that, not when Prescott went above and beyond.

"It's definitely different, but I can make it work." I go to him and wrap my arms around him in a hug. "I'm thankful for everything."

"Ah, hunny." Gracie comes up behind me and gives me a hug. "You know we'd do anything for you."

Prescott pulls his hands out of his pockets and wraps them

around us both. We stand in silence for a moment, but then he starts laughing.

Lowering his hands, he takes a step back. "It's hideous, isn't it?"

I smile at him. "Hideously perfect."

"I'll call a designer and see what can be done," he says.

"That's not necessary." I can't bear for him to do any more than what he's already done. "It's kind of growing on me."

"It's up to you, but you're going to be stuck here for a while," he says. "There's a fine line between wanting to rush the trial and needing to prepare your defense. I haven't had a chance to look at the arson report, but we've got our work cut out for us. Come, let's sit and chat." He gestures back toward the living room.

Gracie and I follow him. Over the next hour, he lays out his conversation with the judge and his plans concerning my defense. I tell him all about the hike, coming up on the scraggly man, and getting knocked out. Gracie covers her mouth when I describe waking up in the middle of the forest fire, my mad dash through the flames, and how I flew over the edge of the ridge falling head over heels down the steep bank. I tell her about the injury to my ankle which healed remarkably fast and why I tunneled into that cleft between the boulders.

"Oh dear," she exclaims. "How did you keep your wits about you? I wouldn't have known what to do."

"I've learned a lot, actually." It's the truth and I'm proud of myself. I've gone from being a ditzy socialite whose biggest concern in life was whether my nail polish and lipstick matched my evening gown, to an independent self-sufficient woman who tackles the outdoors like a professional. When I think of who I was a year ago, and the woman I've become, I don't recognize the vapid waste of breath I once was.

That girl no longer exists.

I shiver wondering where I would be now. I would be married, probably with a kid on the way. My days would be spent relaxing from all my non-existent stress in a day spa to picking out the most fashionable baby clothes and complaining about the stretch marks marring my perfect skin.

Do Gracie and Prescott see the changes? Or do they only see the woman their son would've married? The daughter they never had? Is it possible for them to like the new me rather than the old?

Prescott listens to my story with practically zero reaction. That's not exactly true. He's quiet, but the muscles of his jaw bunch and I'm pretty sure I know what he's thinking.

It's impressive how he's holding his tongue. At any moment, I expect the 'I told you so' to come spilling out of his mouth, but he grits his teeth and lets me continue. He's listening to my account as the lawyer who will defend me in court. He's not taking notes, but I'm sure every word I say is being indelibly stored in that impressive mind of his.

"Well, that is a terrifying story." Gracie pats my knee. "I'm glad everything turned out all right."

It's not all right. I'm facing felony arson charges which can put me away for up to twenty years. Or more.

I've seen that look in Prescott's face before. The challenge of a particularly difficult case. My life is literally in his hands.

"How about we put your things up, get you moved in?" Gracie grabs one of the many bags full of our shopping spree. I wanted simple, she shopped like she always did. Half the things inside these bags will never get worn. This town simply doesn't cater to that echelon of society.

I did manage to get in some sensible clothes, jeans, shorts, cotton panties instead of silk and lace, and an assortment of cotton tee-shirts instead of the designer blouses she insisted I buy. I grab several bags and join Gracie in the larger of the two bedrooms.

"We can move the bed out." She points to the smaller bedroom. "And set it up as an office."

"An office?"

"I know this place isn't what you're used to, but we can make it work. If there's not a gym nearby, we can set it up with what you need."

Yes, I forgot Gracie's life revolves around keeping her model perfect figure.

"I saw several day spas we can check out." She gives another pat to my arm. "We'll find you something suitable."

How do I tell her I don't need a workout room in my home because I get more than enough exercise on the trails? My worry isn't if I'm getting enough exercise, but whether I can consume enough calories not to lose precious muscle mass.

I've always been thin, but now I'm thin and lean. Strong. Self-sufficient. I don't need a day spa home or a fitness center with a coach.

That's not my life anymore.

It is for the foreseeable future, however. Prescott says no more disappearing for weeks at a time. I process what that means as Gracie and I pack the drawers of the dresser with things I don't need and hang all the fancy dresses I'll never wear in the closet.

When we're done, we rejoin Prescott and head out for dinner where our conversation is stunted and filled with awkward pauses. I get it. We've all been through shit and no one is dealing with any of it particularly well. Fortunately, dinner is a quick affair and I'm home before I know it.

They leave me in my new home with no television, no WiFi, and nothing in the fridge. I'll get groceries in the morning when my car arrives. Prescott thought of everything, even down to delivering a car.

For the rest of the night, it's me and my garish little home. I'm so damn bored I could cry.

Spending the day with Prescott and Gracie emotionally drains me. It's been a long, lonely day without Asher. Odd how much I miss him, but I refuse to be clingy. I could call, but I don't.

I don't want him to know how much I'm thinking about him. Or admit it to myself. There must be something I can do to entertain myself.

Not a book in the house?

How is that possible? I've got the most hideous country cute decor and not a single book or magazine? If I had my old phone, I'd read on it, but my new phone is a virgin piece of technology, completely unlinked to my previous phone.

I would download my old phone from the cloud, except after a year of barely looking at my phone, I remember none of the passwords to any of my previous accounts. So, I can't even download the extensive library I'd built up over the years and I'm too damn lazy to start new accounts.

This means asking Prescott for another favor. Hopefully he can restore my phone from wherever its backup is stored. Until then, it's just me, my empty home, and the walls which feel as if they're closing in on me.

Funny to think I feel more comfortable sleeping outside in a tent than under a roof. None of the designer stores Gracie took me to sold what I need for that. Not to mention, I didn't want Prescott giving me the eye. For the foreseeable future, my backpacking is on hold, which leaves me jumpy around all this civilization.

The house creaks and groans, speaking a language I don't understand. I try not to jump at each unfamiliar sound, but I swear it sounds as if there's someone else in here.

My head knows it's nothing, but my nerves are uneasy and restless.

All houses make noise, but I don't know these sounds. I don't feel safe. Which leads me around the house on a mission to check all the locks, inspect all the closets, and look under the beds. There's no one but me, but I can't help feeling as if there's a presence watching me.

Shrugging the feeling off as nonsense, I head to the bathroom where I draw a bath. One thing this ugly house has going for it is a massive clawed bathtub. It looks dreamy. A little soaking and suds sounds like the perfect thing to settle my nerves. And while I have no food in the house, our little shopping trip netted me an entire host of bathroom necessities, along with a box of scented bath bombs.

Water pours out of the copper faucet warming up while I sniff the box of bath bombs. The lilac and rose one smells the best. After testing the water, I plug the tub to let it fill and head back to my room to grab my robe.

A flutter of movement in the living room catches my eye. When I go to investigate there's nothing out of sorts.

"It's just nerves." I say this out loud. If I speak it, it must be true. Honestly, I don't know where this unease comes from. It's almost as if I'm afraid to be alone, which is silly considering I spent most of last year with only myself and the outdoors for company.

Shrugging off the odd feeling, I return to the bathroom, strip out of my clothes and sink into the luxurious tub.

Lilac and rose fill my senses. The hot water lulls my mind and the tight muscles in my legs let go. My arms grow heavy on the side of the tub. My head leans back and I allow my eyes to close. It's been a long time since I allowed myself to let go and enjoy the creature comforts of a home drawn bath. Into this, I let myself float away and doze.

A fit of coughing wakes me, along with an acrid stench and heated air. Black smoke billows into the bathroom and rolls across the ceiling, filling my lungs. Each breath pulls in more of the smoke. Tears pour down my face, brought on by the coughing fit, and the thick smoke.

There are no alarms going off, but there are most definitely flames licking along the carpet and climbing up the wall.

I leap out of the tub and grab my robe as I go to my knees. The smoke is thick, suffocating, and the heat unbearable. The orange flames are garish against the brilliant blues, yellows, and red of the furnishings. Paint bubbles as the intense heat consumes it.

I'm trapped with no way out.

But wait.

My only option is the bathroom window and a twelve foot drop to the yard below. There is no other alternative.

I can't stay here.

Before I put on my robe, I dunk it in the tub, getting it thoroughly wet. I'll need what little protection it gives. My only problem is the window is high, barely big enough for me to fit through, and it's completely covered with smoke. A quick glance around the bathroom and I grab the plunger behind the toilet.

I take in a deep, scalding breath of smoke and superheated air, then stand to bang against the window. The glass breaks and I sweep the shards to the side. Out of breath, I kneel back down to the floor to take in another lungful of air and smoke. I only have one chance.

Already the water saturating my robe is turning to steam.

Using all my strength, I pull myself up and through the window, where I drop down to the ground below. Flames lick along the roofline and all I feel is terrible heat.

The ruddy glow of the fire lights up the night sky. Sirens screaming through the night reach my ears. I race around to the front of the house, breathing hard, and see the brilliant red and white lights of emergency vehicles racing up the hill.

Outside, anxious neighbors gather in the street, huddling with one another as their cellphones capture the blaze. I turn back to the house only to see the entire thing engulfed by the deadly fire. A window blows out and everyone ducks as hot shards of glass shoot onto the lawn. I'm barefoot and naked beneath my robe and feel incredibly exposed.

One of the neighbors rushes up to me. "Are you okay?" He's an older man in his mid to late-sixties. He wraps his arms around me and leads me off the lawn and into the street.

I give a shaky nod.

"Anyone else in the house?" He's concerned, but I shake my head.

"Just me." My heart pounds and I cough from smoke inhalation.

I've done this before. This is the worst déjà vu ever.

What is it with me and fire?

Videos of house fires are woefully inaccurate when compared to the real thing. I've seen footage on TV before: black smoke billows into the sky and flames lick along the wood. But the real thing is much different. For one thing, the heat is intense.

Even standing in the road, the heat scorches my skin. The yellow, ruddy glow fills the sky and the smell of wood and plastic dominates every breath. The flames roar, louder than I think they should, as they devour what was once a quaint, yet hideous home.

As the flames engulf my Art Deco disaster, the surrounding trees curl back from the flames, their leaves singeing in the intense heat. I take a step back, pushed further into the street by the conflagration.

The older man holding me does what he can to console me, but I need Asher and his strong arms. His reassuring words. Instead, I lean on a stranger, unable to process what's happening.

Down the lane, sirens announce the cavalry is here to save the day. I glance down at my robe, at the scorched areas which protected me as I escaped the house and hold back the tears threatening to spill forth.

Once again, everything I own goes up in flame. The house is like a macabre bonfire chewing through my possessions with relentless hunger and the need to destroy.

The siding on the house bubbles and slides down like melted chocolate in summertime. Smoke curls into the sky and rains down dirty ash.

Sirens wail as two firetrucks scream down the street with an ambulance in tow behind them. They pull up alongside the curb and men in heavy protective gear jump out. A couple of them go to man the hoses. One heads right at me.

He places a gloved hand on my shoulder and there's a tender voice which seems familiar. He says something, but I can't focus on the words. All I hear is the roaring of the flames.

My house is burning.

Acrid, chemical infused smoke fills the air as the fire devours my home.

"Evelyn!" The firefighter shouts and gives me a little shake. "Is this your house?"

I tear my attention from the flames and look at the firefighter. I know that face, even if I don't remember his name.

I nod, unable to speak.

"Is there anyone else inside? Is Ace in there?"

My head shakes the other direction. "No. Just me. I was alone."

He's one of Asher's friends. One of the Bingham brothers and his name begins with a G, but for the life of me, I can't remember his name

He says something to the man standing beside me then lifts his arm to wave someone over. Two men carrying a stretcher and bright orange bags come trotting over to me.

"Treat her for smoke inhalation."

That's all I hear as Asher's friend hands me off to the two men. A rush of dry oxygen hits me as they place a mask over my face.

The firefighters train their hoses on the burning house and send jets of water to douse the flames.

More sirens sound down the lane, but these flash blue and white lights. A cop car slams to a halt behind the fire engine and a man climbs out of the vehicle. He goes to the firefighters while the paramedics place me on the gurney and wheel me back to their ambulance.

There's nothing they can do to save the house. When this is done, it'll be reduced to nothing but ash and charcoal. My entire body shakes. I cough into the mask as the paramedics take my vitals. I can't process everything going on and am unable to believe what my senses tell me.

The house is fully engulfed. The firefighters and the paramedics are every bit the heroes I expect. They can't save my home, but they will save the houses on either side.

For me, I'm alive.

I'm still alive. My fingers curl around the edges of my robe, gripping it as I try to process this event.

I need comforting, strong arms, and reassuring words. I need Asher by my side, someone I can lean on and who will protect me.

One of the paramedics flashes a light in my eyes. "Miss, is there anyone we can call for you?"

I give a sharp nod. It's hard to speak. Every word brings a coughing fit, but I spit out what I need to say.

"C-call…A-Asher La Rouge."

The cop comes into view. I know this man too. He's the brother of the firefighter, the one who arrested me.

"I've got this." He places his hand on the paramedic's shoulder, then puts the phone to his ear. "Hey, Ace, something's happened…"

I listen to him as if from a distance. My body is shutting down, going into shock, and I sway on the stretcher.

"Here you go." The paramedic eases me back.

The stretcher is raised, so I'm not lying flat, but rather reclining. It allows me to watch the firemen as they struggle to put out the blaze.

"Yes, a house fire." Officer Bingham rattles off the address. I would thank him, but my mind is disassociating.

21

ASHER

Asher

Benjamin's voice is calm, too steady. "Hey, Ace, something's happened…"

I can't focus on his words and ask him to repeat himself. He speaks in slow, measured tones, the kind that tell a person no matter what he's going to say, they will freak out. I brace and focus on what he says.

"There's been a house fire."

"Okay?" Why would he mention a house fire? It's not my wheelhouse. I'm a woodland firefighter.

"Evelyn is okay," he says.

A sick feeling overcomes me and a knot forms in the pit of my stomach. Benjamin is a pro at giving bad news. His smooth tones allow me to focus and listen.

"I'm on scene now," he says. "You should come."

"Evelyn?"

"She's fine. Not injured, but she could use someone by her side." He rattles off the address. "You got that?"

"I'm on my way." The line goes dead as I hang up on him. I

race around, grabbing my wallet, my phone. What am I missing? "Where the fuck are my keys?" I call out to my brothers.

Brody answers. "Where's the fire?"

"At Evelyn's."

"I was kidding." Brody stands, shock fills his face. "Is she…" He wants to ask, but holds back from saying the words.

"She's fine." My reply is clipped as I try to figure out where my keys are.

Cage looks up from his game. "Seriously? Is she okay?"

"Benjamin says so."

"He's there?" Cage drops his controller and grabs his phone.

"What are you doing?" I ask.

"Coming with you." Cage locates my keys and heads toward the door.

"I'm coming too." Brody doesn't hesitate.

Yet again, I'm thankful to have the most amazing brothers. They always have my back.

We pile into my truck. Cage refuses to let me drive, saying I'm 'too distraught' and he wants to 'get there in one piece.'

The thought of Evelyn in danger twists my guts and my heart lodges itself in my throat. Cage lets the tires spin out and we race down the long drive.

The drive passes in a blur. I barely register the traffic lights or the turns. Brody tells Cage where to go while my fingers drum against my knee. It seems to take forever, but then we see a thick column of smoke colored cherry red. Two firetrucks are on scene, along with an ambulance, and several cop cars. Cage pulls up behind them.

Chemical infused smoke infuses the air and mixes with burning wood. My focus shifts to the scene, trying to find Evelyn.

There she is, in the back of the ambulance, huddled on a stretcher. Benjamin said she wasn't injured. So, what the fuck?

Three men surround my girl.

Among the many thoughts storming around in my head, anger and irritation predominate. I'm irritated for letting Prescott take Evelyn away.

She was perfectly safe with me.

I'm angry because I let her go.

She didn't make it one night before something catastrophic happened. I blame Prescott and I blame myself.

Where is the bastard? I don't see him anywhere in the crowd, but there's Benjamin-fucking-Bingham. He's right beside Evelyn, paper in hand, pen scribbling notes. If he thinks to pin this on her, we're going to have issues. Anger stirs in my belly and I have a hard time tamping it down.

Two engines from Brandon's fire station are engaged in fighting the fire. Several firefighters hold hoses, spraying the base of the fire. Other men douse the roof of an adjacent house, making it less likely for the fire to spread. They look like they have things under control, but the house is a total loss.

Blue lights from the cop cars mix with the red and white flashers of the fire engines. It looks like a damn circus is in town. A growl escapes my throat because Benjamin's questioning Evelyn.

Her attention shifts and her eyes connect with mine across the distance. Immediately, the lines on her forehead ease and her tight expression softens.

I can't get to her fast enough and try to storm off. Only, Brody grips my arm tight and he tugs me to a stop.

"What the fuck?" I glare at my brother. He's between me and my girl.

"I might ask the same." His grip is solid and he's not letting go.

I know that look in his eyes.

He drops his voice low, for my ears only. "You need to take a few deep breaths, then tell me why you're looking at Benjamin Bingham like you want to kill him."

I yank out of his grip, but his words keep me rooted in place. Damn if he isn't right.

"He's the one who arrested Evelyn." I explain how he resorted to cuffing her in the hospital and how I felt it completely unnecessary. "She would've gone quietly, but he had to bring out the damn cuffs. And she had bandages on her arms."

I'm still pissed at Benjamin for that.

"I would strongly suggest you shove that shit far down before storming over there. Evelyn doesn't need you making a scene, and while I wasn't there, you know Benjamin. He's not like that. Whatever happened during her arrest, he had a reason, and you saw what they posted in the Gazette. People are pissed and out for blood."

What Brody says isn't something I can argue against. I take a moment to take three deep breaths. He's right, even if I don't like it. Evelyn needs my support, which means standing by her side, not stirring up shit and creating problems.

"You good?" Brody bodily turns me until I'm facing him.

The bright blue strobe lights from the police vehicles put me on edge, but I give Brody a nod.

"I'm good."

"You sure?" The bastard can be persistent.

"I'm sure."

"Good. Now, go get your girl while Cage and I figure out what the hell happened. Try not to bite Benjamin's head off. He's not the enemy for Christ's sake."

There's no arguing with that. The Bingham and La Rouge families have always been close. Genevive Bingham and my mother bonded when we were little, commiserating over the challenges of raising three boys and not having the blessing of daughters to spoil.

We spent many weekends at their house, and they rambled around our vineyards growing up. It's where Brandon and Bradley learned to ride dirt bikes and sat behind the wheel of a car for the very first time. Benjamin was older. As children those few years felt like decades, so I'm not as close to him. Not like Brandon. We all looked up to Benjamin and he always had our backs. Brody's right. Benjamin isn't the bad guy.

As I rush up, Evelyn's soft voice reaches out to me.

"Asher." Wrapped in a blanket, she looks smaller than I remember, frail and scared. Her wide eyes hold mine and in them I feel her fear.

Benjamin spins around. When he sees me, he takes a step back. "It's good to see you, Ace."

"Benjamin." I give him a clipped nod.

Evelyn's eyes shimmer with tears. Her cheeks are streaked with soot and dirt, and she's wrapped in a soiled white robe. I wrap her in my arms, not giving one fuck about her soot-covered mess. She buries her face against my chest and sobs.

"Shh...I'm here." Fuck if I'm ever leaving her alone again. "What happened?"

Evelyn says something, but between her sobs and her sniffling it's a blubbering mess. I hold her tight. All she needs to know is that I'm here and that I'll never let anything bad happen to her again. She may not realize what that means, but I have no intention of letting her go.

"What the fuck happened?" My question isn't for Evelyn, but rather Benjamin.

Unlike Pete Sims, Benjamin is a persistent bastard. I'm glad he's here. His investigations are thorough and he likes to listen to a witness's account several times, paying attention to things they didn't include the first time, tiny details that will help him crack the case.

He tells me what happened, giving me a chance to absorb the details. I grip Evelyn tighter when I realize how incredibly close she came to not making it out. The flames had been in her room.

People don't realize how incredibly effective a simple door can be to stop a fire, or slow it down. It can mean the difference between life and death, but she didn't have the protection of even that thin barrier.

Asleep in the tub? She's lucky the carbon monoxide and other noxious gases didn't knock her out. Yet again, I'm impressed by her ability to keep her wits in an emergency. Dunking her robe in the bathwater probably saved her life.

"Do you need anything else from Evelyn?" I want to get her out of here.

"If I do, I'll let you know. I assume she'll be with you?"

"You bet." My response is immediate.

"Can I speak with you for a moment?" He eyes the way I hold Evelyn, perhaps sensing I'm not about to let her go, but the urgency in his expression is enough to get me to release Evelyn. I kiss the crown of her head. "Give me a second, okay? I'll be right back."

She gives a shaky nod. As I release her, Brody comes to stand beside her, taking my place. He reaches out and takes her hand. We don't say a word, but I know he'll be by her side until I return. Brody can be a royal pain in the ass, but he's got my back.

Benjamin pulls me away from the ambulance. Cage comes with us. We stand behind the line of firefighters and stare at the destruction.

"What's up?" That uneasy feeling in the bottom of my stomach is now a gaping bottomless pit. He's got something he needs to tell me.

"This isn't an accident." He says the words I've been fearing.

"And you think Evelyn set it?" I can't help my fingers from curling into fists.

Cage puts his hand on my shoulder and his fingers dig in. It's a not so gentle reminder to keep my shit in gear.

"I didn't say that." Benjamin scratches the back of his neck.

"But it's what you're thinking." I can't help it. I'm ready to pounce on Benjamin and his fucking assumptions about my girl.

"It's absolutely not what I'm thinking." Benjamin fixes me with a stare. "Don't be a dick, Ace. I didn't pull you aside to tell you I think she set this fire."

"Then why?"

"Because someone else did."

"Someone else?" He says it with such confidence that I reel with the sudden shift from what I was expecting.

"Something isn't adding up, and I'm rethinking the other fire too. I took a look at Pete's report, and you're right. It's sloppy in execution. I need to speak to Evelyn about her account." He glances over to the ambulance. "But this may not be the best time."

I agree. She's distraught, more fragile looking than the strong, resourceful woman I carried out of a forest fire. That woman had been incredible. Now? Evelyn looks broken.

"What changed your mind?"

"Nosey neighbors." He points to the crowd. "Someone left the house a little before the fire started. I need to question the neighbors further, but the only people Evelyn says were at the house were her in-laws."

Benjamin's right about one thing. Something isn't adding up.

"They're not her in-laws, just friends of the family."

"Well, someone saw a younger man. At first, I thought it must've been you, but…"

"Yeah, I wasn't here."

"Exactly. I thought about the fire on the ridge and the man she claims assaulted her."

"Do you think someone is targeting her?"

"I'm considering a lot of options. Establishing motive escapes me at the moment. I can understand kidnapping her, but murder doesn't make sense. I don't see what the end-game would be?"

I must be doing a stellar job hiding my shock, because Benjamin doesn't pick up on my confusion. Several questions come to mind. I begin with the easiest.

"Why did you mention kidnapping?" My gut squeezes thinking about anyone wanting to harm Evelyn.

"Ransom is far more lucrative, especially considering her estate. It's a strong motive. Although, maybe there's something to murder considering what happened to her family."

My head spins. I'm not following Benjamin.

"What do you mean, considering her family?"

"The crash?" He looks at me like I should know this, but shit if I don't.

"I'm not following."

"The plane crash?" He looks at me like I know what he's talking about. "It killed everyone on board except for her. She's the sole survivor. Her entire family was on that plane."

And I bet her fiancé was too. Shit, the grief she must be dealing with has to be intense.

"This may be a third attempt on her life. I need more information, but I'm concerned."

He's concerned. My entire world feels as if it's been turned upside down. Someone is hell bent on killing Evelyn? I can accept one fire. But two? And a plane crash on top of that?

"Benjamin…" Not sure exactly what it is I want to say, I let my words trail off as I try and absorb what this means.

"I know." He gives a shake of his head. "I don't believe in coincidences."

"What about Pete's report? The fingerprints and the receipt?"

"It muddies the picture, for sure, but…"

"I want to help." Then it hits me. "That receipt. It has the name of the store where the accelerant was purchased, right?"

"I don't know."

"If it does, it'll have credit card information. That should help."

"Unless cash was used."

"Then we go to the store and see if there's any record of Evelyn even being there. If she wasn't, it should clear her of the arson charge…right?"

Benjamin gives a slow nod. "Definitely. It's a place to start."

"We shouldn't have to do anything. That was Pete's job. He's a fucking slacker."

"I hear you. Let's get through tonight. I'll come by La Rouge tomorrow and we'll figure out our next step. In the meantime, I'm going to look at the report." He places his hand on my arm and gives my bicep a squeeze. "We'll figure this out. I know you were pissed with the arrest—I'm sorry for that, but my hands were tied. Now that we know more, we'll get to the truth. I need to question her further, establish a timeline, but I don't think bringing her to the station is the best thing for her right now."

"She's coming home with me." Evelyn's not leaving my side until I sort shit out and get answers.

"I'll give you a call and arrange for a time to come over. I'm also going to call a few people and see what we're missing. Everything about this feels wrong."

I cock my head, interested in what he's saying. For the first time since arriving, I don't want to punch Benjamin in the face. He's not out to arrest Evelyn, or pin this fire on her. He's doing what he does best, looking to solve a crime; perhaps multiple crimes.

"Is that it then? We're free to go?"

"As long as the paramedics clear her, but I'm done with her for now."

Cage is quiet during our entire exchange. His supportive presence is the only thing keeping me from losing my shit. So many questions tumble in my head, things I need answers to, but they'll have to wait until I get Evelyn alone.

"Let's go." My comment is for Cage. I spin my heels and march back to the ambulance.

With soot and grime covering her face, and that god-awful robe wrapped around her body, she looks like she's been through the ringer. Brody sees us and helps Evelyn down to the ground.

She folds into my arms and ducks her head beneath my chin. I look to the paramedics. "Is she cleared, or does she need to go with you?" Please say No.

"Her vitals are stable. There's no sign of residual smoke inhalation. Of course, we recommend she be seen at the hospital—"

"No hospital." Evelyn clutches my shirt. "I don't want to go back there. Can you please just take me home?"

I like the way she says home.

We pile into my truck. Cage takes the wheel again, and this time Brody sits up front in the passenger seat. I'm in the back with Evelyn clutched tight against me. She huddles in my embrace, keeping her head down, and alternating between soft sobs and unintelligible muttering.

It takes twice as long to get home as it did to get to her house. I didn't realize how fast Cage had been driving. When we pull up outside the house, mother is there. Her little red corvette is parked off to the side and she waits on the porch.

Brody helps Evelyn out of the truck, then hands her back to me after I get out. When we climb the few steps up to the porch, I'm blown away when Evelyn practically launches herself into Mom's arms. Her weeping turns inconsolable and I'm left not knowing what to do.

My mother gives a little jerk of her chin. "Why don't you boys go inside while I get Evelyn situated?"

I'm not sure what it is, whether it's a woman thing, or a motherly thing, but I understand the power of a mother's embrace. I follow my brothers inside and slump down on the couch.

Cage sits across from me and kicks his ankle across his opposite knee. "So—that was an interesting way to spend a Saturday night."

"You don't say." I lean back and pinch the bridge of my nose, overwhelmed by everything I've learned.

Brody disappears into the kitchen while my mother ushers Evelyn inside. She gives a slight shake of her head, telling me she has everything under control, and gently guides Evelyn down the hall.

Brody returns with three beers and sits down beside me. He tosses one to Cage, who catches it, then hands me the other. "To one fucked up night."

"No shit." Cage takes a sip while I sit and cradle the beer in my hands.

I keep looking down the hall, feeling like I need to go to Evelyn, but I trust my mother. Evelyn needs time and space to collect herself before I start badgering her with the thousand questions running through my head.

Brody and Cage try engaging me in conversation, switching from topic to topic trying to get me to bite. When I sip sullenly at my beer, they give up. Brody asks Cage about his latest assignment, and I kind of zone out as Cage talks about polar bears, ice caps, and other things I don't care about.

Finally, my mother returns. Alone. She waves me over and places her tiny hand on my bicep. "She's been through a lot. This may not be the best time to ask a ton of questions. Sometimes, a woman simply needs to know her man is there and cares for her. I left her in the shower. Give her a minute before you go in." She grabs her purse and keys. "I'll be back in the morning. Goodnight, boys."

Brody and Cage jump to their feet and give her a kiss goodnight. They argue about what game to play. I stand in the middle of the hallway with my hands shoved in my pockets until I can't stand it anymore.

My feet are on the move. I need my girl.

22

ASHER

ASHER

Not surprising, Evelyn is still in the shower. I knock softly on the door.

"Evelyn? Can I come in?" I've seen the woman naked, fucked her on nearly every surface in my bedroom, and against the wall, yet I worry about invading her privacy? It doesn't make sense, but somehow, seeing her this vulnerable feels like crossing a line.

"Y-yes." Her voice sounds incredibly small, nothing like the self-assured woman I know.

Slowly, I open the door. Steam billows out into the hallway and sweat beads up on my brow. The heat is stifling and fog completely covers the mirrors. It's a large bathroom with a shower enclosure built for two. Multiple shower heads make it one of my guilty pleasures. There's a rain shower overhead. Two shower heads built into the opposite sides of the enclosure, and two rows of water jets which provide the most amazing massages. Evelyn has all of them turned on, and from the thickness of the steam, the heat is cranked.

"How're you holding up?" Like the mirrors, the glass door is fogged over. Her blurry outline is all I can make out. She's sitting, knees pulled up and tucked tight to her body.

"Surviving."

Without thinking about what I'm doing, I toe off my shoes and strip out of my clothes.

She needs me, but she won't ask me to join her.

Somehow, I know this, just as I know she needs me by her side.

This isn't about sex. It's about connecting, comforting, and providing solace in a world that doesn't make sense. When I think about everything she's lost, my heart gives a crushing squeeze that stops me in my tracks.

I'd give anything to ease her pain.

I open the shower door, step inside, and sit beside her. Mirroring her pose, I draw my knees to my chest, wrap my arms around my legs, and prop my chin on my kneecaps.

"It's foggy."

She gives a soft laugh. "Yeah, I like the steam and after the way my bath turned out…"

After she nearly died…

Benjamin's arson investigation may turn into an attempted murder instead.

I reach for her hand and ignore the stirring of my dick. Evelyn naked is too much for it to resist which means I'm going to have to be on my best behavior. This is about being present to support Evelyn, not fuck her brains out.

That serves my needs, not hers. Although, I'd like to think she kind of enjoys the fucking too.

"I like the steam," I say.

"You do?"

"Brody and Cage tease me when I take long showers. They think I'm jerking off, which is mostly true…" I give a soft laugh, trying to lighten the mood. "But sometimes I just need to sit. It helps clear my head."

She peeks up at me. "I do the same thing, or I did before I started backpacking. The clearing my head part, not the…the other thing." Her smile brightens my entire world and her little joke tells me she's going to be fine.

This woman has been through hell and back. I know about the

plane crash, but only because Benjamin mentioned it and I hope she'll open up and tell me.

I want to be the person she shares the ugly bits, the painful parts, and the happy times of her life with.

"Tell me about backpacking. Is it something you've always done?" Getting her to open up will be tricky as I tread the line between interest and overly inquisitive. My goal isn't to pry.

"Actually, I never did anything outdoorsy growing up, except summer horse camps, but we didn't exactly rough it. We stayed indoors and had housekeepers and chefs."

"Horse camps? Housekeepers?"

"Didn't I tell you I'm a spoiled rotten brat?"

"I don't know about spoiled," I tease. "You seem pretty self-reliant."

"You wouldn't have said that a year ago. I was pretty self-absorbed."

"How's that?"

"All I cared about was superficial crap that doesn't matter."

"That's pretty harsh. Why do you say that?"

"Because I was a rich spoiled brat and didn't have a clue what that meant until..."

"Until what?"

"Until I realized none of that mattered." She tucks her chin behind her knees. "There's a lot you don't know about me. I want to tell you everything, but some of it is pretty ugly and some is incredibly sad."

I lean against her shoulder. What I want is to wrap my arm around her and pull her tight against my body, but I can't do that. I'm already long, hard, and aching for her.

This is not about sex.

It's a time to listen and not give in to the base urges which are more than willing to take this shower talk to its most logical next step.

"I'd love to know more. You're a kick ass woman, who's not afraid of the outdoors and is incredibly good at surviving both forest fires and house fires."

"I'm cursed."

"Why?" It's killing me, dancing around what I know, but coming at her directly about the plane crash feels all kinds of wrong.

"Not that it's exactly the best thing to do, considering who you are to me, but can I tell you a little about Justin?"

Who I am to her?

Shit, all I want is to know what she thinks I am to her. Does she consider me her lover? Her boyfriend? Something more? Her forever? Because I'll take all of it.

My mother says I'll know, and damn if she isn't right. I'm head over heels in love with Evelyn. I'm already imaging sharing my life with her and I don't give one fuck what that says about me.

"Sure." My response is shorter than I'd like, but sincere. I want to know everything about her, even the painful bits.

"We were engaged."

"You mentioned that."

"But I didn't tell you what happened. Or how I wound up in the middle of that forest fire."

"I want to know everything about you. All the good stuff, the bad stuff, and the stuff in between. I'm completely and utterly fascinated by you." I love you.

That's not something I'm ready to throw out there, but it's the truth.

"Even if it's tragic?"

"Especially if it's tragic."

"My family is wealthy, more like wealthy elite." Her body stiffens as if searching for my reaction.

"Go on." Her hesitation worries me, but I'm not afraid of her wealth. It doesn't change anything for me.

"Our destination wedding was supposed to be the social event of the season. We leased a private island in the Caribbean and arranged to fly all the guests out for the day. Family and close friends were to stay on the island. As the island had no airstrip, we flew everyone in on seaplanes. Justin, wanted to make our entrance spectacular." Her voice kind of chokes up, but she presses on. "We flew everyone in over the course of the day and ours was to be the last trip. My entire family was on the plane, my parents, my brother, and Justin."

"What about his parents, Prescott and Gracie?"

"There were only six seats on the plane. They flew in ahead of us."

"Okay?"

Her lower lip trembles and she places her forehead on her knees. Her next words come out a muffled mess.

"Our destination wedding became a life-altering disaster when the plane went down. They said it was mechanical failure, something about the engine overheating. We stalled out on landing. The plane flipped end over end in the lagoon." Her grip on her knees tightens. "I was the only one who survived."

"Evelyn…" I don't know what to say and decide to pull her into my lap. My eager dick deflates as the horror of that accident hits me. "I'm so sorry. I can't imagine what that must have been like."

"The only reason I survived is because I wasn't buckled in. My dress…" She waves her hand in the air. "Anyway, I was thrown clear while the plane came apart. At least that's what everyone says happened. I was knocked out and nearly drowned. The only reason I didn't is because some of the guests ran into the water and saved me. There I was, my wedding day, getting fished out of a lagoon, while my entire family died. It was life altering."

"I don't know what to say." Benjamin mentioned an accident, but listening to Evelyn relive the disaster puts a lump in my throat. I lost my father years ago and still feel the loss. Some days are better than others. It's not something a person ever gets over.

If I lost Brody and Cage, and our mother all in one fell swoop, I don't know if I could stand living without them. I embrace Evelyn as she takes a deep breath.

"Every day, something reminds me of what I lost. There's no getting over that kind of grief. But I had to do something, my grief was slowly suffocating me. Each day it felt like I was the one slipping away. Instead of living, I was slowly dying inside."

I stroke her head, threading my fingers through her wet hair, and breathe in the humid air. Not knowing what to say, I let my hands speak for me with a gentle caress to her shoulder, fingers kneading the tight muscles of her neck, all light touches to let her know I care.

She takes in a deep breath and it's unclear if she's crying or simply taking the time to pick her words.

"That crash set me on a path of becoming someone I admired. To get there, however, I first had to face the kind of person I was."

"And what was that?"

"A vapid, narcissistic, privileged bitch." Her soft laugh sounds forced. "It just hit me one day. I was alone in the family home, wandering the halls, feeling sorry for myself. I looked down at my engagement ring and had an epiphany. Everything we had…it was just stuff, stupid, meaningless stuff, and I realized something else."

"Go on?" I rub her shoulders, which I hope encourages her to continue.

"I was marrying Justin because it was expected, not because I loved him." She looks up and touches my cheek. "I didn't love him and that hurt more than I ever thought it could."

"That's sad."

"It's pathetic, but there's more. I wandered into my closet and looked at all the ball gowns I'd only ever worn once, the shoes I only wore once a year, and I got sick of it. I got sick of all the stuff. The more time I spent in that house, the more I hated the materialistic over-indulgence that was my life. It was suffocating and I suddenly knew I needed to get away from it, get away before I did something I'd regret."

"And what was that?" What would she do that she'd regret? Was she suicidal?

"I ran away." Another soft laugh escapes her and she shakes her head a little. "I turned my back on all the daily reminders of everything I lost, and everyone I knew. The only thing I had left was stuff. My friends weren't really my friends. None of them stuck around as I wallowed in grief. No one wanted me around because I reminded them of what happened the day of my wedding. I reminded them life was short and I don't think they liked it."

"People can be cruel."

"It was eye-opening, but only because I was no different from them. I realized I couldn't stand the person I was and decided to become something new. I needed a fresh start. Everything I had, I no longer wanted. I took the ring Justin gave me and gave it to Gracie. I told Prescott to manage the estate and to sell off all the stuff my family had accumulated over the years. All the trappings of wealth sickened me and I wanted no part in it. But also, I couldn't stand all the little reminders which held the ghosts of the people I lost."

"So you started backpacking?"

"I read a book about a woman who found herself while hiking the Sierras. Something about her story resonated within me and I thought if I could just get away from it all, then maybe I'd figure out who Evelyn Thornton was, because I honestly didn't know. For me, a fresh start literally meant starting out with everything new. I was a high society city girl who turned to the wilderness for solace."

"You don't strike me as a city girl."

"I'm a spoiled heiress who never lifted a finger to help herself, let alone anyone else. Now?" She takes in a deep breath and lets it out in one long sigh.

"And now?" I encourage her to continue, fascinated by her words. Never in a million years would I have thought Evelyn Thornton was an heiress.

"Now, I forage and hunt for my own food. I set my campsite, make my fires, and source my own clean drinking water. In the past two months, the only person I relied on was me."

"I'm here." Rely on me.

"Yes, and I'm really happy for that, but I want you to know a little more about me, so you can understand where I'm coming from and why there are things I need to do for myself."

I get it, even if it's a truth difficult to swallow. In rescuing her from the fire, I inadvertently took something precious. I took away some small part of her independence and self-reliance.

"You can be quite intimidating. Tell me, how did you go from socialite to a solo backpacker?"

She glosses over my comment about being intimidating,

becoming more animated as she tells me about her journey of self-discovery. I admit she intimidates me, but it changes nothing about how I feel about her. I've dated my fair share of self-absorbed, helpless women who don't think to do anything for themselves.

The strength of Evelyn's character is what draws me to her, her confidence, her self-reliance, and the way she keeps her head on her shoulder in times of crisis. It's because of those qualities that I hold such deep respect for her as a woman. And it's probably the lack of those same qualities which kept me from feeling this way about any of the women I dated in the past.

"I didn't just start backpacking. I bought books, researched, and started small; overnights in campgrounds where I learned to pitch a tent. I talked to whoever would talk to me, picked their brains, and learned everything I could. I started hiking, short trails to start, then day hikes, then my first overnighter. The peace and quiet…" Her voice turns wistful. "The solitude? I don't know how to explain it, but it felt good. And I was learning. I learned all kinds of things, but most importantly, I learned how to do things for myself. I learned how to depend on myself. I kept my brain engaged in surviving rather than grieving."

"That's an incredible story. It takes a lot of inner strength to do what you did." It's not possible, but I find myself loving her even more.

"I tackled so many things outside my comfort zone, because keeping busy, having a mission, and needing to rely solely on myself kept me from reliving the accident. It kept my grief at bay and silenced the terrible guilt I live with being the only one to walk away."

"I can't imagine how horrifying the accident must have been, except I'm glad you're here." I squeeze her tight.

"I wouldn't have met you if I hadn't left everything behind. My outlook on life is different now. Not that I believe in fate, but I think we're destined to meet certain people in our lives."

"You getting philosophical with me?"

"Maybe? I'm tired and scared. I'm having to rely on Prescott again and that's…difficult. I don't want to become that person again, and I'm really afraid it'll happen if I don't watch out. Does that make any sense?"

"It makes a lot of sense, but I have something to say."

"What's that?"

"I don't want to lose you, and I'm going to fight this with you. If I over-step, promise you'll say something. I'm wired to protect and help others. It's who I am. I'll probably cross some lines with you, trying to help, just let me know when to back down, because I won't know when I need to."

"That's the most honest thing anyone has ever said to me."

I give a soft laugh. "You know, I have this picture in my head of a ditzy socialite and I'm trying to figure out how that woman is the same one I carried out of a forest fire."

"I'll take that as a compliment. As for that ditzy socialite, I figured if that woman could do it in the book, I could do it too. Anytime I thought something was too hard, too difficult, or impossible, I checked my assumptions and thought of that woman. There was a lot to learn, but I focused on learning one thing at a time. My single overnight hikes turned to weekend adventures and then I decided to head west. Eventually, I wound up here." She leans against my chest and reaches up to wind her fingers in the hair at my nape. A shiver works its way down my spine and my dick gives a little twitch.

She stills, then relaxes into my hold. "I'm supposed to be in the Sierras now, hiking the John Muir trail. It's kind of my opus, two-hundred plus miles of back country backpacking, the ultimate solo-escape. This was supposed to be my resupply stop, but then the fire happened."

Such a simple statement, that fire changed everything. "That fire brought you into my life."

"It did." She smiles at me. "I'm really glad we met."

"How did Prescott and Gracie handle you leaving like that?" I begin to understand their relationship better.

Evelyn grew up with their son and the expectation they would marry. Prescott's overbearing paternalism makes more sense.

"Prescott hated it. He refused to do as I asked, but we sorted things out."

"I can only imagine how that conversation went." I huff a small laugh. Thinking about Evelyn and Prescott going at it is something I would've paid money to see.

"Well, there was a lot of screaming on my part, words I wish I could take back. I wasn't very nice and threatened to cut them out of my life if he didn't do as I asked."

"Ouch." I run my fingers through her hair. "Evidently, you sorted things out?"

"A lot of my anger came from my grief and with trying to control me...well, he was a natural outlet. Gracie forced us to talk it out and I was able to get him to understand."

"They were going to be your in-laws. I suppose they see you as their daughter-in-law. It has to be hard on them too. They lost a son and then you walked out on them. I can't imagine how hard that was for all of you."

"You're right. Prescott saw me as his daughter and tried to parent me. Once we got past that, he backed off and I backed off. I understood he wasn't the enemy and was only trying to do right by his best friend's daughter. I was so self-absorbed, I forgot he lost not only a son, but his best friend, my father. He'll do anything for me, and I don't want to cut them out of my life."

"I'm glad you didn't. And I'm happy you realized you didn't lose your entire family in that crash. You still have them."

"I do. We're finding our way." She tilts her head and looks at me for several seconds. "I also found you. I thought my life stopped after the accident. My head went to some pretty dark places. I'm only just now realizing there's so much more living left."

I hesitate to bring it up, but Benjamin's suspicions fill my head. "Evelyn?"

"Yes?"

"Is there any reason to think the accident wasn't an accident?"

"What do you mean?"

"Just a thought, but the accident, the forest fire, and the fire tonight. It makes me wonder."

"You think someone is trying to hurt me?"

Not hurt, but murder.

"I don't know what to think. It was Benjamin who actually brought it up. He's coming by tomorrow to speak with you, but can you think of anyone who would benefit from your death? Or anyone with a grudge who would want you dead?"

Her brows pinch together. "I never thought of that. Honestly, I figured I was cursed, but no. I can't think of a single person who'd want to hurt me, or see me dead. And to be honest, there are no beneficiaries on the trust but me. Prescott's been on me to fix that."

"I don't understand."

"If I die, there's no one who the trust passes to. He wants me to designate a charity, or him, because otherwise everything goes to the government."

A strange feeling stirs in my gut. Is it possible Prescott has something to gain from her death?

It doesn't make sense. He wouldn't kill his own son, and Evelyn says Prescott and her father were the best of friends.

There must be someone else with a vendetta against the Thornton name, or Evelyn herself. A spurned lover?

I want to ask, but those questions are best left for Benjamin to uncover. With my hand wrapped around the back of her neck, I massage the tight muscles. Her eyes close and my dick stirs.

Her lips part on a sigh and I can't help but lean down and take advantage. The kiss isn't something I push. In fact, I leave it to the briefest touch. I want so much more. It's not my fault she's a knockout. My dick's had about enough of my iron-willed restraint and instantly hardens beneath her buttocks.

But it's late and she needs rest.

"How about we get you out of here and tucked into bed?"

"I'd like that."

Before my dick changes my mind, I lift her out of my lap. We both climb to our feet and rinse off. Several minutes later, I tuck her into my bed.

"How's that?"

"Dreamy," she says. "You're pretty amazing, Asher La Rouge. Do you know that?"

When she says my name like that, my heart just about bursts.

"If you say so."

She pats the side of the bed. "Aren't you coming to bed?"

"There're a few things I need to take care of first. I'll be back in a bit. Just close your eyes and try to get some sleep. You're perfectly safe here."

There's nothing more in the world that I want but to crawl under the covers with her, but there are chores which need to be done, like mucking out Knight's stall and checking on our mares in the pasture.

Evelyn's ability to walk away from her life shows incredible force of will, an adventurous streak a mile wide, and impressive character. I'd love to follow in her footsteps, but La Rouge Vineyards requires constant attention. If it's not harvesting the grapes, producing our next vintage, or prepping for the next crop, there's still La Rouge Stables which requires attention.

Our small herd of plodding mares don't require much care, but they still need tending. Knight and I need to patrol the pasture fence, find and fix any holes that would let the mares out or the rare predator in, and make sure the feed and watering troughs are full. The work never stops.

"I feel safe…I…" Whatever it she was going to say is lost as she snuggles into the blankets and eases into sleep.

I head back to the living room, too wound up to sleep. I'm thinking about who might want Evelyn dead because there's no doubt in my mind someone is going to great lengths to make sure that happens.

My brothers sit with me while we discuss what to do. I tell them Evelyn's story, but there's no way to know who might want her dead. For that, I need to speak with Prescott. He'll know more about who might have a grudge against her family, or who might benefit from her death. Although, he's still on my list of suspects.

"Well." I stand and stretch, "I'm going to lock things down." A deep yawn escapes me.

"Want some help?" Cage places his game controller down on the coffee table.

"I'd love help." It keeps slipping my mind, Cage is here for the next few weeks. Too used to doing everything myself, it never occurs to me to ask for help.

"Well shit." Brody sets his controller beside him on the couch. "I'm not sitting around while the two of you are working." He'll be headed back to the city once the weekend ends. A busy man, he tries to help when he can, but usually only makes it out here one, maybe two weekends a month.

The three of us head outside and saddle our horses. It's late, night fell hours ago, we should be getting ready for bed ourselves. I should be in bed with Evelyn.

Truthfully, the work can wait for daylight, but I'm restless and agitated. There's little I can do to help Evelyn, and I'm not used to not being able to fix things.

Not knowing how to help Evelyn, other than stand by her side, kills me. One thing is clear, however. From here on out, she's under my protection

Evelyn

I wake to sunbeams spilling into Asher's room. The man is not one to stay in bed when there's work to be done. Not ever having worked a day in my life, his dedication is something I admire.

Stretching in bed, my toes curl, my back arches, and my arms reach high over my head. I luxuriate in the sensation and roll to my side where I clutch his pillow and take a deep breath. His scent fills my nostrils and I can't help but close my eyes and draw him deep into my lungs.

Exhaustion pulled me under last night. He wanted to do more. There was no way to ignore his arousal in the shower, but he didn't push. Instead, I found myself carried to bed and tucked in with a feather light kiss to my forehead. The only reason I know he slept in the bed at all is from the depression in the mattress and the toe curling scent of him swirling all around me. I take a moment to simply breathe him in.

How lucky am I to have found a man like him? Frankly, I could stay in bed all day, but I feel a little guilty laying around while he's outside working. There are so many questions floating around in my head about La Rouge Vineyards. The whole process of making wine fascinates me and I want to know more.

I get up, determined to find him. As I head to the bathroom to relieve the pinching in my bladder the events of last night hit me. I stagger and press my hand against the wall to keep from tumbling to the floor.

The flames and choking smoke. The acrid stench. I'm overwhelmed and need a minute to simply breathe.

For the second time, I've lost everything.

The third time if I count the loss of my family.

I literally have nothing.

That includes the clothes on my back. Asher let me borrow one of his shirts before putting me in bed last night. There's nothing on beneath it.

All the new credit cards, the lovely clothes and shoes Gracie and I bought, even my new phone, all went up in smoke.

My search for Asher ends in the kitchen where he's cooking with Brody and Cage. They turn as one, an odd sight, and I'm greet by three devilishly handsome smiles.

"Hey, you're up, sleepy head." Asher hands the spatula to Brody —I think that's Brody, it's hard to tell Brody and Cage apart. As for Asher? I know exactly which one of the three identical brothers is mine. It's a feeling deep in my gut and tucked inside my heart.

"It smells wonderful." I give a little squeak as Asher comes over and lifts me off my feet. He gives me a kiss before depositing back on the floor.

"We're making waffles and eggs." Brody flips a couple eggs while Cage turns a cast iron waffle pan over the gas burner. "I hope you're hungry."

"You've been busy." There must be enough food to feed an army, but I have a sinking suspicion the three brothers will eat every last bite. "Is there anything I can do?"

"Nope. Just sit back and relax. Food's almost done." Asher leads me to the dining table. He rocks a pair of denim jeans which hang low on his waist and hug him in all the right places. "Coffee?"

"Yes, please."

With a kiss to the top of my head, he leaves me to fix a steaming mug of coffee. I greedily watch every flex of muscle and the way the denim shifts over that glorious ass.

He returns to me with a twinkle in his eye. "A penny for your thoughts?"

"Nothing." I glance at Brody and Cage.

Asher presses the tip of my nose with the pad of his finger. "I have a feeling nothing is a whole lot of something."

To keep from having to fess up to the dirty thoughts swirling in my head, I bring the coffee cup to my lips. One sip and I'm in heaven.

La Rouge Vineyards is officially my favorite place on earth. Breakfast is amazing. I haven't eaten this well in months, more used to a handful of trail mix as I break camp for the day. My offer to do the dishes is politely declined, something about guests not doing the dishes. I always thought the opposite was true, guests should clear the table and clean up.

Not that I've ever done that in my life.

My life is—or was—a life of excess. We had cooks and maids who did all that stuff for us. It didn't matter if we were the hosts or the guests, I never once lifted a finger to help out.

I'm not proud of that.

With nothing to do, I head outside to take in a gorgeous morning. There's a slight chill in the air which will be gone as soon as the sun climbs a little higher in the sky. A gentle wind stirs the dust on the ground and birds flit from bush to bush. I watch a squirrel get into a fight with the birds, chattering angrily back at them as it races around the bushes. They bring a smile to my heart.

The coffee in my hands is getting cold. A year ago, I would've turned my nose up at it for not being of high enough quality. My tastes changed, however, on the trail.

One of the creature comforts I brought backpacking is—was—a

small percolator. The coffee was rough, unfinished, but some of the best coffee I ever drank.

There's something about doing things for yourself, a sense of accomplishment, which makes the foulest coffee turn into the best in the world. I miss my morning trail-coffee, even the tiny grounds which slipped through the filter and always seemed to get caught in my teeth.

I'm reminded of my complete lack of earthly possessions. All I have is my robe, which is now in the trash. Asher gave me one of his La Rouge tee-shirts and I've already decided I'm never taking it off. His mother returned sometime during the night and dropped off a pair of her jeans, socks, and shoes. I'm a size smaller than her, but with Asher's belt the jeans stay in place.

There's another shopping adventure in my near future, but this time, I'm not going to let Gracie steer me toward clothes I no longer wear. I don't need name brand. Functional is my brand of choice and I'm going to re-kit myself out for the trail.

A restlessness grows within me to head back into the wilderness. Not sure how long it'll take me to hike the John Muir trail, I anticipate a couple weeks at least, but it's exactly what I need to clear my head.

The door behind me opens and Asher comes outside. He sits beside me.

"How're you holding up?"

I place the lukewarm coffee down on the side table and smile at him. "It's beautiful."

He glances out from the house and takes in the deep blue of a nearly cloudless sky. We're smack dab in the middle of paradise.

"You think you're up for a ride?" Asher asks.

"I'd love a ride." My gaze shifts down to his crotch and the corner of my mouth curves into a smile. He's asking about riding horses. I'm thinking about riding him.

He follows the direction of my gaze and gives a low laugh. "Dirty girl, what am I going to do with you?" Generous to a fault, Asher is an amazing lover. We've officially broken in every surface in his bedroom, and are working on the walls.

I'm new to wall sex. Raw and brutal, there's nothing soft about getting fucked against a wall. Asher has more than enough strength for it, and stamina. The man is a glorious fucking machine. In his arms, I feel light as a feather. There's a small bruise forming at the base of my spine, the aftereffects of Asher unglued. I love the way he unleashes his inner beast as I wrap my legs around him and simply hold on for the ride.

Squeezing my legs together, I bite my lower lip. Thoughts of sex with Asher turn me into a needy, horny, ravenous bitch.

"I enjoyed it very much." I'm thinking about the one thing we haven't really done, or rather what I haven't done. Asher's tasted me, but I've yet to return the favor. I lick my lips in anticipation of bringing him to his knees.

Well aware that Brody and Cage are inside, my attention shifts toward the horse barn. There's one other thing we've yet to do. Something else I've never done before, and I'm excited to explore it with Asher.

I'm not used to the carnal aggression Asher brings to sex and I'm pretty sure his filthy, deviant mind is working on broadening my horizons.

"Damn…" Asher shifts in his seat. He grabs at his crotch and makes an adjustment. "I don't know what the hell just went through your head, but you have my attention."

"I was just thinking about a couple things."

"Things?"

"Yes—things." I look toward the barn. "What do you think of showing me a little of your rope work?"

His head tips back and he clutches at the hardness pressing behind the zipper of his jeans.

"Fuck, I think I'm going to come right here. You interested in getting tied up, little backpack?"

I nibble at my lower lip. "That depends. Will I be going for a ride?" Leaning forward, I place my hand over his and give a little squeeze. He's fully erect and squirming in his seat.

"Oh, I'll take you for a ride, but I'd rather put you on your knees."

I lean back and lick my lips. "Too bad your brothers are here."

"Fuck that." Abruptly, he stands and lunges for me. I shrink back, but then give a little squeak when he lifts me out of my seat and slings me over his shoulder. He locks me in with an arm around my legs and heads for the barn.

"I'm perfectly capable of walking."

"Oh, I don't doubt that, but I don't want you running off."

I playfully slap his back and he rewards me with a swat to my ass.

"Stop that, little backpack." The tonal registers of his voice shift to a low, throaty growl. "Or you'll wind up over my knee."

Holy fuck, that's sexy.

A man on a mission to fuck, Asher marches with single-minded determination to the barn.

I think he's going to put me down and we're going to have sex away from the prying eyes of his brothers. I'm not prepared for the fire in his eyes, the command in his voice, or the way I yield to his desire.

He takes me to the back of the barn where he deposits me on my feet then presses down on my shoulders. His intent is clear.

I fall to my knees as he flips the button of his jeans and lowers the zipper with a rasp. His eyes are hooded. Lust blows out his pupils, turning his green eyes nearly black. He frees his cock, then palms the back of my head.

There's no asking.

No sexual banter.

This is Asher in the raw, focused on one thing. Damn if I don't find that sexy as hell.

"Open that sexy mouth."

With his hand on the back of my head, it's not like I have much choice. He practically yanks me onto his dick.

"That's right...swallow me whole." His hips rock forward and I take him in.

A needy throb lodges itself between my legs. I'm terribly turned on by this side of Asher. My place is clear and it's all about serving Asher's pleasure.

Why does that excite me as much as it does? I don't know and frankly I don't care. My mouth opens and I do exactly as he says.

He groans as I take him in.

"Fuuuck, I've wanted this since the first time I saw you. You on your knees. Me standing over you. You taking me in and swallowing me whole." His fingers tighten in my hair and his hips jerk forward as he tries to shove himself deeper in my mouth.

I work to take him in, to open my mouth and drown him in sensation. I'm not sure if I'm giving him a blowjob or if he's taking it from me. All I care about is the crazy way he makes me feel, the way I respond to his demands, and how fucking hot all of it is.

"You drive me insane. Do you know what the sight of you on your knees does to me? Do you know all the filthy things I want to do to you?"

With my mouth full of his cock, it's impossible to answer, but I look up at him and our gazes lock.

I imagine what he must see. Me on my knees. His dick buried in my mouth. It's got to be fucking erotic as hell.

His grip tightens and I'm fully at his mercy as he pulls out of my mouth and slams forward. There's no easy rocking back and forth. There's no slow drag as I slide my mouth up and down his cock. My control is non-existent as he takes his pleasure.

Asher's head tips back. The muscles in his neck draw tight with strain as he moves in and out of my mouth. His body shakes as he fucks my mouth.

"I want to tie you up. Smack that perfect ass. Fuuuck...I want to control you. I want to fuck you until you beg. I want to watch you come apart for me."

I may not have control of my head, but I do control my hands. I yank his jeans down, exposing his ass, and wrap my arms around him. His breath hitches and I wonder if he knows I've given myself to him.

Whatever he wants—it's his.

Whatever he needs—I'll give.

"Look at me." His command snaps through the air and my gaze

lifts to meet his. "You're fucking gorgeous." Strain fills his voice. His legs shake. "Fuuuck, I'm going to come."

He releases his grip on my head and I understand what he's saying. I can pull off and he'll shoot his load onto the straw around us. Or, I can take him in and swallow him whole.

I dip my head forward, taking him all the way to the back of my throat.

"Ev-e-lyn…" Taut with strain, his voice waivers as he makes sure this is okay.

I draw back, using my tongue to stimulate him and let him know I want this too.

He reaches down, taking my head in his hands. "I need to move… Fuck, I need…"

I know exactly what he needs. Asher can be a soft and gentle lover, but this is who he really is. He's a man willing to take as well as give. I want him to have it all.

I give the slightest shake of my head, granting him permission to do what he needs.

A growl escapes him as he releases the last of his restraint.

I gag as he goes deep and ramps up his pace. This is no blowjob and I'm just holding on for the ride.

23

ASHER

Asher

I've never seen a woman as beautiful as Evelyn on her knees. God, the sight of her lips wrapped around my cock. The way her tongue strokes me. The warm, wet heat of her mouth taking me in. It's enough on its own to make a man go insane, but what really drives me over the edge is the desire in her eyes and the permission she gives for me to unleash the last bit of my restraint and chase my release.

I can be kind and gentle. Some of the best sex is when I take things slow, one hundred percent focused not on me, but the needs of my partner. I love the power which comes with that.

But I like this too. The taking and claiming. The freedom to let a willing partner give me what I need.

And I take that now.

My hips jerk erratically and my body gives a shudder. I come with a low, throaty, growl as my release rushes through me. It's powerful. A toe-curling explosion of lust and heat coursing through my body.

And Evelyn?

She's goddamn sexy on her knees. The trust in her eyes warms my heart. Her willingness to give so that I might take turns me inside out. She's perfection.

I let the wave pass, panting against the sensation before dropping to my knees and taking her in my arms.

"That wasn't too…" As much as I enjoyed coming unglued, I worry about it being too much. I especially worry about scaring her off.

Shit, I told her I wanted to control her while blinded by my lust and driven with need. That kind of shit tends to scare people away.

She buries her head against my chest. "That was…"

Scary? Distasteful? Overbearing?

Wrong?

Her arms encircle my waist. "Asher…" She says my name on a sigh, then looks up at me. "That was incredible."

My insides clench because incredible sounds fantastic.

"That was fucking hot as hell." I brush aside the hair from her face as she places a hand over my chest.

Like a rush of heat, all the tension leaves my body.

Hot as hell?

I like that.

"About some of what I said…" I take in a stabilizing breath. She peeks up through her lashes then dips her head. That's the hesitation I fear.

She presses her palm against my chest, right over my heart. "Whatever you want, Asher—it's yours."

I choke at her words. She keeps her chin tucked, but damn if I need to see the truth in her eyes.

"Evelyn…"

Her grip tightens and she presses her cheek to my chest. Her fingers draw a circle over my heart.

"Whatever you need—take it."

Shit, that's not a fucking circle. That thing she's tracing over my heart? It's a goddamn heart.

"Was that too rough? Did I hurt you?"

"No." She gives a soft laugh.

"Did I scare you?"

Where the fuck is this insecurity coming from? This isn't me, Ace La Rouge takes what he wants, but it seems Asher La Rouge needs Evelyn's reassurance.

What a fucking pussy.

I'm not happy but it's the truth. We're still brand new. Everything is shiny and bright, exciting and filled with intense emotions. I'm blind to the hazards and if I'm not careful, I'll fuck this up before we really have a chance to begin.

"You didn't scare me at all." She finally looks up at me. "Exactly the opposite."

"Really?" I want to believe her, but I'm cautious. She's not some chick I want to fuck and leave. Evelyn is part of my future, which means I need to be careful and not fuck shit up by going all caveman and scaring her off.

She reaches for my chin and drags a finger along my jawbone. "That was…" Her voice trails off and I hang on her every word.

It was what?

What was it?

"Hey, Ace!" Cage calls out from the front of the barn. "We've got visitors and your phone is going bat-shit crazy."

Evelyn breaks away from me. She rubs at her mouth and chin, removing the evidence of moments ago, then she drags her fingers through her hair finger-combing it straight.

"Shit." I pull my pants up and tuck my dick inside. It's spent but eager for more.

"It's Evie's friends." Cage isn't dumb. He knows exactly what's going on in here, which is why he yells from the door.

"Be there in a sec." I lift Evelyn to her feet and give her a once over.

She takes a look at her clothes. "How do I look?"

"Perfect." My shirt looks fucking amazing, especially with her nipples practically drilling a hole through the fabric.

She's turned on and I can't help but wonder which of the many things I said had an effect on her. We will finish what I started in here, and I'm going to find out exactly how interested she is in more of it, like a little rope work.

We head out and Cage meets us with a shit-eating grin. Yeah, he knows exactly what we've been up to. Fortunately, he keeps whatever thoughts are swirling in his head to himself.

He thrusts my phone out at me. "Smokey says you need to go."

"Shit." I turn to Evelyn. "Sorry, I gotta call him back."

"Anything wrong?"

"Smokey is my crew chief." I dial his number. "If he's calling, it's for a reason."

Cage jerks his thumb over his shoulder and speaks to Evelyn. "Your friends are here. They're waiting on the porch."

Evelyn peeks around Cage's broad form and I follow the direction of her gaze. Sure enough, Prescott and Gracie wait on the porch.

Smokey picks up. "Hey, Ace."

"What's up?"

"We're spinning up. Fires down in San Rios."

Shit. "I'm on my way."

Evelyn doesn't go to meet her guests, choosing to remain by my side. "Anything wrong?"

"My helitack team is spinning up. I'm really sorry, but I gotta go. I don't know how long I'm going to be away." I look to Cage.

"Don't worry, Ace. We got her."

"What does that mean?" she asks.

I take Evelyn's hands in mine and lean in for a kiss. My dick wants much more than that, but there's no time.

"I don't know how long I'll be gone. It could be a few hours, a few days…" Or weeks. I don't tell her this. "Brody and Cage will look over you. I want you to stay at La Rouge while I'm gone."

I glance over at Prescott. Evelyn wasn't safe when I turned her over to him, and he's still on my list of suspects.

"Okay," she says.

"I mean it. I need to know you're safe, and I can't do that if I don't know where you are. Stay here. My brothers will keep you safe."

She squeezes my hands. "I will. You have to go now, don't you?"

"I do, and Benjamin Bingham is planning on coming over to talk with you. Please be here when he arrives."

"I won't go anywhere." She lifts up on her tiptoes and whispers into my ear. "I like your bossy side."

"Do you?"

"Hmm, yes, I think I do."

"Then you'll stay?"

"I promise."

Holy fuck, my dick takes note of that.

"I'll stay right here until you get back." She gives me a nod and a soft smile brightens her face.

I suppress a low groan because all I'm thinking about now are all the filthy things I want to do when I get back. But I need to leave.

"Keep her safe for me." I slap my brother on the arm and race inside to grab my gear and head out. When I exit the house, Cage and Evelyn are talking to Prescott and his wife.

I hear Evelyn tell them about the house fire as I race to my truck. All I want is to stop in my tracks, turn around, and go to my girl. But I don't.

I hop in my truck and head off to meet my team.

Last to arrive, they're gathered around the table, leaning over a set of maps.

"What's up?" I ask, a little out of breath.

"San Rios fires," Smokey says.

"How bad?"

"Bad." Smokey takes my hand in his and gives an abrupt shake. "This is going to be a tough one, ladies. They're spinning up the entire state for this one."

Shit. That doesn't sound good.

A text flashes across my screen. I hope it's Evelyn, but it's Brandon instead.

Brandon: You headed to San Rios?

Me: Yes.

Brandon: They spun up the fire station. Maybe I'll see you there.

It's got to be a bad fire for them to pull local assets like that. If

Brandon's going, it leaves the township unprotected, which tells me we're getting ready to fight one hellacious bitch of a fire.

Me: We're pushing out now. Be safe, brother.

Brandon: Ditto.

"Grab your gear, ladies. Time to go." Smokey's command gets us in motion. We grab our gear, our tools, and head out to the helipad where our ride waits for us.

We pile in and secure our mass of equipment. Anxious energy floods the air as we get ready to face the unknowable.

Every fire is different. Each with its unique energy, power, and risk. Fear swims through me, not the paralyzing kind, but the adrenaline spiking kind. It's going to be a grueling few days and we'll all soon be running on fumes.

I live for this.

We spend the next hour double-checking our gear as we fly towards the fire. I would do this full time if I didn't have La Rouge Vineyards to maintain because this is what I love.

It's a passion burning in my veins and I approach each fire without hesitation. Already, a familiar trancelike state falls over me. It's a single-minded existence where I lose myself and focus on the task at hand. The outside world fades away as I become laser focused on only one thing.

Fighting fire.

We head to the high Sierra's where we'll tangle with a snarling bitch of a beast. She's hungry and on a rampage, but we're determined to stop her in her tracks. As it is, this bitch doesn't give up without a fight. Soon, she turns into one of the worst fires in California history.

24

EVELYN

It's hard watching Asher go. He exposed a side of himself I find fascinating, something I'm eager to explore. I've never had sex like that and my mind is blown.

I want more.

But that needs to wait.

Of course, Prescott wants to take me away from here. He's devastated about the house fire and goes on and on about how California isn't safe. I need to go with him, where he can keep me safe, but I'm not willing to leave. There's a promise holding me to this place, to La Rouge Vineyards and the man who calls it his home.

Gracie wants to take me shopping again, but I'm not up for another trip purchasing clothes I won't wear. I apologize, using Benjamin Bingham as an excuse and eventually get Gracie and Prescott to leave.

I don't wait long.

Benjamin shows up within the hour with a sharp knock on the front door.

Cage gets up from the couch. He and Brody are playing something on the gaming system, while I read a book.

"Hey, Benjamin."

"Is Ace here?"

"Nah, he got called in."

"What about Evelyn?"

"She's here."

"Mind if I come in?"

My expectation is Cage will leave Benjamin and I alone, rejoining Brody in whatever it is they're playing, but he doesn't. In fact, Brody joins us in the living room. They take their responsibility for watching over me seriously. It comes as a surprise, but what's more surprising is how much I need that show of support.

"Do you mind if I ask you a few questions, Miss Thornton?"

"No, and please call me Evelyn, or Evie."

He shifts in his seat and pulls out a pad of paper. "I have a few questions about the fire."

My lips twist. "Which one? I seem to be a fire magnet." I'm sitting in the middle of one of the large leather couches. Brody and Cage bracket me on either side. Cage shifts closer and places his hand over mine. My hands are clasped in my lap, fingers twisting with unease.

"Well, that's what I want to discuss. Being involved in one fire is rare enough, two pushes the laws of chance."

"Are you arresting me for that fire as well?" I can't stop the indignation rising in my voice.

"Not at all." Benjamin leans back. "I'm working another angle."

"And what is that?" Brody shifts closer. I'm in the middle of a La Rouge brother sandwich, protected and supported by them both.

"Did you see anything suspicious last night?"

"No." I shrug.

"Can you walk me through what you remember?"

"What are you getting at Benjamin?" Cage squeezes my hands. He doesn't have to say it, but I know he's doing his best to stand in for his brother's absence.

Benjamin looks between Brody and Cage. "Look, I want everyone to take a breath. I'm not arresting Evelyn, and I'm not looking to implicate her in anything."

"Then what are you doing?" Brody asks.

"Trying to put the pieces together."

"What do you mean by that?" I ask.

"I'll answer your questions. I promise. But first, let me ask mine. I have a process which never fails. Do you think you can do that?"

Our first meeting didn't go well, but I sense Benjamin is on my side.

"Okay."

"Good. Let's start with last night. Walk me through what happened."

"What do you want to know?" His question confuses me.

"Let's start with whether you noticed anything unusual."

"Nothing really comes to mind. Prescott and Gracie brought me home. We'd gone shopping and Gracie helped me put everything away. They left and it was just me. I remember feeling anxious and bored. We didn't have time to set up internet and all I had was my phone."

"Your phone." Cage shifts in his seat. "Ace said you had pictures of the guy on it."

"Which guy?" Benjamin asks.

"The one who started the forest fire. I remember that really well. He gave off a bad vibe and I figured I'd snap a picture."

"Why would you do that?" Benjamin asks.

"Because I figured it would help Prescott if…well, if things didn't go well."

"Were you afraid for your life?"

"No, it was nothing like that. I'm used to coming across people on the trails, most are friendly, but this guy, something just seemed off with him. I told him I was taking selfies for my 'social media followers.' I figured if he knew I had people checking in on me, and that I had a photo of him, he'd be less likely to do something to me. I was going to camp at that campsite but figured I'd go to the next one."

"Then what happened?"

"I tripped. I wasn't watching where I stepped. Next I knew he attacked me, hit me in the head with a rock. When I woke up there was fire everywhere."

I tell him about my escape through the fire, my tumble down the ridge and Asher rescuing me.

"Evelyn, if you took a picture it'll be uploaded to the cloud." Cage releases my hand. "Where's your phone?"

"Which one?" I give an awkward half-laugh. "I lost both of them. I thought about that too, but I don't remember any of my passwords. I can't log in. That's one of the reasons I took a bath last night. I had nothing to do without television or internet. No books on my phone, because I couldn't remember my password to that account either. But I don't think it matters because there was really poor reception up there. I didn't have a signal."

Benjamin taps his chin. "That's actually very helpful."

"How's that?"

"We don't need your passwords. Do you know what email address you used for your account?"

"Maybe. I use several."

"Well, that's good news. I can get a warrant for an attempted murder investigation."

"A murder investigation?" His words turn my blood cold. "What do you mean?"

Benjamin lifts his hand and begins ticking off his fingers. "There's the house fire, the forest fire, and the plane crash."

"What plane crash?" Cage leans forward and my stomach clenches. Asher's brothers don't know about that.

Fortunately, Benjamin explains. His account of the accident is surprisingly accurate, leading me to wonder how much investigating he's done.

"You think someone wants me dead?"

"I'm investigating all angles right now, but that does seem to be the case."

"But I'm a nobody."

"You're an heiress to a hundred million dollar fortune. At first, I thought maybe someone was targeting your father, and that may still be the case. My assumption is they didn't expect anyone to survive that crash. Since you did, all Thornton assets passed to you. Are you aware of anyone who would benefit from your death?"

"No one." I shake my head and return to my finger twisting. "I really am nobody."

"I think there's more." Benjamin scratches at his chin. "Tell me how you came to be on the trail."

I start to explain, but he holds up his hand. "One moment, back up please. Where were you before coming here?"

I tell him about camping in Colorado and hitchhiking to Napa.

"Do you remember your route?"

"Kind of, but to be honest I wasn't paying attention."

He takes out his phone and pulls up a map. "Do you mind taking your best guess?"

I take his phone and stare at the map, exploding and zooming in on the screen as I need to. Benjamin gets up from the couch and sits on the coffee table as I lean forward and show him my best guess.

"I'd like to have you sit with a sketch artist. It might help if we have a solid description of the man who attacked you."

"I can try, but I don't know if it'll be any help."

"You'd be surprised what a trained sketch artist can do. I'll get it set up and arrange for it sometime next week. Does that sound good?"

"Sure."

We talk for a little longer. He thanks me for my time and excuses himself.

As he opens the door, I call out. "Detective Bingham…"

He turns and gives me a smile. "You can call me Benjamin."

"Um, okay. You asked if there was anything weird last night."

"Yes?"

"I remember feeling like someone was watching me, like a presence. It was really strong. So strong that I made a circuit of the house, checking the locks, looking in the closets." I give a soft laugh. "I even checked under the beds. I don't know if that means anything, or if it was just me being nervous in a new house."

"That actually helps. I'll be in touch." He heads outside and Brody and Cage follow, leaving me alone with my thoughts.

Benjamin's theory about someone trying to hurt me doesn't feel right. My father was well liked. My mother was loved by practically everyone. The terms of the trust are rather specific. Everything went to me and my brother. There are no other heirs. With my brother's death, I'm the sole heir.

Benjamin's theory doesn't hold up. Something else is going on.

While Brody and Cage are outside with Benjamin, Abbie drives up in her little, red corvette. She takes one look at my state of dress and shakes her head.

"Girl, you and I are going shopping."

I think about Gracie offering to do the same and hold back a groan. I'm not up for a shopping trip, but somehow she gets me to not only go, but allow her to foot the bill. Until Prescott gets my cards reissued, I have no access to my money.

We spend the afternoon riding with the top down in her corvette. I relax beneath the sun and let the wind whip at my hair. We ride in silence as I take everything in, processing Benjamin's theories. And then we talk. Nothing of substance at first, but then I tell her everything, spilling my life's story as we drive through Napa Valley. Instead of fancy designer stores, Abbie takes me to the super-store Asher mentioned.

We spend two hours inside where I pick up an entirely new wardrobe for the second time in less than a week. Unlike the clothes Gracie and I bought, these are practical. I load up on comfortable jeans, tee-shirts, shorts and lightweight sweaters. I forget about shoes until Abbie reminds me. I grab a pair of boots in addition to sneakers while I'm at it.

If I'm going to stay at La Rouge, I plan on helping out. No longer a helpless socialite, I'm ready for hard work and know exactly how I can help the La Rouge brothers out.

The four of us spend the rest of the day together at La Rouge. Abbie and I join forces in the kitchen, kicking her boys out, and whip up a feast of burgers and hotdogs. I'm pretty helpless in the kitchen. Not a required skill for a socialite, but I'm eager to learn and Abbie is an excellent teacher.

After dinner is put away, I ask Cage if I can help him in the barn mucking out the stalls.

The day passes, then another. The San Rios fires dominate the news. It's a challenging fire season in California, and the San Rios fire looks to be the worst fire in recent history. I don't begin to worry until the fourth day when we get the news one of the fire crews was overrun by the fire.

Brody and Cage tell me not to worry, but that's impossible, especially with the strain in their expressions. They're putting on a brave face for my benefit, but they're worried about their brother.

25

ASHER

Fire snaps all arounds us, crackling as it chews through dry tinder. Summer, and the long drought, have not been kind to the land. Everything is dry, ripe kindling to feed a voracious fire, and we've got the beast of all fires marching over the mountains.

Hundreds of acres have fallen and we're dead set on saving what we can. This bitch of a forest fire, however, mocks our efforts to put her out. She roars with fury all around us and spits at our pathetic attempts to contain and control her voracious appetite.

Every county in the state lends support. We even have several hotshot groups from out of state involved in the effort.

My friend, Brandon is somewhere in this mess with his team. As for me, my helitack crew rappels in and out of trouble spots, where we help to hold the line.

This fire is officially large enough to be called a true firestorm, meaning it draws in enough fresh air that it's develop its own weather system.

We're in the middle of a vortex and losing ground. Brandon's out there with his team, cutting the line, fighting the fire with grit and determination.

We've been fighting this fire for four days and ease into the fourth night. It's been over a day since I last spoke to Brandon. Two since I spoke to Evelyn.

Brandon sounds much like me. He's tired and running on fumes. Evelyn is supportive, but worried for my safety.

Right now, my team and I stare down a ridge. In the darkness, flames are all we see. Small breaks in the smoke give us glimpses of the night sky. Stars shine down on us, oblivious to the battle we wage. Shifting winds place us all in danger. We've already had one team overrun, but so far, no lives lost.

A tree explodes somewhere down the ridge, splintering from the inside out as the sap inside of it superheats. There's a flash of orange which marks the spot. A terrible roar rumbles in the air, fire chewing through vegetation, sucking in oxygen, drawing in more fuel to sustain its burn.

Smokey takes a call over the radio. His expression flattens, turns grim. "Another team has been overrun."

It's what we all fear, getting caught in the middle of the flames. Our kits include fire blankets designed to protect a man caught in the open. They give us five minutes to survive. Three-hundred seconds of harrowing fear while we pray the fire rolls through and past.

Life is measured in a matter of heartbeats. We all train with the blankets, using warehouses to simulate fire. I hate those drills. The intense heat and suffocating breath is a slow, painful way to die.

I send a prayer for the team caught in the fire.

"Who's down there?" I turn to Smokey, certain he knows which team is overrun.

Smokey gives a slow shake of his head. "Men from Fire Station 13."

Our entire team stops what we're doing. Fire Station 13 serves our town. Brandon is on that team.

I look down the ridge and into the inferno. My best friend is down there and there's shit I can do.

I've never felt so helpless.

The radio crackles, HQ asking everyone to report in. Smokey answers the call giving our position and stats.

An explosion rips through the air. Not the sound of a tree being ripped apart from the inside out, but what sounds like a bomb going off. I know what that sound is from. It's the sound of a gas tank exploding and we're not that far from it.

We all exchange looks. The same thought goes through our minds. Brandon and his team are hunkered down somewhere down there.

How much time do they have? Not long.

"Over there!" Dice points down in the valley. "Gasoline explosion. Our boys are down there."

We gather together. Tarzan and Highball stand beside me. Dirt, soot, and sweat cover our faces, turning them black. We're thirty-four hours into what should've been a twenty-four-hour shift. We would stop, but we can't. If we don't hold the line, this fire destroys everything.

In the middle of the firestorm, a tendril of black smoke marks the spot of Brandon and his team. They're completely surrounded by a raging inferno.

"Smokey, we have a location." I point toward the fire, trying to distinguish landmarks in the darkness which will help.

No one questions the next step. We need to get to those men.

The wind howls all around us, drawn in toward the flames. Adrenaline flows through me as does the sickest feeling. There's nothing we can do to get to those men except to wait for a break in the fire.

"If they survive." Smokey's never one to mince words, "They'll need to cut their way out." He draws his finger across the landscape. "We'll head there. Try to meet up with them. If they make it out."

We all know the likelihood is slim. I pray the fire blows through quickly, and keep count in my head.

Five-minutes.

Three-hundred seconds.

That's all the time Brandon and his team have to survive.

"Come, we're heading out." Smokey gathers us together. He

calls in to HQ, telling them what we plan. After he gets the go-ahead, we head down into the blaze.

The stifling heat only grows more oppressive as we near the leading edge of the fire. Smokey leads us off to the left, along a line he thinks Brandon's team will follow. We've got a long hike ahead of us.

The minutes stretch and we pass the five-minute mark. Smokey calls in, but there's no word from Brandon's team. Either their coms are down or the entire team is dead.

Hour after hour, we work the line. Backbreaking work that makes our muscles ache and steals our breath. Hours during which I think about Brandon, wondering if he and his team survived, and hours to think what would've happened if that had been me.

I'm not ready to say goodbye. Not after finding Evelyn. It's a sobering thought. When it was just me risking my life, I didn't worry about death. Now, there's someone I want to come home to.

What has she been doing these past four days? Did Benjamin stop by like he promised? Did he follow up on that receipt like he said he would?

Are Brody and Cage taking good care of my girl? There's at least one question I know the answer to. My brothers won't leave Evelyn's side.

Dawn is upon us before we know it. We're eager to find Brandon and his team, but we're hampered by vegetation. We cut in fire prevention lines as we go. The work never stops.

No radio calls come in from Brandon's team. Not that radio silence means shit. They could've lost their coms in the fire.

It's frustrating work, no matter how hard we work, hot spots flare around us, delaying us as we stop to put them out. Smokey keeps shouting at us to 'keep the line' and we do the best we can. We're coming up on forty-hours with no sleep. Adrenaline can push a man only so far.

It feels as if we've stepped into hell with fire and brimstone all around us. The smoke is so thick we practically push it aside as we advance. Orange flames lick their way up the bark of trees and red embers fade and flare on the ground. It looks like the fire is breathing.

Out of habit, I take a swig of water from my hydration pack. There's not much left. We need to resupply, but that will pull us off finding Brandon and his team.

Smokey holds up a fist and we pause. He taps his ear, telling us he heard something and we pause to listen. All I hear is the crackling of fire and the roar of the wind. But then I hear it. "Balls to the wall, boys." The deep voices of men respond.

Smokey calls out into the smoke. We pause and hear a response. My heart lifts because I know that voice.

"Brandon-fucking-Bingham are you alive?"

"Ace? Holy mother of God. It's fucking Ace La Rouge."

Our teams find our way to each other, calling out through the dense smoke. There's seven of them and six of us.

Brandon emerges out of the smoke. When he sees me, his face spreads into a huge grin.

"Goddamn nice to see you," I say.

"It's good to be seen." We clasp each other and thump each other's backs. This is repeated all around until Smokey's clear voice rings out.

"HQ, we found them."

I don't know how long Brandon's team has been on the mountain, but they look strung out and exhausted. Their eyes are haunted from the firestorm which nearly took all their lives. But I see relief, resilience, and that dogged determination to stare death in the face and survive.

Nobody speaks about what could've happened. There's no place for that kind of shit in our line of work.

"Okay ladies," Smokey says, "we've got some dirt to put behind us. Base camp is sending a truck up to the fire road, but it's still gonna be a hike."

We hump well over two clicks. HQ guides us to a fire road where we meet up with our transportation and cram into the open bed. We bump and jostle our way down to base camp while the fire rages on the ridge behind us.

New men will hold the line.

For us, the day is done, but not the fight.

It takes ten more days before I get to head home. Two weeks since I left Evelyn. I'm both excited and nervous to see her again. I've been out of touch, with no idea how things are going.

26

EVELYN

To fill my time, and avoid thinking about Asher and the danger he's in, I revert to my comfort zone.

Oddly, it's a mix of old and new.

Some of my favorite memories growing up revolve around the horse camps I attended as a girl. There's something wildly freeing about being on the back of a powerful animal yet completely in control.

Mostly in control.

There's a fine balance between the will of the horse and that of its rider.

I spend the first four days of Asher's absence working with Cage in the barn, taking care of the horses, mucking out their stalls, and spoiling Asher's stallion rotten with treats of carrots, sugar cubes, and apple cores. He's an amazing animal with a summer coat of the sleekest midnight black. And he's tall, much taller than the horses I'm used to riding.

Mornings, we spend in the small fenced pasture behind the barn. Cage reminds me not to let Knight join the mares in the main pasture, and watches over me. I must pass some kind of test, because after the fourth day, Cage leaves me to tend to the horses alone while he and Brody meet with La Rouge Vineyard's foreman to discuss the upcoming harvest and what to do with the burned acreage.

I've yet to see the damage and have been itching to explore for days. I spend most of my time outdoors, because the house feels like a cage. The call of the outdoors is too strong to ignore, and the new me isn't one to let that go unanswered.

I'm getting a little stir crazy. It's time to get out.

Knight gives me a look when I take him out of his stall and tie him up beside the tack room. It's easy to figure out which saddle is his. It's the one that's most worn. He stamps his rear foot when I cinch down the saddle, but quiets to the soft cooing of my voice.

I'm comfortable around horses and can tell he's a bit high-strung. That's fine by me. I won't push him and let him know I'm no threat. I'm also not so stupid that I take him for a long ride the first time out. We're still in the 'getting acquainted stage' where we're building mutual trust.

Knight and I get to know each other better in a small fenced ring. We begin the morning with him wearing his saddle and me encouraging him to trot in a circle around me. I spoil him rotten, more with verbal praise than the sugar cubes he can't seem to get enough of. He knows where I hide them and nibbles at the pockets of my jeans.

By noon the fifth day, I mount him for the first time. His eyes roll and he stamps nervously, but I coo to him and rub at the soft spot he loves behind his ears. That first day, all we do is trot in circles inside that small enclosure. He tries to buck me off, but I hang on and keep up my soft cooing, reassuring him that I won't hurt him.

The next day, I take him to the smaller field. He almost throws me again, but I continue in soft, reassuring tones telling him how amazing and wonderful and awesome he is. He eats it up and I'm confident he'll let me ride him without him unseating me.

Today is the perfect time to put our new friendship to the test.

Brody and Cage aren't around. They're busy, waking at the ass crack of dawn and returning long after dusk deepens to night. My days are mine to fill as I please and I'm ready for an adventure.

"Okay, Knight, do you trust me enough to be good?" I reach down and pat the side of his neck. He gives a rumbly nicker, a low vibration coming from his throat which says he's excited. I lead him through the gate of the small enclosure we've been running around the past few days and he prances with excitement. Giving a sharp snort, he can't wait to stretch his legs.

I'm comfortable enough with the lay of the land to head out on my own. Navigating a vineyard is easy compared to a forest trail. Knight and I are off and ready for an adventure.

He's excited to be out of the barn.

I'm excited to be away from buildings.

We're perfectly matched.

And the vineyards are nothing short of breathtaking. The vines sit heavy with grapes. They're so tempting. I want to reach out and snag a cluster, but hold back. I tried a grape a few days ago and wine grapes are nothing like supermarket grapes. I spat it out with a grimace while Brody and Cage laughed their asses off. They're not here to make fun of me today, but I learned my lesson.

The burnt fields are sobering. Knight slows, making me think he knows something bad happened here. A horse's sense of smell is greater than a human's, as is their fear of fire. He gives a little whiney, shakes his head, and snorts, all while stamping at the ground.

"It's okay, boy." I give another pat, trying to soothe him. Fortunately, he likes the sound of my voice and calms down.

We reach the end of the burnt field where I briefly consider heading back home. But there are still a few hours left before I lose the light. My curiosity is at an all-time high and I know exactly where I want to go.

Pretty certain I can find my way, I do a quick search on my phone for the trailhead. I'm right. It's less than a mile down the road.

"How about a little climb, boy? You up for a nice, long walk?"

With a snort, he stamps at the ground again.

I take this for a yes and guide him to the trailhead. He doesn't need my assistance, however, and seems to know exactly where to go. That's when it dawns on me that this must be where Asher takes his La Rouge Stables clients on what he fondly refers to as his plodding mares.

I assume Knight is very well acquainted with the trail and let him have the lead while I sit back and enjoy the day.

It doesn't take long before we pass familiar landmarks. That outcropping of boulders is where I took Prescott's call. They're one of the only things I recognize. The forest I hiked through is nothing but the charred skeletal remains of what used to be a breathtaking wilderness.

We round a bend and I peer around the curve. Right where I expect it to be is the fire pit with its rocks. Everything is covered in black soot and char marks.

There's hope, however. It's been a few weeks since the fire, and it's impressive to see a burst of new life. Green shoots poke through the charred dirt. Even in fire and devastation, nature is resilient, creating new life from the ashes of old.

That's what I wish for myself, to be able to rise from the ashes of my previous life and become something new. I'm more certain now than ever before that I don't want to return to my previous vapid life of a socialite. I'm much more than the number of zeros found in my bank account.

I'm on a mission, eager to find the remnants of my cellphone. Concerned about my missing revolver, I climb down from Knight's back and hobble him while I stretch my legs. It's been well over a year since I've ridden a horse, and years since I've sat in the saddle for that long. I'm going to be sore when the morning comes.

Knight paws at the soil and nibbles at new shoots of grass. They must taste especially sweet, because he seems to be enjoying himself. I place my hands on my hips and take a moment to simply take it all in.

It's too quiet and nothing like the blazing inferno I woke to. Impossible to stop myself, I trace an imaginary line from the fire ring to the edge of the ridge. I don't know if this is where I catapulted myself into thin air. It's impossible to tell, but I see the grouping of boulders in the ravine where I took shelter.

Did I really think those would protect me from a firestorm?

Desperation does crazy things to one's mind.

With Knight happy munching on baby grass, I make a circuit of the campsite, kicking at the sooty earth, hoping to find evidence of my cell phone and pray I find my revolver.

But they're nowhere to be found.

A breath of frustration whooshes out of my pursed lips. It was a fool's notion to think I'd find my revolver. This place was picked over by whoever did the arson investigation, but I'd hoped to find something.

The jangle of tack grabs my attention.

I'm not alone.

A man on a pretty chestnut mare comes up the trail. I shield my eyes against the sun and squint at the stranger. He pulls to a stop.

"Good afternoon." He tips his cowboy hat in a welcoming salute. His lips curve into a panty-melting smile. "Don't I know you?"

"Um, yeah." I know who this is. "We met at the bar."

"That's right, you're…" He points at me. "Don't say it. I never forget a beautiful woman's name." He pauses dramatically then snaps his fingers. "Got it. You're Evelyn Thornton."

"That's me."

Honestly, anyone within fifty miles knows my name by now. I remain the most hated stranger, vilified on a daily basis by the local gossip magazine, although I'm no longer front page news. It's one of the reasons I haven't left La Rouge Vineyards since Abbie's mega shopping trip to the local superstore.

"Well, it's nice to see you, you're a pleasant surprise. I'm—"

"Felix." I supply. "I remember you." How could I not? I'm no stranger to the flattery of men. On the surface, Felix is like many of the men who tried to steal me from Justin. He knows his worth. He's good looking, has a great smile, and knows how to flirt.

But I'm taken.

And cautious.

The tension swirling between Felix and Asher that night at the bar was palpable. I don't know Felix, but I trust Asher.

"Whatcha doing up here?"

I glance around and take in the devastation. "I guess I wanted to see what it looked like."

"Is what they say in the papers true?" The tone of his voice shifts.

It's subtle, something I would normally miss except I'm paranoid. The last time I was up here with a strange man, he tried to kill me.

"If you're asking if I set the fire, then no. It's not true."

"Then how did it start?"

"There was someone else here, a man who knocked me out. He started the blaze."

"Oh no. Have they caught him? I haven't heard anything."

"No. I wish, but no luck so far."

"Well, if that's the case, you're getting raked over the coals in the Gazette for no reason."

His reference to getting raked over the coals hits too close to home. "Soon enough, they'll catch the guy who really set the fire."

"You think that's likely?"

"If I can find my phone it will be. But the cops are looking into other angles."

"Your phone?"

"I lost it, along with everything else." I cast about the campsite. "But I can't find it."

"Don't you have iCloud backup or something?"

"I wish that were the case. If so, I could get them to drop the charges, but no luck."

"Just get a new phone and download, or upload, whatever it is. You know restore your phone from the cloud?"

"Thought of that, but I don't know any of the passwords. I can't restore it, which is why I'm up here."

"I guess they won't find the guy then."

I shrug. "I don't know. Benjamin Bingham had me sit with a sketch artist. I don't remember much, but it's something."

"A sketch artist?" His upper lip twists and he shifts in his saddle.

His grip on the pommel tenses. "Kind of a long way for a pretty woman like you to be alone."

"I'm used to it." Not interested in pointless small talk about my innocence, or presumed guilt, it's time to wrap things up. "Well, it is getting late. I should be headed home."

"Home? Now where would that be? I thought they said you were from out of town?" He leans over the pommel of his saddle. "Honestly, I've been looking for you. You know, kind of hoping to run into you again, or have you run into me. Felt like we had a connection."

Definitely no connection.

Felix's clean-shaven appearance probably draws the kind of women who are more than eager to drop their panties with one well-timed blink and that fabulous smile.

Not me.

I've got something better.

"I'm staying at La Rouge Vineyards."

"Ah…" He cups his hand over his heart like he's wounded. "I've lost you to a La Rouge triplet. Ace, I presume?" Giving a slow shake of his head, he looks appropriately disappointed. "He always had a way of stealing the best girls. I guess you and Ace…" He leaves the rest for me to fill in, but I'm feeling too jumpy to react to his comment.

"They've been really nice to me, stepping in to help." I walk over to Knight and release his hobble. "Anyway, it was nice seeing you, but I need to be heading back. They get upset if I'm not back for dinner." Cage and Brody roll in long past supper, but Felix doesn't need to know that.

"Such a shame." His eyes pinch. "We could've watched the sunset together. The view from up here is phenomenal."

"Maybe another time." I place my foot in the stirrup and lift myself into the saddle.

It feels a bit abrupt leaving so quickly, but Felix is right about one thing. I'm alone, far enough from civilization that no one will hear me scream. Not that Felix is a threat, but the last time I was up here with a stranger things didn't turn out very well for me.

"Maybe another time, Evelyn." The way he says my name sends a shiver down my spine, and not the good kind.

I urge Knight into a canter and head back the way we came. For a split second, it feels as if Felix might join us, but I look over my shoulder and breathe out a sigh of relief.

It's me and Knight all the way home. When we get to the barn, I intend to reward Knight with a treat, but I'm the one who receives the best surprise imaginable.

"Evelyn?" Asher calls out as we come into view. "How the fuck did you get him to let you ride him?"

There's no time to answer. I practically levitate out of the saddle in my rush to jump into Asher's arms. My legs wrap around his hips and my lips lock to his.

"You're back!" I bury him in a flutter of kisses and hug him tight. If it weren't for Knight, I'd fuck Asher right there, but Knight needs to be rubbed down after our ride and Brody and Cage are home early. They watch from beneath the covered porch

And yes, they both have shit-eating grins on their faces because they know exactly what went through my head. I'm practically dry humping their brother in front of them.

Not that I care.

Asher is home.

27

ASHER

ASHER

It's been nearly two weeks without Evelyn in my life, in my arms, and wrapped around my cock. She clings to me like life itself and I admit to loving every minute of it.

Funny how before I met her, I thought Erin was the woman I wanted to spend my life with. I'd been so blind.

Evelyn feels like a breath of fresh air. We kiss and I'm practically dizzy from lack of oxygen. Our lips lock. Our tongues tangle. My dick gets hard. Damn, I need to sink inside her wet heat and feel her tight pussy clench around my dick.

Unfortunately, my brothers snicker from the porch and Knight snorts with indignation because I'm ignoring him. Unlocking my lips from Evelyn's, I reach out and pat his neck. He's hot and lathered in sweat, as if he's been working hard.

I want to be hot and lathered in sweat, but only because I can't wait to fuck Evelyn's brains out.

Crude. I know.

But it's true. I'm long, hard, and aching.

"Where did you take him?"

Evelyn squeezes her legs around my hips. Damn, but I can feel the heat of her pussy through our clothes. She climbs off me and places her feet back on the ground. It sucks, because I liked her hot pussy pressing against my greedy cock.

"I need to fuck you and soon." Low, gravelly, my voice rattles with need.

"Definitely." She smiles up at me, soft, seductive, and irresistible. "I missed you."

I missed her more than I'm willing to acknowledge.

"I can't believe you rode Knight." A low cough escapes me as I switch topics.

"Why?" She grabs his nose, gives him a kiss, then leans over to scratch his special spot behind his ear. Nobody knows Knight's ticklish spot, but she seems completely at ease with him, and more surprising, my horse appears to be utterly and completely infatuated with her.

"He never lets anyone ride him but me."

"Oh, we had plenty of time to get to know each other. He's really just a big push over." She turns her attention to Knight. "Aren't you, boy?"

Knight, totally out of character, gives a little whinny.

A whinny.

He's flirting with her, fucking bastard.

"Where did you guys go?"

Evelyn looks at the ground and traces a half circle in the dirt with the toe of her boot. "Through the vineyard."

"Through the vineyard?" She's lying. I can tell by the way she refuses to look at me. "That's it?"

"Well, I wanted to see the burned area."

"And..." I know my horse. A quick ride around the vineyard doesn't bring that much of a froth to his coat. "Where else?" A sinking sensation in my gut tells me I know exactly where she went.

"I took him up on the trail."

"The trail."

"Yup, the trail."

"Where you almost died?"

"Where you saved me." She lifts on tiptoe and props her forearms on my shoulders.

Her fingers twine in the hair at my nape, sending shivers down my spine and bringing a nod from my dick.

I like her hands on me.

The idea of Evelyn out all by herself doesn't sit well with me. I'm very well aware she's able to take care of herself, but that doesn't mean I have to like it. To hide the anger stirring within me, I grab Knight's bridle and lead him inside the barn.

I have no right to be angry, but I've been away for nearly two weeks. I'm tired. Exhausted. And pissed. She has no regard for her safety. But I'm not too far gone to make the mistake of voicing those thoughts out loud.

Knight provides the perfect distraction. As does Evelyn. We head into the barn while my brothers dismiss themselves and retreat into the house. This leaves Evelyn and me alone to reconnect, a.k.a. fuck, while they do whatever the fuck they need to do without us.

If there's one thing I've learned over the years, it's to never take Knight for granted. As much as I need to reconnect with Evelyn, I take the time to properly care for my horse. While I do, there's plenty of time to talk myself down from the anger stirring in my belly.

I have no right to be mad at Evelyn for heading back up to the ridge, but damn if it doesn't gnaw at me. While she's comfortable in the wilderness by herself, I'm not okay with it.

Funny how that's one of the things I love most about her, even when I don't like it. Too much of a protector, I'm not used to a woman who's able to take care of herself. I'm not used to a woman with the balls to go hiking alone.

"Why did you go up to the ridge?" I'm curious.

"I wanted to see if I could find my phone."

"We went to look for it, but didn't find anything."

"I know. I guess I just needed to go myself. I was also kind of hoping to find my revolver."

"Your what?" This is news to me.

"My father gave it to me and I kind of lost it."

"What do you mean by lost?"

"I had it when I hiked up there and didn't have it after...well, you know."

After that asshole knocked her out and left her for dead. Yeah, I know all about that.

"Is it possible he took it?"

"Considering the arson investigator didn't find it, that's kind of what I'm assuming. It's a shame because it's the only thing I really have left of my father."

"How can that be?" She told me her story, but still. Did she really get rid of everything?

"Just is. Anyway, California gun laws are strict, and I kind of didn't want that laying around."

She's right about that. It's harder than shit to get a gun permit in California, and concealed carry for an out of state visitor? Impossible. I'm not sure what kind of laws she broke, but understand her need to recover the weapon.

"Brody, Cage and I spent an entire afternoon up there looking for your phone. If there'd been a revolver we would've found it."

"I appreciate that." She shoves her hands in the pockets of her jeans. "I guess I needed to see what it looked like up there after the fire. It was a sobering experience."

It's a fire she very nearly didn't survive. I suppose I understand her need to revisit the scene of the crime, as it were.

"Did Benjamin come by and talk to you?" My shift in topic may be abrupt, but I haven't had a chance to speak with Benjamin. I need to know what he's found.

"He did." She twists a lock of hair around her finger. "He had me sit with a sketch artist to get a picture of the man I saw."

It shouldn't surprise me. Unlike flakey Pete, Benjamin is a thorough fucker. He'll chase down every lead until it reaches a dead end. I'm glad he's working her case.

With Evelyn helping me, we unsaddle Knight and give him a rub down in half the time it normally takes. I slide the bolt to Knight's stall closed and turn to find her playing with a length of rope.

She glances toward the door, then turns her attention back to me. A shit eating grin spreads across my face. I love the direction her thoughts are going.

"Whatcha got?" I tease.

"Nothing."

"Doesn't look like nothing." I prowl toward her, harder than ever. My dick has a mind of its own and it wants her. I'm happy to oblige the fucker, but first that barn door needs to close.

It faces the house and there's no way I'm giving my brothers a show.

Evelyn isn't going to get fucked in some stall. That rope she's holding is going over the main support beam stretching over her head.

It's been two long weeks of backbreaking work fighting the San Rios fire and I'm ready to let lose a little steam. This is something I intend to savor.

Instead of coming at her directly, I keep a wide berth and walk around until I reach the barn door. We generally keep it open for ventilation, closing it only during the chilliest nights in winter. Which means it makes one hell of a screeching noise as I pull it shut.

As expected, there's movement in the windows of the house. My fucking brothers were watching. We're going to have a conversation about that later. For now, my attention returns to Evelyn.

"Have you ever been tied up during sex before?"

She takes a step back and clutches the rope tight to her belly. Her lower lip rolls in as she nibbles on it. Such a fucking turn on. I know what that mouth of hers can do. Too nervous to speak, she gives a tiny shake of her head.

This is a first for her and damn if I'm not happy about that.

She's willing, but nervous, which means I need to take this really slow. My dick is pissed about that. It wants to rut and fuck and bury itself deep inside her hot pussy. Fortunately, I'm not so far gone that I listen to my dick.

Yes, I want to fuck, but I'm more interested in making this an

ELLIE MASTERS & USA TODAY BESTSELLING AUTHOR

experience Evelyn will never forget. I hold out my hand and shift my voice to a lower register.

"Give that to me."

Her eyes widen and she takes another step back. I close the distance, and she takes another step back. The corner of my mouth curves up, because this is going to be so much damn fun.

On my fourth step, she backs up against one of the support posts. It's actually the perfect place. I thought to loop the rope over a beam and torment her nice and slow, but there's a peg at the top of the post that'll do just fine. I can't wait to tie her hands over her head, tease her until she screams, then fuck her against the post.

Yes, this will do just fine.

"Are you trying to run from me?"

She can't find her voice and gives another shake of her head. Attuned to everything about her, I take my cues from the way her cornflower blue eyes blow out with lust. Her pupils fully dilate and there's only the faintest rim of blue left. The way her breath accelerates turns me on. That damn nibbling of her lower lip drives me fucking crazy. Her eyes lock to mine, testing my resolve, a little uncertain, but determined to see this through.

"I fucking missed you." The crotch of my jeans tightens as my arousal grows. I avoid adjusting myself. I want her full attention on me not my cock.

At least for now.

I take another step and she presses her back against the post.

I reach out. "Hand me the rope."

Careful to make everything a command, instead of a request, I set the tone for our little experiment. If this is something she likes, I have so many other things I want to show her.

With some degree of trepidation, she hands over the rope.

"Hands together, little backpack."

Her lips curve into a smile at the crazy nickname. It's unusual, but I love it. Every time I say it, I'm reminded of the day we met.

She places her hands out, wrists together. Now I'm the one biting my lip because damn if her trust isn't the sexiest thing in the world.

Silence falls between us as I wrap the rope around her wrists. It's snug, not tight, and if she really needs to, she should be able to wriggle her way free. I'm hoping she doesn't try and allows herself to really sink into what's happening here.

I press her against the post and stare down at her wide eyes.

"Do you trust me?"

She gives a nod. Still no words. She's willing but unsure. Going slow is my motto.

I lean into her, pressing the length of my body against hers. No way she doesn't feel my dick. One hand is around her wrists, over the knot I tied. The other presses against the post as I kiss her slowly. Reverently. Desperate for more.

But I don't take more. Not yet.

I break apart and slowly lift her wrists over her head, watching her expression the entire time.

No fear.

No hesitation.

Exactly the opposite. Her breathing accelerates and she licks her lips.

I raise her hands over her head, then force her on tiptoe to slip the loop I made over the peg jutting out of the post.

She's completely at my mercy.

A quick glance at her heaving breaths and I realize a mistake. I should've taken her shirt off first. Too eager to begin, I didn't think everything through.

That's okay. I'll make it work. Slowly, inexorably, I lift the hem of her shirt, taking my time to expose her bra.

She giggles as my fingers tickle her ribs and bites at her lip.

I hold back a moan.

"You're so goddamn sexy, little backpack." I nuzzle her neck, sucking gently as I decide whether or not to leave a mark. I decide not to, because my fucking brothers will only tease me about it later. I can take the heat. I'll throw it back at them, but I don't want to make Evelyn uncomfortable.

She dances beneath me, squirming and shifting her feet as I

nibble my way to her collar bone and back up to gently suck on her ear lobe.

She only just now realizes she's at my mercy. With her hands over her head, I can do whatever the hell I want. My attention shifts to her amazing tits.

"Asher!" Her sudden shout stops me in my tracks. "Watch out!"

I pull back, see the whites of her eyes. Her mouth opens on a scream.

Something hard slams against the back of my head.

Evelyn's scream is the last thing I hear as I slump to the ground.

28

EVELYN

Felix watches Asher collapse. With his chest out, shoulders back, his angry glare turns to me. I stare at him, eyes wide, shocked by this turn of events, then it hits me. It slams into me like a sledge-hammer and I don't know why I didn't notice before.

Those copper-colored eyes? His rugged good looks? His barrel chest and broad shoulders? Throw a beard on him. Grow his hair out shoulder length…

It's all right there, something I should've seen. Something I can't forget.

I've seen him before, and it wasn't at the bar.

I look at the rope binding my hands, the peg far over my head, and thrash trying to get free.

It's hopeless.

I'm stuck.

"Felix, what are you doing?"

Maybe I can reason with him.

Anger flashes in his eyes and he fixes me with an unblinking stare. Placing his hand on his hips, his attention shifts to Asher and his lips twist into a snarl.

"Ace-fucking-La Rouge, who knew he'd be such a pussy."

267

He squats down and rolls Asher face down in the dirt. Yanking Asher's arms behind his back, Felix turns his smug expression back to me. He yanks out a long, black zip tie from his back pocket and secures Asher's hands behind his back. Felix stands and his attention shifts back to me.

"You're one tough bitch to kill." He shoves his hands in his pockets then pulls them out and pinches the bridge of his nose. "I thought I got rid of you on the ridge, but no, you survived."

"Felix…"

He holds up a hand. "I got them to pin the fire on you. Figured it was an open and shut case, but no." He jabs a thumb at Asher's unconscious form. "Your boyfriend has to go crying to the cops. Which made them dig." He points at me. "Fuck the La Rouge triplets. Thorn in my fucking side my whole damn life. They always bounce back no matter how hard I knock their asses down."

"I don't know what this is about, but we can talk about it."

"Talk?" He huffs with indignation. "I'm done talking. I'm done trying to take what's mine. This time, Ace is going down and La Rouge Vineyards is going up in flames."

I try again to free my wrists, but I'm effectively trapped.

"Felix…what are you doing?"

His grim smile stretches wide as he looks around the barn. I see the can of gasoline the moment he does and my insides go ice cold.

"Felix please, you don't have to do this. We can talk it out."

"Talk it out? Do you have any idea what that bastard did to me? What his family took from mine? This is our land. Ours! And he forced those girls to tell those filthy lies. He stole from my life."

What girls? What lies? I twist in my bonds. I try to jump, hoping to get the loop of rope to slip over the peg. Nothing helps.

Felix grabs the gas tank and gives it a shake. The sloshing inside tells me it's nearly full. He unscrews the nozzle and watches me.

"Please…" I beg, but his maniacal grin doesn't waiver. He tips the can and a dribble of gasoline flows out onto the dirt of the barn floor.

I release a blood curdling scream, hoping Asher's brothers come running.

Felix puts the gas can down and marches over to me with a sour expression fixed to his face. He pulls out a rag from his back pocket and shoves it in my mouth.

I spit it out and scream, louder this time

His eyes pinch as he picks up the dirty rag. Very deliberately, he yanks Asher's belt through the belt loops of Asher's jeans until it's free. Narrowing his eyes, he scrunches the rag into a ball, pries my jaw open, and shoves the cloth inside my mouth, pushing it as deep as it'll go. I gag against it and tear up as he ties Asher's belt around my head and mouth.

"No one is coming to save you. Not this time. By the time Tweedle-Dee and Tweedle-Dumb out there figure out what's happing in here, I'll be long gone and you and your boyfriend will be nothing but a crispy mess."

Why?

What does he have against me? Against Asher?

Other than me being the only person who can identify him. The only person who can testify he started that fire.

I know why he wants me dead, but what I don't understand is what he was doing up on the ridge starting a forest fire in the first place.

I scream against the gag, but it's garbled and too low for anyone to hear.

With the barn door closed, Asher's brothers won't intrude. They think Asher and I are doing something else in here rather than fighting for our lives.

My attention shifts from Felix to Asher. Is Asher breathing? I can't tell. Holy shit, is Asher dead?

Felix hums as he wanders around the barn shaking gasoline over the hay and at the base of the barn walls.

I wring my hands and desperately try to unhook the damn loop from the peg over my head.

Each time Felix looks at me, he bares his teeth and sneers. Then he follows that with a dismissive shrug. His lips twist as he turns away. To him, we're already dead.

But what does he get out of this? I don't understand.

My eyes narrow as I try to puzzle it out. I try to unhook myself for what feels like the hundredth time, and fail.

Felix finishes his circuit of the front part of the barn. He runs out of gasoline and tosses the empty can to the side. Knight sticks his head over his stall door and gives a nervous whinny. Felix is not only going to burn Asher and me, but all the horses as well.

Son of a bitch!

Still no movement from Asher. I can't tell if he's breathing, but I'm hopeful. A knock to the head shouldn't be lethal.

I think.

Hell, I survived Felix knocking me upside the head. I call out Asher's name, but the gag prevents anything intelligible from leaving my mouth.

Felix returns. He reaches out and cups my breast. My insides twist as he squeezes the sensitive tissues.

"You picked the wrong guy. You should've gone home with me." He kicks Asher in the ribs. "I guess you'll die with him."

He backs away with a feral grin. When he gets to the horse's stalls, he looks back at me. "Shame about the horses."

With those words, he reaches into his chest pocket and pulls out a box of matches.

A blood curdling scream erupts from my throat, but it comes out a low rumbly mess.

Everything slows as he lights the match and tosses it onto a bale of hay. I watch the match arc through the air, land on gasoline fueled straw, and ignite. Flames lick at the straw.

With a slow wave, Felix turns and runs out the back of the barn.

The fire spreads like lightning, filling the barn with smoke.

I struggle, but can't free myself. When I slump in defeat, the tip of my boot touches Asher's shoulder.

"Ungh!" My scream of frustration rips through my throat and goes nowhere, but Asher rolls toward me with a groan.

He's alive.

I toe him with boot, kicking harder until he stirs. He rolls over and slowly opens his eyes. I'm the first thing he sees and his brows pinch in confusion. Then he jerks, realizing his hands are tied behind his back.

His nostrils flare when he smells the fire, then his attention snaps to the rope around my wrist. He staggers to his feet.

I give a shake of my head. We're running out of time. My eyes flick to the ground and I lift my foot. I have no idea if he understands and repeat the gesture, mimicking climbing a step.

His eyes widen and he goes to his knees at my feet. I step onto his back, which gives me the height I need to finally lift the loop of rope off that damned peg.

Jumping down, I yank the belt from around my face and pull the rag from my mouth.

"We gotta get out of here," he says.

I pat my jeans. "I don't have a knife." There's no way I'm opening that barn door myself.

Flames lick up the sides of the barn, growing more ferocious by the second. The horses scream, terrified of the smoke and flickering light of the flames.

"Back pocket." He leans back on his knees.

I reach inside his back pocket and draw out his pocket knife. It takes but a second to slice through the sturdy zip tie, but he's free.

Asher runs to the barn door and leans his bodyweight into pushing the heavy door open. The rails screech and it slowly slides on its tracks.

Knight kicks against his stall in terror. The smoke and flames engulf the walls and reach the roof. The acrid smoke makes it difficult to breathe.

Asher gets the door open just enough to squeeze through. He waves at me. "Evelyn come. Get out of there."

"Not without the horses."

They're behind us, behind a curtain of flame with no escape. Asher gives one look over my shoulder, nods, then leans into the door widening the gap.

I don't hesitate. Turning around, I search for a gap in the flames. I'm getting good at getting out of fires. Let's hope my luck holds out.

Knight's stall is the furthest back. I want to get to him, but the chestnut mare and Arabian are closest. I grab a bridle and put it on the chestnut, then do the same for the Arabian. I need to lead them through the flames and they're going to fight, too terrified of fire and incapable of understanding they must go through the flames to survive. I rip off my shirt and wrap it around the Arabian's head, blinding it. Then I grab a blanket and throw it over the chestnut mare as I leap onto her back.

I'm an accomplished English rider, trained for years in riding horseback, but I've never ridden bareback before.

Where is Asher?

I can't leave Knight to die.

But then a shape appears through the flames, Asher covered in a thick horse blanket. He glances at me, gives a nod, and races to open Knight's stall.

I don't hesitate. The crackling flames reach the ceiling, licking along the wood. Blinding smoke fills the barn and I can't see my way out, but I know if I head straight I'll hit the barn door.

Hopefully, that door is open. That has to be what kept Asher.

The chestnut mare stamps her feet, but I dig into her flanks and force her into a gallop. The Arabian's lead yanks my arm and my shoulder nearly dislocates. I hold on to the Arabian's bridle, and he follows the lead.

Blinded, the horses can't see the flames, but they hear the crackling and smell the smoke.

We charge forward and I brace for the wall of flame, hoping the horse beneath me pays more attention to the pressure of my heels against its flank than the heat of the fire.

Intense heat consumes me, singing the hairs on my arms, but it's over in a heartbeat.

We barrel through the opening of the barn and into the dark night.

I cough and sputter as the horses come to a stop. Brody grabs the reins of the Arabian and Cage helps me down from the chestnut mare.

We're out.

We're safe.

But where is Asher?

I spin around and can't believe my eyes. The entire structure is engulfed. It went up so fast.

"Asher!" I cry out.

Cage grabs my waist, keeping me from running back into the burning building. My eyes fill with tears and I try to yank free.

As I struggle, a shadow of the deepest black appears in the flames.

Knight leaps through with Asher on his back. They breach the opening as the barn roof collapses behind them.

Asher comes to a stop, leaps off Knight and slaps at the flames burning Knight's tail. Brody and Cage rush to help, the three brothers put out the burning hair.

I hold the reins of the other two horses who paw at the ground and rear up on their hind legs. Their eyes roll back, white with fear.

Asher and his brothers pat down Knight, then Asher hands the reins of his horse to Cage.

He rushes to me, strips the shirt of his back and hands it to me.

No words are spoken as he pulls me into a hug. There's a light tap on my wrist as Brody takes the reins of the horses from me.

I wrap my arms around Asher and weep.

29

ASHER

ASHER

I came to with a ringing in my ears, and the worst headache of my life, not knowing what the hell happened. I still don't know, except I woke to flames.

Evelyn's quick thinking saved not only our lives, but the horses as well. I can say I never want to lead a terrified Knight through a wall of flame anytime soon.

I wrap my arms around Evelyn as sirens sound in the distance. Their red and white lights flash in counterpoint to the flickering light of the flames and the pounding in my chest.

We nearly died. I almost lost everything.

"What happened?" I hold Evelyn tight. I still don't know why I was knocked out or came to inside a burning barn. I expect her voice to be shaky, terrified, but she speaks clearly.

"It was Felix."

"Felix?"

"Yes." She steps away as a firetruck pulls up.

Men from Fire Station 13 pile out of the fire engine. I'm not sure what they can do. The barn is a complete loss.

I turn my attention back to Evelyn. "Are you sure?"

"He was crazy. He hit you on the head, then set the barn on fire."

"Felix has always been trouble, but why would he want to hurt you?"

"Because he's the one who started the forest fire. He's the man I saw on the ridge."

"How's that possible?"

"I don't know, but he looks different now. He cut his hair and shaved. That's why I didn't recognize him."

She repeats everything Felix said to her and my gut twists. There was never anyone out to hurt Evelyn. It was always about me.

She was merely collateral damage. Which means the plane crash really was an accident. I feel like a tool for the way I've been treating Prescott.

One of the firefighters walks by dragging a hose. He gives a nod. It takes a second before I realize it's Brandon Bingham.

Over the next hour, they fight the blaze.

Benjamin arrives and pulls us to the side. "What happened?"

"I don't know." It's the truth. Other than escaping the fire, I have no memory of Felix.

"Damn, I'm really sorry." He pulls out a grainy photograph and turns to Evelyn. "Do you recognize this man?"

She peers at the photo of a scraggly man with a beard at a hardware shop.

"That's him." She points excitedly. "That's the man I saw on the ridge. It's Felix."

Benjamin's lips twist. "That's what I was afraid of." He tucks the photo back into its folder. "Needless to say, the arson charges against you are being dropped."

"And what about Felix?" I want to go after the bastard, wring his neck, kick him in the balls, then toss his ass off a cliff.

"There's a warrant out for his arrest. I've sent people to his home, but we're not likely to find him there."

"How did he think he could get away with this?" Evelyn looks as confused as I feel. None of this makes sense.

"I don't know, but we're going to find him." Benjamin shakes my hand and heads out.

There's a manhunt underway for my high school nemesis. I take Evelyn with me to the porch where we sit and I hold her hand. My brothers took the horses to the back pasture with the mares and just returned. They sit down beside us.

"So, Felix-fucking-Franklin?" Brody picks at his fingernails and shakes his head.

"Looks like," I say.

"The fire on the ridge?" Cage runs a hand through his hair and joins Brody in the head shaking thing. "What the fuck was he thinking?"

"Do you think he lit that fire thinking it would hit your land?" Evelyn curls her fingers in mine.

"You mean start a massive forest fire out of spite and hope it reached our vineyard?" I try not to do it, but damn if I'm not shaking my head too.

"It's possible." She shrugs. "If he knew about the wind."

"I don't think Felix is that smart—although the way the wind pushed the fire that day, it kind of makes sense. It spilled right down the hills toward us."

"You think he really tried to burn us out?" Brody props his elbows on his knees. "That fucker is whacked in the head. First, he tries to steal our land, then burn it to the ground?"

"It would be the end of La Rouge Vineyards." I tilt my head back and stare at the stars. "Maybe that's what he wanted? To put us out of business. He'd be able to come in with a low-ball offer and bail us out." It sounds reasonable, but who knows what the fucker is thinking.

The fire raging across from us burns the barn down. Thank fuck Brandon and his team are here. If not for them, we would've lost the vines as the fire spread.

"You think that's what he wants? To put us out of business for good?" Cage's lower lip curls inward. "He tried that when dad died."

I scrub my hands over my face and let out a long breath. We talk for a bit, coming no closer to a reason behind Felix's actions.

Exhaustion pulls at me as my mind drifts away. A light touch on my palm draws me back. It's Evelyn tracing a heart on my palm.

I stand and pull Evelyn into my arms. "I almost lost you."

For the first time, I know what my future holds. The future of La Rouge Vineyards may be up in the air, but my future is set. It belongs in the arms of my beautiful little backpack.

Her hair is a mess. The long curls singed at the tips. The rest of her hair is a knotted mess. Soot covers her face, broken only by the tracks of her tears. Like me, she reeks of woodsmoke. It permeates her clothes, her hair, and her skin.

A firestorm brought us together. The fire at her house brought her to me. But this last one?

It forged our future.

I pull her up the steps. Brody and Cage glance at me and give a nod. It's the triplet thing. They know I've found my forever. And unlike Erin, they approve my choice.

"Come on. Let's get you cleaned up." I gesture inside.

Evelyn looks at her dirt and soot-stained clothes. Her soft smile looks like heaven and settles inside of me where it lodges in my heart.

She's the most beautiful sight I've ever seen and encompasses everything I want in a woman.

Soft and tender.

Fierce and indestructible.

Her strength is uncompromising.

Her will to survive undeniable.

I can't wait to get her inside and tell her I intend to stay right beside her wherever she chooses to go.

She's not from around here and we agreed to no strings, but damn if there's not something binding us together. If she chooses to leave, at least she'll walk away knowing exactly how I feel. What I'm willing to give up to be right by her side.

We barely make it through the front door before her grip tightens and she pulls to a stop.

Our gazes lock, communicating without words, the fear we faced, working to free ourselves, and making it out of the barn alive.

She's suddenly in my arms. Legs wrapped around my waist. Lips press against mine. I'm right there with her, running my hands along her back, cupping them beneath her gorgeous ass as I carry her through the house.

"I thought we weren't going to make it."

I thought the same thing, but she was alone with Felix. She watched him take me out, pour gasoline around the barn, light it on fire. The horror she endured is something I wish I could take away. The helplessness she felt tied to that post isn't something I ever want her to feel again.

"But we did." I feather kisses over her mouth, her cheeks, the tip of her nose and over her eyelids.

"Yes, we did."

"You're here, little backpack, and I'm never letting you go." Does she understand what that means?

"Promise?" She leans back to gaze into my eyes.

Our tongues meet as I press her up against the wall. I fucked her against this wall and I'm seconds from doing that again. I need to be buried deep within her, physically reconnecting, as I bind her to me.

She wraps around me. Arms draped over my shoulders. Legs wrapped around my hips. Her hot pussy pressing against my hungry cock.

No way in hell am I ever letting her go.

I press her against the wall and brace my hand beside her head. My other hand reaches between us, flicking open the button of her jeans, lowering the zipper. Getting frustrated because her jeans aren't coming off like this. A low groan escapes me.

She breaks her lips from mine and glances toward the front door. If someone comes through, they'll see everything.

"Fuck," I say. "Shower or bed. You pick."

She nibbles her lower lip and smiles. "I love where your mind's at."

"You'll love even better where my cock is going to be."

My heart swells with the look in her eyes. So many unspoken words linger between us.

I gently lower her down, my heart filling with so many emotions as I pull her to my room.

Once inside, I close the door and push her against it. Leaning forward, I slow things down and kiss her nice and slow. Then I rest my forehead against hers.

"You have no idea what you do to me," I say.

"Show me."

"I'm happy to oblige." I press the long, hard length of my dick against her hip. "But first we need to talk."

"Talk?"

"Yes. Change the parameters of our agreement."

"What does that mean?"

"We said no strings, but damn if I can't imagine not having you in my life. I want to tie you to me, Miss Evelyn Thornton. I want you to stay."

"Stay?"

"If you can't, I understand, but you need to know one thing."

"What's that?"

"I'll be right by your side."

"You can't leave La Rouge." Her eyes widen.

"For you, I'll do anything." I run the pad of my thumb along her cheek. "I'll do anything to be with you, but I won't fuck you if you're going to walk away. I can't do no strings anymore."

"I would never ask that of you."

"You don't have to, but if we do this, you need to know there are strings. I'll tie you to me, my little backpack, and never let you go."

"Asher…"

My pulse races waiting for her to say more and let me know I haven't just made the worst mistake of my life. Every molecule in my body surges, waiting for her to say yes.

"When I came to…back in the barn…all I could feel was fear. How I couldn't bear to lose you. I know it's selfish to make you choose, but if you're going to walk away, I need you to do it now."

She nibbles her lower lip. "There's so much we haven't talked about. My life's a mess. I've been so busy running from my past, I can't imagine my future."

"Then close your eyes."

Her brow quirks up.

"Trust me."

Her eyes close.

"There's nothing except you and me. I'm standing in front of you, watching you undress, devouring you with my eyes."

"Asher..." Her eyes flicker open and I shake my head. Obediently, her eyelids close.

"You let your hair down, and in that moment, you lower all your defenses, letting me in."

"I feel weird." Her words hit me, make me worry, but she keeps her eyes closed.

Trusting me.

"Your gorgeous hair spills all around and covers us both. I take you in my arms and make love to you until you come apart in my arms. You come for me. You run right into me and I pull you close, easing your pain. You don't have to go through life alone. Not when I'll be right by your side."

Her lids flicker and she looks at me. Her voice is soft. "You promise?"

"Do you know what you do to me?"

"No."

"You make me shake, send shivers down my spine. You fucking bring me to my knees. That's what you do to me. I want to spend my evenings tracing the lines of your body with my fingertips until you feel them stirring your soul, knowing that's exactly where I belong."

"You make it sound amazing."

"Stay with me."

She gives me a long look, and while the words don't come, the answer's in her eyes.

"Stay at La Rouge. Give me time to show you what we're meant to be."

She wraps her arms around my neck. "You don't need to show

me anything. I never thought when I ran from my past that I would run into you."

Her words hit me where it counts, right in my heart, where they sink and settle in like a slow, simmering burn. My pulse races and I can't speak. Too many emotions run through me.

Tears fall from her eyes and when I press my lips to hers, the salt of her tears fill my mouth. But there's more. I taste her love mingling with hope.

"I love you, my little backpack, and I never want to let you go."

Evelyn comes apart in my arms. She cries and laughs as she kisses me.

"I love you too, Asher La Rouge, and if you'll have me, I want to stay. I never want to leave."

"Thank fuck for that." I lift her into my arms.

"Speaking of fucking." She pulls reaches between us and places her hand over my hard length. "If you're going to tie me to you, you'd better start now."

"I never thought you'd ask."

I never thought I'd hold the whole world in my hands, but I have that and more with Evelyn.

She's the future I've been chasing.

The forever I want to make.

The slow fire burning in my heart.

Evelyn is my future and I'm her beginning.

And for the next few hours, we communicate without words, showing each other how hot our love burns.

———

Enjoyed reading about Asher La Rouge?
If so, you're in for a treat!
More La Rouge magic is on its way.
Grab your copy of Brody's book HERE.

30

BONUS CHAPTER

―――――

"You ready, little backpack?" Asher looks at me, eyes brimming with excitement. His expression is full of adventure. We stand at the beginning of the John Muir trail, over two-hundred and twenty miles of backcountry wilderness lies between us and the end.

But the end is not our destination.

Instead, the journey is what we look forward to, a time for the two of us to be alone and see if this thing between us is strong enough to endure a lifetime of adventure.

I already know the answer to this. I'm simply waiting for Asher to catch up and get on board.

I shift my backpack on my shoulders, loving the fit of my brand-new pack. Its weight settles on my hips, and I adjust the shoulder straps for comfort. My boots are new, although I've spent the last month breaking them in on the trails behind La Rouge vineyards. I'm ready, eager, and excited to tackle something I never thought I could do.

"I'm ready."

"Let's do this." He waves me forward. It's a grand gesture. He wants me to be the first to step foot over the official beginning of the trail. Asher knows what this hike means to me. In many ways, it forms a bridge between my past and future.

Considered a grueling test of a hiker's skill, this trail isn't for the faint of heart. We'll be hiking far from civilization, cut off from all the creature comforts for two to three weeks. My original plan was to attempt this trail on my own, determined to prove something to myself, specifically that I'm no longer the vapid socialite of my past.

But I'm not alone, and there's nothing to prove. I'm happy and content. I'm proud of who I am.

The most handsome man in the world is by my side. He leaves La Rouge Vineyards at the height of the fall harvest. It's a crucial time for his business, but I'm more important. I was willing to put this off, but winter is coming, and the trail will become impassable. It's now or wait for early summer to arrive. Asher didn't want to wait.

And it's not like we left La Rouge Vineyards to flounder. Cage stays behind, working with George, the vineyard's foreman. Together, they'll bring in the harvest and begin the crucial first steps of producing the next award-winning La Rouge vintage.

Asher and I have all the time in the world to disappear.

Not that we are…disappearing that is. Our progress will be tracked.

We cave into Cage's demands, and Prescott's as well. We'll travel with a satellite phone which will be used to call in each and every night. Our journey will be documented, chronicled as a feature article for Cage's outdoor magazine.

We've been given assignments and tasks along the way, and honestly, I no longer mind the intrusiveness of it all. Instead, I feel overwhelmingly loved. I belong to a family greater than myself.

I found a new home filled with Asher's love, the affection of his adorable brothers, the admiration of a woman I hope to one day call 'Mom,' and the joy of knowing Prescott and Gracie will always be a part of my life. They tie me to the past I wanted to forget, a past that should never be forgotten. They remind me of what it means to love unconditionally.

The woman I am today comes from that past, and honestly, I'm happy to have them in my life.

Prescott's mind is at ease. We've sorted out survivorship of the trust, which holds the net worth of the Thornton name. If something happens to me, he knows exactly how to distribute my wealth. It'll go to the charities my mother and father supported while they were alive. In that way, their memory lives on. We also decided to set aside money to form a foundation in memory of Prescott's son, Justin. It's a small thing, geared toward encouraging underprivileged youths to consider the law as a career. It's something Justin would be proud to have in his name.

With Brody's financial help, we've restructured my assets, and I no longer look upon my inheritance as a burden. Instead, I see it as a tool I can use to do incredible things.

For the first time, I'm happy. I've embraced my past and discovered a bright future awaits me.

Not that everything is wonderful. Ghosts haunt our future, specifically Felix Franklin. All charges of arson against me were dropped, but Felix remains free. Benjamin Bingham organized a manhunt, but Felix is gone, disappeared until he surfaces again to cause trouble with the La Rouge triplets.

His feud with Asher and his brothers comes from accusations and convictions of attempted rape in high school and beyond. Asher, Brody, and Cage stood with the girls Felix assaulted. Those charges sent Felix to jail for eight years. It should've been much longer, but prisons are crowded. They must have commuted his sentence and released him early. Which brought Felix and my lives crashing together on a ridge overlooking Napa Valley.

Benjamin Bingham assures us, once Felix is caught, he'll be charged with several counts of felony arson and two counts of attempted murder. He'll go away for the rest of his life.

Until then, we'll be careful and vigilant. I never recovered my father's revolver, but I carry a new one in the pack at my waist. This time, I'm legal, with appropriate concealed carry documentation to keep me within the law.

"Goddamn, but you take my breath away." Asher's words wash

over me, stopping me in my tracks. I turn around, a smile fixed to my face, but then gasp when I see him on one knee.

Instead of following me up the trail, Asher holds a velvet box in his hand.

"Little backpack, I love you, and I always want to be by your side. I want you to be my wife. Once we finish this trail, that's exactly what we'll be; husband and wife. It's all set up. All I need is for you to say yes." He pops open the top of the box, revealing a slender ring with a diamond propped on top. "What do you say? Wanna get hitched?"

I stare at the ring and gape. The last time I wore a ring, it ended in disaster, but this time everything will be different.

His brows draw together. "Don't leave me hanging, little backpack, answer the question, and make me the happiest man on earth."

A smile fills my face and tears pool in my eyes. I stretch out my hand and wiggle my fingers. "Yes! Absolutely, yes!"

"You're pretty when you blush." Asher gets off his knee and slides the ring on my finger. Sunlight glitters off the diamond. While I stare at it, he cups my cheeks and presses his lips on mine.

I belong heart and soul to Asher La Rouge and can't wait to begin our new life. Hand in hand, we take the next step. It's the first step of two-hundred and twenty miles of backcountry trails and the first step of the rest of my life.

———

T HE END

ELLZ BELLZ

ELLIE'S FACEBOOK READER GROUP

If you are interested in joining the ELLZ BELLZ, Ellie's Facebook reader group, we'd love to have you.

Join Ellie's ELLZ BELLZ.
The ELLZ BELLZ Facebook Reader Group

Sign up for Ellie's Newsletter.
Elliemasters.com/newslettersignup

ALSO BY ELLIE MASTERS

The LIGHTER SIDE

Ellie Masters is the lighter side of the Jet & Ellie Masters writing duo! You will find Contemporary Romance, Military Romance, Romantic Suspense, Billionaire Romance, and Rock Star Romance in Ellie's Works.

YOU CAN FIND ELLIE'S BOOKS HERE:
ELLIEMASTERS.COM/BOOKS

Military Romance
Guardian Hostage Rescue Specialists

Rescuing Melissa

(Get a FREE copy of Rescuing Melissa

when you join Ellie's Newsletter)

Alpha Team

Rescuing Zoe

Rescuing Moira

Rescuing Eve

Rescuing Lily

Rescuing Jinx

Rescuing Maria

Bravo Team

Rescuing Angie

Rescuing Isabelle

Rescuing Carmen

Rescuing Rosalie

Rescuing Kaye

Cara's Protector

Rescuing Barbi

Charlie Team

Rescuing Rebel

Rescuing Stitch

Military Romance

Guardian Personal Protection Specialists

Sybil's Protector

Lyra's Protector

The One I Want Series

(Small Town, Military Heroes)

By Jet & Ellie Masters

EACH BOOK IN THIS SERIES CAN BE READ AS A STANDALONE AND IS ABOUT A DIFFERENT COUPLE WITH AN HEA.

Saving Abby

Saving Ariel

Saving Brie

Saving Cate

Saving Dani

Saving Jen

Rockstar Romance

The Angel Fire Rock Romance Series

EACH BOOK IN THIS SERIES CAN BE READ AS A STANDALONE AND IS ABOUT A DIFFERENT COUPLE WITH AN HEA. IT IS RECOMMENDED THEY ARE READ IN ORDER.

Ashes to New (prequel)

Heart's Insanity (book 1)

Heart's Desire (book 2)

Heart's Collide (book 3)

Hearts Divided (book 4)

Hearts Entwined (book5)

Forest's FALL (book 6)

Hearts The Last Beat (book7)

The LaRouge Triplets

Asher

Brody

Cage

Billionaire Romance

Billionaire Boys Club

Hawke

Richard

Contemporary Romance

Cocky Captain

Romantic Suspense

EACH BOOK IS A STANDALONE NOVEL.

The Starling

~AND~

Science Fiction

Ellie Masters writing as L.A. Warren

Vendel Rising: a Science Fiction Serialized Novel

BOOKS BY JET MASTERS

If you enjoyed this book by Ellie Masters, the LIGHTER SIDE of the Jet & Ellie writing duo, and aren't afraid of edgier writing, you might enjoy reading BDSM themed books written by Jet, the DARKER SIDE of the Masters' Writing Team.

The DARKER SIDE
Jet Masters is the darker side of the Jet & Ellie writing duo!

Romantic Suspense
Changing Roles Series:
THIS SERIES MUST BE READ IN ORDER.
Book 1: Command Me
Book 2: Control Me
Book 3: Collar Me
Book 4: Embracing FATE
Book 5: Seizing FATE
Book 6: Accepting FATE

HOT READS
A STANDALONE NOVEL.

Down the Rabbit Hole

Light BDSM Romance
The Ties that Bind

EACH BOOK IN THIS SERIES CAN BE READ AS A STANDALONE AND IS
ABOUT A DIFFERENT COUPLE WITH AN HEA.

Alexa
Penny
Michelle
Ivy

HOT READS
Becoming His Series

THIS SERIES MUST BE READ IN ORDER.

Book 1: The Ballet
Book 2: Learning to Breathe
Book 3: Becoming His

Dark Captive Romance

A STANDALONE NOVEL.

She's MINE

ABOUT THE AUTHOR

Ellie Masters is a USA Today Bestselling author and Amazon Top 15 Author who writes Angsty, Steamy, Heart-Stopping, Pulse-Pounding, Can't-Stop-Reading Romantic Suspense. In addition, she's a wife, military mom, doctor, and retired Colonel. She writes romantic suspense filled with all your sexy, swoon-worthy alpha men. Her writing will tug at your heartstrings and leave your heart racing.

Born in the South, raised under the Hawaiian sun, Ellie has traveled the globe while in service to her country. The love of her life, her amazing husband, is her number one fan and biggest supporter. And yes! He's read every word she's written.

She has lived all over the United States—east, west, north, south and central—but grew up under the Hawaiian sun. She's also been privileged to have lived overseas, experiencing other cultures and making lifelong friends. Now, Ellie is proud to call herself a Southern transplant, learning to say y'all and "bless her heart" with the best of them. She lives with her beloved husband, two children who refuse to flee the nest, and four fur-babies; three cats who rule the household, and a dog who wants nothing other than for the cats to be his best friends. The cats have a different opinion regarding this matter.

Ellie's favorite way to spend an evening is curled up on a couch, laptop in place, watching a fire, drinking a good wine, and bringing forth all the characters from her mind to the page and hopefully into the hearts of her readers.

FOR MORE INFORMATION
elliemasters.com

f facebook.com/elliemastersromance

X x.com/Ellie__Masters

◎ instagram.com/ellie_masters

BB bookbub.com/authors/ellie-masters

g goodreads.com/Ellie_Masters

CONNECT WITH ELLIE MASTERS

Website:
elliemasters.com
Amazon Author Page:
elliemasters.com/amazon
Facebook:
elliemasters.com/Facebook
Goodreads:
elliemasters.com/Goodreads
Instagram:
elliemasters.com/Instagram

FINAL THOUGHTS

I hope you enjoyed this book as much as I enjoyed writing it. If you enjoyed reading this story, please consider leaving a review on Amazon and Goodreads, and please let other people know. A sentence is all it takes. Friend recommendations are the strongest catalyst for readers' purchase decisions! And I'd love to be able to continue bringing the characters and stories from My-Mind-to-the-Page.

Second, call or e-mail a friend and tell them about this book. If you really want them to read it, gift it to them. If you prefer digital friends, please use the "Recommend" feature of Goodreads to spread the word.

Or visit my blog https://elliemasters.com, where you can find out more about my writing process and personal life.

Come visit The EDGE: Dark Discussions where we'll have a chance to talk about my works, their creation, and maybe what the future has in store for my writing.

Facebook Reader Group: Ellz Bellz

Thank you so much for your support!

Love,

Ellie

DEDICATION

This book is dedicated to you, my reader. Thank you for spending a few hours of your time with me. I wouldn't be able to write without you to cheer me on. Your wonderful words, your support, and your willingness to join me on this journey is a gift beyond measure.

Whether this is the first book of mine you've read, or if you've been with me since the very beginning, thank you for believing in me as I bring these characters 'from my mind to the page and into your hearts.'

Love,
Ellie

THE END

———

Made in the USA
Monee, IL
04 August 2025

22597672R00184